INVERSION III

THE LIGHTER SHADES OF GREYS

BY PAUL STANSBURY

First Edition
2020

Sheppard Press

Sheppard Press
461 Boone Trail
Danville, Kentucky 40422

Printed in the United States of America
ISBN 978-0-9986516-7-5 paperback
ISBN 978-0-9986516-8-2 e-book

Cover Graphics by Paul Stansbury

CONTENTS

INTRODUCTION

Inversion III, The Lighter Shades of Greys, is my third volume of speculative fiction stories. If you are unfamiliar my interpretation of what is speculative fiction, you will find the introduction to *Inversion, Not Your Ordinary Stories*, in the Appendix.

As you might guess from the title of this volume, the stories deal in some fashion with beings from other worlds. There may be one or two characters you will encounter whose origins may be in question, but take it from me, they are not from this neck of the woods.

If you are looking for creepy alien abduction yarns, these stories are not for you. Nor will you find cataclysmic invasions of vicious, flesh eating space monsters on the menu. As the subtitle for this volume indicates, these stories are on the lighter side perhaps even humorous. The beings you will encounter here are most certainly of a kinder, gentler variety, although not too sweet. I hope they suit your taste.

Some of these stories have been previously published, either in print or online. I would like to express my appreciation to those editors who were willing to publish my work.

I would also like to thank the members of the Danville Writers Group, who have read many preliminary drafts of these stories and offered their feedback and assistance.

Finally, I would like to thank Joan Stansbury, affectionately known as the *Queen of Commas*, for her editorial assistance.

Paul Stansbury

LITTLE GREEN MEN?[1]

Little green men ain't green and ain't necessarily men. At least that's what Maggie Jean, Dougie and me found out during the dog days in Kentucky between senior year and college. The three of us spent most of that summer hanging out and counting down until we could leave Buckhorn far behind in search of our dreams. Maggie Jean and I were enrolled at Eastern Kentucky. Dougie was off to the Nashville Auto Diesel College because he wanted to be a diesel mechanic. He had wanted to go Eastern with us until he found out there were no classes for diesel mechanics. After that, he tried to convince Maggie Jean and me to switch to Middle Tennessee. I would have gone, but she had her head set on Eastern and when she set her head, there was no changing it.

We had been friends since first grade – that is to say me and Dougie. We were just a couple of goofy country kids. Liked to fish, didn't play sports, got ordinary grades. Maggie Jean showed up in third grade. Her family had moved into town over the Summer when her daddy got the job as manager at the state park. First day of school, she just sat down at our table in the lunchroom and from then on it was us three.

In grade school, before hormones started complicating the normal state of affairs, girls and boys could be friends without much effort. By junior high that started to change. Maggie Jean was a full head taller than me and Dougie, freckled, with green eyes and a tousle of auburn hair. Me and Dougie remained ordinary with just a bit of baby fat left clinging to our cheeks. She was very popular, especially with the boys. That began to weigh heavily on me and Dougie, too. Everyone pestered her to go out for cheerleading. However, all that attention didn't seem to matter much to Maggie Jean. Why is beyond me, because she could have hung out with the

---

[1]"Little Green Men?" was published as a digital media product by *The Society of Misfit Stories of Bard and Sages Publishing,* 12/16/2016. It was subsequently selected to appear in *The Society of Misfit Stories Presents... Volume One* published by Bard and Sages Publishing, 12/2017.

cool kids if she wanted. Everyone liked Maggie Jean and she was always friendly with everyone. Lots of guys tried to get her attention, but try as they might, she never paid them much mind. Maggie Jean was like that.

In high school, about the time I had grown tall enough to look Maggie straight in the eye, we became sweethearts. It's not that suddenly one day it happened. It was more like a natural progression. Me and Dougie remained best friends despite the fact he had a huge crush on Maggie Jean. I could tell by the way he looked at her when he didn't think I was paying attention or how he hung on her every word. How do I know he was my best friend? He never let his feelings come between us and he always respected the closeness Maggie Jean and I shared.

Dougie just couldn't seem to find the right girl. He wasn't a bad looking guy even though he was only 5'4" with a scraggly beard and an already receding hair line. As my Mom said, "He's got a nice personality and there is no reason the girls shouldn't want to go out with him." He had his fair share of dates, but never seemed to date a girl more than once or twice. Sometimes, I thought it was because in his mind no other girl could quite match up with Maggie Jean. On the other hand, it could've been because Dougie was on the short side, or he was going bald or he would have rather worked on an engine than go to a dance. He did have the well deserved reputation as the best shade tree mechanic around. He would work on anything. Given his druthers, he would happily work on a motor than do about anything else. By senior year, Dougie had saved up enough money to buy a Ford F650 with all the bells and whistles as well as pay for all his tuition at the Nashville Auto Diesel College.

Our summer flowed along like a lazy stream through flat bottomed fields with hardly a ripple to be seen. Maggie Jean ran the rental boat concession for her daddy at the marina. She convinced him to hire me to mow the golf course and let Dougie do the mechanic work on anything that needed fixing. It worked out real sweet. We all had paying jobs without having to drive all the way into Hazard. We all got to swim in the park pool for free on our time off and if there was a boat not in use, we could take it for free as long as we filled the gas tank.

It was two days before the big 4th of July picnic, concert, and fireworks show at the park. Dougie and I were greasing the gang mowers I towed behind the John Deere to cut the fairways. I asked Dougie if he had asked anyone, meaning a girl, to go.

"Naw," he mumbled, without looking up.

"What do you mean 'naw'? It's only the biggest thing going on all summer! The Roswells are playing. I thought you were gonna get a date and go with Maggie Jean and me. You know, this might be the last time we all'll have the chance to celebrate the 4th together."

"Well," Dougie said, "I mean I'm still going with y'all, but jus' not with anyone else an' y'all."

"Have you even asked anyone?"

"Well, it's like this –" he started.

I cut him off mid sentence, "That means you haven't asked anyone, don't it?"

"I guess you could say that. It's jus' that I'm particular about who I ask out. An' when I do find a girl I would like to take out, seems she's particular too – but not about me. I've gotten tired of hearin' excuses. The polite ones say they already got other plans and the rest just say 'no'. I'm just tired of gettin' my hopes up."

"Hell, Dougie," I consoled, "the right one is out there, you jus' got to keep pluggin' away. You can't give up now."

Dougie got a sheepish grin on his face, "You think Maggie Jean could find me a date?"

"I figured this would happen, so I already asked her to see what she could do, but no promises."

"Thanks," Dougie said, as he hung the grease gun on the nail by the mowing shed door. "I'll see you later. Gotta a job." That meant he was off to work on someone's car or truck.

I hitched the gang mowers to the John Deere and set off to mow the fairways. It was late afternoon when I returned to the shed. On days she worked, Maggie Jean had to stay at the dock until the last rental boat came back. After I locked up the shed, I slipped into the life guards' shower and cleaned up. Then I headed around to the back of the kitchen. The cook had already sacked up some food from the buffet. I walked down the gravel ramp to the marina where Maggie Jean was waiting with a couple of cold sodas from the cooler.

We ate while she waited for the last of the rental boats to meander back. We had just finished tying off the last of the rental boats and sat down on the bench overlooking the now still water of the Marina to finish off our Nehi Grape sodas.

"Dougie finally asked me to ask you if there isn't someone you know that you can get to go with him to the fireworks," I said to Maggie Jean.

"So that means he hasn't asked anyone."

"To make a long story short – yeah."

"Don't you think Dougie needs to find his own date?"

"In a perfect world, sure. But this is Dougie we're talking about. He's not the best at findin' when it comes to girls. You want a motor or a transmission, he can find it in the dark during a rainstorm. But findin' a date is like asking him to fly a spaceship – it'll never get off the ground."

"Well, there's LuAnn who works the front desk. She's real nice."

"Maggie Jean! Doesn't she have a kid in 3rd grade?"

"Of course not, he's not even in preschool."

"I don't think that's gonna work. There's got to be someone else," I pleaded.

"Why can't you let him just tag along like always?" Maggie Jean said in a pensive tone.

"I didn't say I didn't want him to go with us – and I know he wants to go with us. It's just he won't say it – but I can tell he would like his own date – I can see it in his eyes when the three of us are together – you know, someone other than you and me to share experiences with – like the fireworks – fireworks always look better – well you know– with someone special – like you – but I don't mean you, that is – I mean – bein' special for Dougie – hell, I'm not making any sense dammit – you know what I mean – you're a girl."

"Yes, last time you checked, all the necessary stuff was there," she giggled, leaning over to give me a kiss. Then her voice turned serious. "But Dougie's got to find that person – you or me can't do it for him."

"I know that. I'd just like to help him along." Our conversation was interrupted by the growl of Dougie's F650 hauling down the gravel boat ramp, kicking up a mighty dust storm. His custom horn blasted the UK fight song as he locked up his brakes and slid to a stop just inches short of the water. He waited inside the cab watching the dust wash over the truck and out across the water. Then, he hopped out and joined us on the dock.

"Y'all won't believe it!" he called out, as he pulled off his ball cap and wiped his forehead with his handkerchief.

"Believe what?" I asked.

"What I just saw,"

"And what would that be?" Maggie Jean teased. "Let's see, you happened to be out bird watching with your binoculars when a rare bird landed in a tree right where the Buxton twins were skinny dipping in the creek?"

"Come on Maggie Jean," Dougie said, his voice betraying a hint of embarrassment. He furrowed his brow and looked at me for sympathy.

"Don't look at me, your reputation precedes you. You want something to eat, there's some left." I offered, pointing to the paper sack on the bench.

"It's bigger than the Buxton twins put together," Dougie blurted out.

"Well, I'd like to see that," I shot back, not expecting the sharp poke in the ribs Maggie Jean delivered before I could close my mouth.

"Serves you right," Dougie chortled. He eyed us both for a few seconds until he was satisfied we were ready to listen. He furrowed his brows, "Now, if you two are finished, I got something important to tell you." Satisfied, he continued, "I was over to Krypton working on Bunk Taylor's '73 Firebird. You know the one I put a big block 427 in last year."

"So you want us to look at Bunk Taylor's engine?" I asked.

"Shut up!" Dougie said, throwing his cap to the ground. "No, I don't want you to look at Bunk Taylor's engine. Besides, I was putting him in a new rear end. Well – not him, his Firebird. But that ain't important. It's what happened on the way back here that I want you to see. I decided to take that old logging trail that runs off KY 28 to check out the new suspension I put in my truck."

"You want us to go look at logs?" Maggie Jean asked. It was her way to slow Dougie down.

Dougie closed his mouth and took a deep breath. He could get madder than hell over the slightest provocation, but never with her. He pulled at his scraggly beard. "No Miss Maggie, not logs." 'Miss Maggie' was what he called her when he thought she was teasing.

"Good, 'cause I really can't think of any log that you could get me this excited about."

"Is it OK to go on?" Dougie asked.

"Please do," she said, nodding her head.

"The loggin' trail goes over the ridge and comes out on the back side of Grover Mill's farm. Well I was just clearing the woods, still in low gear, when I heard this strange buzzing and the truck started shaking. I thought my engine had broke loose or my rear end had gone shot. I cut the engine off, but the buzzing and shaking didn't stop. That's when I saw it."

"Saw what, Dougie?" I asked.

"That's just it, I don't rightly know what I saw."

"Dougie, you been smoking something? Did Bunk pay you with cash or did he trade something for your services?"

"Well yes and no."

"What do you mean 'yes and no' Dougie Luttrell?" Maggie Jean barked. She took a step forward so their faces were mere inches apart. "And don't be thinking of lying to me, 'cause I can tell when you're lying, and if you tell me a lie, you'll never forget what I'll do to you." Dougie could bend the truth like a bow and make you think it was the arrow, but he never tried it with Maggie Jean.

"OK, OK. Bunk paid in cash with a little bonus gift. But honest, I ain't smoked nothin'.

"Dougie, you know I don't hold with those kind of doings," Maggie Jean said sternly. "What was this bonus gift?" He reached into his pocked and pulled out a small plastic bag holding it up for her to see. "Just as I thought. Dougie Lutrell, fooling around with weed is going to get you in trouble. I mean it."

"But Maggie, I couldn't refuse a gift from Bunk. He gets a little touchy if he thinks you've insulted him."

"Dougie!"

"Alright, Maggie Jean, I promise I'll get rid of it. "

"Right now. You dump it right there in the water. You understand?"

"Yes." Dougie said, quickly prying open the bag and shaking out the contents. "Satisfied?"

Maggie Jean stared at Dougie with her *this conversation is over* look.

After a few seconds dragged by, Dougie looked at me and asked, "D'ya ask Maggie Jean about that thing I asked you to ask her about?"

"Yes, and we'll get to that directly. What about what you saw over to Grover Mill's farm?"

"Oh yeah. Like I said, I don't rightly know what I saw, but I sure saw it. It looked like a big ol' bubble – like we used to make by blowing through that ring thing you dipped in a bottle of bubble stuff – only a lot bigger – I mean a lot bigger – about as big as that fake hot air balloon Stuart Allen flies over to the Chevy dealership. An' man, was it shiny like a new set of chrome valve covers with those rainbow lookin' colors swirling all around – but you could still kinda see through it. – an' it was floatin' down from up in the air." He paused to catch his breath. "It had three little legs poking out – old man Mill's cows were running for the hills. Well, no sooner did it set down than one of its legs gave way and it tipped over. Well the all the buzzin' and shaken quit, so I cranked up the motor and came straight here."

"You didn't wait to see what happened?" Maggie asked.

Dougie stood there with a blank expression on his face. 'I come back to get a trailer so I can haul it back to the shed."

'Why is that?" I asked

"It's obvious somethin's busted on it and rather than take all the tools out to Grover Mill's pasture, I thought it would be easier to hoist it up on a trailer and bring it back here to work on."

"Well, that's a plan if I ever heard one." I said, looking at Maggie Jean. "Think we ought to go see what this is all about?"

"Wild horses," she laughed.

***

7

Dougie picked out a pontoon boat trailer and hitched it up to his truck. We piled in and set off. In a few minutes, we turned off the main road through a beat–up farm gate and bumped along a dirt path through the scrub trees and undergrowth until we emerged into a field tucked between the wooded area and the side of a ridge. Just as Dougie had described, about two thirds across the field sat his big ol' iridescent bubble. From where we were, we could see the sphere resting on two legs, like a dog sitting on its haunches. Mr. Mill's cows, true to their nature, had quickly forgotten what had frightened them and were milling around the contraption as if it had been there all along. Dougie pulled his truck about half way across the field then turned a 360, lining the trailer up for loading. He backed up until the rear of the trailer was about 15 feet from the sphere.

"You're the man with the plan,' Maggie Jean said to Dougie. "Now what?"

"Let's load it up!" Dougie responded, throwing open the door and jumping to the ground. Maggie Jean and I got out and joined Dougie.

"Dougie, do you even know that this thing is?" I asked.

"Could be a weather balloon, or some air force experiment, but most likely its some sort of alien spaceship."

"I don't think balloons have landin' legs, Dougie, an' I think this place would be swarmin' with the military if it was some sort of experimental aircraft. That only leaves the other alternative."

"I guess," said Dougie,

"Don't you think you might want to see who or what is inside?" Maggie Jean asked. "They might not be as anxious as you to have this thing drug up on a pontoon boat trailer and hauled away."

"You might be right," Dougie said. At that moment, a soft whir emanated from the sphere as a ramp glided to the ground from an opening portal. Dougie dropped the cable, turning to look. "I told you it was aliens. I think we're about to meet the most advanced beings in the universe." We watched in silence until the ramp was fully extended and firmly resting on the ground. To our utter amazement, a small cow in an ill–fitting shiny grey jumpsuit emerged.

Maggie Jean giggled, "Who would have guessed that the most advanced beings in the universe would turn out to be Guernseys!"

"Now it makes perfect sense why it landed in this cow pasture," Dougie said, ignoring Maggie Jean.

"Whadda we do now?" I asked.

Dougie shouted, "Hold on, I got this!" He rushed forward, holding up his right hand, fore and middle fingers separated from ring and little fingers in a 'V'. He gulped down a breath and said, "Glad To Burrito Nicole." The cow, now half way down the ramp, stopped dead in its tracks.

I called out to Dougie, "What in the world are you doing?"

Dougie turned his head slightly and whispered, "Shhhhhh, I'm communicatin' with the bovine alien in the universal galactic language. I think it means 'Don't kill us'. I saw it in that movie where the alien told the little boy's mom to say that to the robot to keep it from destroying the earth."

"That doesn't make any sense at all," I said, "an' what's with the Vulcan secret handshake?"

Dougie dropped his hand, "Couldn't hurt nothing'."

A nasally voice cut short our conversation. "I think it's cute, although I don't think those were the exact words Mr. Klaatu used."

"Hot damn," Dougie yelled, slapping his thigh. "Who'da thought galactic Guernseys could speak American?"

"I make it a practice to master a practical proficiency in the predominate language of the planet I am visiting, if indeed, it is populated with sentient beings. I am Mar Ti Jovan Vheeffaar, an ecologist, studying life and living systems throughout this galaxy. I am neither a Guernsey, as you have incorrectly identified, nor a Red and White Holstein which is the actual breed of these bovines which I have emulated. I am a Dohi. Allow me to change into something more comfortable."

All of a sudden, the little cow stood up on it's hind legs. It's head began to quiver like feed sack full of frogs. The cow features melted away and were replaced by a human looking face and hands. Well, human looking except for the fact its eyes were way big, its ears were almost non existent, and it had kind of a lavender colored skin with grey speckles. Other than that, you couldn't tell the difference.

"Look at that!" Dougie shouted. "Marty's one of them shape shifter's. Don't that beat all." Then he spoke to the Dohi. "You don't mind if I call you 'Marty', do ya? I can't remember the rest of your name, much less say it."

A smile broke across the Dohi's face, "The pseudonym is acceptable."

Dougie gave us a perplexed look.

Maggie Jean smiled, "It means OK."

***

We took the time to make introductions and exchange pleasantries. We found out Marty's job was to study life on all habitual planets in our neck of the galaxy. Marty assured us that, contrary to all the alien abduction conspiracies, galactic ecologists did not abduct folks or engage in vivisection on living creatures. It seems that Dohi were particularly suitable for that kind of work because of their unique ability to take on the essence of any living creature. As Marty explained, a Dohi could take on the appearance of any creature simply by seeing what it looked like. Moreover, under the right conditions, Dohis could actually transform into an exact copy at the cellular level. That was how most of their research was conducted. Marty went on and on in great detail on how all that transformation stuff worked, but most of it was way over my head, so to be polite, I just nodded like I understood. It didn't take much time for us to tell Marty about high school, renting boats, mowing fairways and the finer points of pulling a motor. We came to a lull in the conversation.

It was then Maggie Jean asked, "How long do you expect to stay here?"

"I had already visited most of the locations on my itinerary for this planet," Marty started. "This was to be my last stop before departing. Unfortunately, my lander was damaged during touch down and I am incapable of effecting repairs, I will have to wait until a rescue vehicle can be dispatched."

"I thought somethin' like that happened", Dougie piped up, "when I saw your ship thing tip over. That's why we brought this here pontoon trailer. I thought I could haul that thing," he said, pointing to the lander, "back to the mower shed and see if I could fix 'er up. How long's it gonna take for your boys to get here?"

"I estimate it would take 75% of one of your planet's solar rotations."

"Oh, sometime tomorrow," I chimed in, "That's not too bad."

"I think that means sometime next year," Maggie Jean corrected. She looked at Marty, "Am I right?"

"Yes, "

"Have you called for a tow yet?" Dougie asked. I could see that look on his face when he was thinking of a scheme.

"No, the truth is that I am somewhat embarrassed. You see, this is my first expedition and I did so want to accomplish my mission without mishap."

"I know what you mean," Dougie said, "First time I rebuilt an engine, I was scared to death to try an' start it for fear it'd blow up. Can we go take a look at what happened?"

"Yes."

We followed Marty around to the far side of the lander. There, the hull rested on the third crumpled leg, a couple of feet off the ground. Dougie crawled under the under the iridescent sphere to examine the damage more closely. After a minute or two, he wriggled back out and rejoined us.

"Jus' like I thought,' he said, with a 'I knew all the time' smile, "set right down in a ground hog hole. Happens more'n you would think. That is with tractors and such, not spaceships. Look, I got an idea. We already got the trailer here. Why don't we haul it back to the shed and see if I can fix it for Marty."

"Don't be silly." I chided. "Working on an old Chevy is one thing, but this is something altogether different. You can't possibly think you are equipped to work on a space ship."

"I don't know," said Maggie Jean, "let's hear what he's got to say."

"Thank you." Dougie paused, giving me the stink eye. "Look here, we can't let Marty here run around old man Mill's farm looking like a cow. An' what about that space ship? Sooner or later somebody's bound to see it, then all hell will break loose. The way I figure, the only chance Marty's got is to let us haul it back to the shed and let me try and fix it. I'll know by tomorrow if I can or not. If I can, Marty can blast off in a day or so, if not, we'll keep it hid in the shed and call the galactic Triple A – no harm done."

"What'll we do with Marty?" I asked.

"LuAnn is working tonight, I'll get her to let me have a key to one of the lodge rooms. Marty can stay there at least until Dougie figures out if he can fix the lander or not. If he can't fix it and a rescue ship has to be called, we'll set up a trailer in the campground."

"There you go!" Dougie chirped, clapping his hands together. "I'll get the trailer."

I held up both hands. "Hold on. Aren't you forgettin' something?"

Dougie furrowed his eyebrows. "What?"

"Don't you think we should see if Marty is on board with this plan of yours before we go snatching up spaceships that don't belong to us?"

"I agree, we shouldn't do anything unless Marty is OK with it," added Maggie Jean.

"Well?" said Dougie looking at Marty. "Are you in?"

Marty paused for a moment then said, "The strategy is ratified."

Dougie pursed his lips, then turned to me and asked in a whisper, "What does that mean?"

I clapped him on the shoulder. "It means OK."

Dougie backed the trailer right between the space ship's two good legs until it nestled up against the hull. As Marty used a remote control to retract the legs, the space ship tipped forward, eventually rolling onto the trailer far enough to free the damaged leg. Dougie chocked it in place, then covered it with a large tarp. The stars had come out by the time we got back to the lodge. Maggie Jean got a key from LuAnn and took Marty to a room at the far end of the lodge, while Dougie and me took the space ship to the mowing shed.

The next day, Maggie Jean got one of the other marina attendants to take her shift so she could stay with Marty. I was scheduled to work until noon digging holes for the Buckhorn Volunteer Fire Department. They were in charge of the following day's fireworks extravaganza. Dougie was waiting at the shed when I showed up to get my digging tools. At lunchtime, Dougie and me went to Marty's room and knocked at the door. We expected Maggie Jean to open the door. Instead, a beautiful young woman poked her head through the opening.

"Oh, sorry, ah, we must'a got the wrong room," I stammered, checking the room number. "I coulda sworn it was this one."

"Howdy," said Dougie.

Just then, the door swung fully open and there stood Maggie Jean laughing her head off. "Well, come on in you two. Don't let all this fine air conditioning outside." She and the young woman who answered the door stepped back for us to enter.

Dougie and me bumped shoulders as we both tried to step through the doorway, which prompted more laughter from inside. Knowing Dougie, I stepped aside in hopes we could avoid a Three Stooges scene.

"I hope you had more success with the lander than you have had trying to get through the door," Maggie Jean teased.

"There ain't no way I can't get it fixed," said Dougie, eyes fixed on the young lady. "A little straightenin', a little bendin', a little weldin' an' Marty can blast off tomorrow."

"An' speakin' of that, who's this," I said, nodding toward the young lady, as I followed Dougie in, "an' where'd you do with Marty?" I studied the young woman as my eyes adjusted to the inside light. She could have been Maggie Jean's twin sister, except for the fact she had long raven hair, violet eyes and porcelain skin. She was dressed in Daisy Dukes and a Buckhorn State Resort Park t–shirt.

"I haven't done anything with Marty," Maggie Jean shot back. Then she made a grand flourish toward the young woman. "She did it all herself, with only a little technical assistance from me. Boys, this is Marty, or should I now say – Marty Jo." You could have knocked the two of us over with a feather. I don't know how long we stood there, gawking like a couple first timers in the belly dancer tent at the county fair. "Take a breath before you faint," Maggie Jean said, "and we'll explain it all."

"Well, yeah," I said. Dougie just kept looking at Marty Jo, who was beaming.

"It occurred to me that Marty Jo couldn't go around looking like a Dohi or a cow, or anything suspicious, specially if she was going to have to stay with us a while. Seemed like a no brainer for her just to take on a human appearance and pretend to be a guest at the lodge."

"Sounds like a good plan." I said.

"Well, in theory – yes, in practice – not so much. At first, we looked in some magazines and Marty Jo tried out a few looks. I soon found out when she did it from a photo, her front looked OK but her backside didn't change. Then there was the issue of looking slightly out of focus and shadows on the face in the photo stayed in place for Marty Jo's copy. We tried the TV, but she ended up glowing. I was just about at the end of my rope when I asked her how she did such a good job with the cow."

"Yeah," Dougie finally said, "that looked pretty real."

"Well it was then Marty Jo reminded me that the Dohi can make an exact copy of something if they go through this thing called merging."

"What's that?" I asked.

"I believe I explained that yesterday," Marty Jo said.

"Oh, yeah, right. I remember, but I think we need to go over it again for Dougie."

"Better let me handle this," Maggie Jean said. "This merging thing is kind of like getting scanned, except the Dohi don't do it with a machine, they do it with themselves."

"I don't follow," I said.

"Well, its kinda like a Dohi gives you a big hug."

"Go on."

"But you can't have any clothes on and neither can they. Then they just kind of melt through you and come out on the other side. Then presto! They become your carbon copy."

"I'd like to have seen that," Dougie said, eyes still focused on Marty Jo.

"Shut up Dougie, before I knock you into the middle of next week," I shouted. Then, I looked at Maggie Jean. "You mean to tell me the two of you were in here huggin' buck naked." I was devastated at the thought of it. "How could you do that, Maggie Jean? I thought you loved me."

"I do love you, and it's not at all what you think."

"What am I supposed to think? I come to find out you and this fella have been in here all morning running around naked, doing this merging stuff and I don't know what else."

"Sure don't look like a fella to me," quipped Dougie.

"First of all, according to Marty Jo," Maggie continued, "Dohis in their natural state are neither male or female, so they don't do the boy–girl thing, so to speak."

Dougie laughed, "That don't sound like much fun."

"Put a cork in it," I growled, "before I knock you into the middle of next week!"

"Both of you be quiet," Maggie chided, "and let me explain before you jump to anymore silly conclusions." She eyed us both with her sternest look. "OK. This merging thing is simply how they gather the biological information necessary to become an exact copy. I don't know how it felt to Marty Jo, but I can tell you that for me it felt like that time of the month, only all over my whole body. It was more like going to my GYN for an exam than anything else, and I don't think you'd be getting your hackles up over a visit to the doctor. Would you?"

"Not when you put it like that," I mumbled, feeling embarrassed.

"Next time, don't be so quick to judge without all the facts."

"So if Marty Jo is supposed to be an exact copy, how come she's got black hair?"

"After Marty Jo finished, she was just like me, right down to the last freckle. And after I checked, I can assure you she's a 'she' in every way. Then, it occurred to me that her looking just like me could create some confusion if people saw us together, seeing how I don't have a twin sister. I was explaining this to Marty Jo when she said that it was easy enough for her to change some things so as not to appear to be my twin. I thumbed through the magazine till I came upon that Elizabeth Taylor perfume ad. I asked Marty Jo if she could change her eye and hair color to match the lady in the photo. In no time at all, I was looking at Liz except with freckles. I decided the freckles had to go, so I told Marty Jo to make her face look like my derrière."

"What's a dairy air?" asked Dougie.

"It's French for 'you don't need to know'," I snorted.

Maggie Jean continued, "If you must know, it's the one place I don't have freckles. Anyway, it took two tries because the first time, I failed to explain I meant skin tone only."

"What d'ya do then?" asked Dougie.

"I went up to the gift shop and got Marty Jo some clothes. The rest of the time, we've been engaged in girl–talk."

We piled into Dougie's truck and drove into Buckhorn for lunch at Blue Mooney's Grille to see how folks reacted to the new and improved Marty Jo. She got some looks, but nothing out of the ordinary for an attractive young lady wearing Daisy Dukes. It's a sure bet, whether you're in the Hazard Walmart or Blue Mooney's, you will run into dozen or so people you know. That day was no exception. Maggie Jean nonchalantly introduced Marty Jo as her new friend from somewhere up North. No one so much as raised an eyebrow. We left satisfied that Marty Jo could pass muster.

We piled back in the truck and Maggie Jean instructed Dougie to swing by her house so she could pick up some clothes for Marty Jo. When we go there, she told us to stay put while she and Marty Jo disappeared through the front door. About 15 minutes passed before they appeared with a couple of suitcases. I tossed the suitcases in the bed, wondering what could possibly weigh so much. From there, we drove straight back to the park. Upon arriving, Maggie Jean herded me and Dougie to the shed to finish up on repairs to the lander, while she and Marty Jo set out to change into some bikinis and head to the swimming pool for some sun and girl–talk.

I didn't do much more than hand tools to Dougie as he worked away on the lander. Along about 5 o'clock, he finished touching up the fresh welds with some John Deere green paint and pronounced the job completed. "Of course we can't test it until we get it out of the shed," he said.

I put the paint back in the locker. "There's room enough behind the shed to set it up. No one'll see it. We can bring Marty Jo over later tonight to check it out. If everything is OK, she can blast off."

"Well, I guess," Dougie said wistfully.

"What's the matter?"

"Well, it was kinda fun hanging around today. Guess I didn't think she'd be leaving so soon."

"Maybe the lander leg won't work."

"Naw, it'll work."

"Maybe we could unwork it a little," I suggested. "You know, kinda put things off another day or two."

"What, an' ruin my reputation? No way." Dougie said indignantly. He drew in a deep breath. "'Sides, wouldn't be fair to hold her up just on account of me."

"What're we gonna do then, chief? It's up to you."

"We'll test it out tonight."

***

After we got cleaned up, Dougie and me went over to the lodge to pick up Maggie Jean and Marty Jo. We explained the plan to them and we all decided to go get some supper before heading back up to the shed. The Starlight was crowded as usual. We sat outside and talked on one of the long pews that had been salvaged from some old church. Marty Jo looked completely comfortable and natural in Maggie Jean's pale blue sundress. No one would take her for anything other than an attractive young woman spending a summer evening with her friends. Dougie, for his part, was uncharacteristically quiet.

We ate, then Dougie suggested we head over to the Milky Way Dairy Bar for some ice cream. After Maggie Jean explained that ice cream came from cow's milk, Marty Jo was very anxious to try some owing to the fact she had recently been a cow herself. We sat in the truck and ate our cones while the sun drifted toward the treetops.

Dougie popped the last of his cone into his mouth and said, "Think I'll get me an Ale 8 One. Anybody else in the mood? I'm treatin'."

"Not for me," I said, "but thanks all the same."

"Me neither," added Maggie Jean.

"What is a late one?" asked Marty Jo.

"Oh it's a local drink," answered Dougie. "ginger ale. You want me to get you a bottle?"

"May I sample of your beverage?"

"Sure, if that's what you'd prefer."

Marty Jo smiled, "That will suffice."

"Well, OK then. Be back in a jiffy."

Dougie hopped out of the truck and trotted up to the counter and placed his order. The attendant handed over a green bottle which Dougie rolled across a stack of napkin–like papers neatly covering its slippery surface. He use the opener beside the window to pop off the cap. On the way back he took a big swallow. He climbed back in the truck then smacked his forehead with his free hand and said to Marty Jo, "Golly, I'm sorry. Guess I'm not too used to sharin'. I took a swig before offerin' it to you. Wait here, I'll go get another."

"No need to expend resources on redundant supplies," Marty Jo said, extending a hand for the bottle.

"I think that means 'don't bother'," Dougie smiled. "I'm startin' to understand." He handed the bottle to Marty Jo who took a drink. He waited a moment then asked, "What d'ya think?"

"Unbelievable," came Marty Jo's reply. She sat very still for a moment before turning a bright fuchsia. We barely had time for a collective gasp before she flickered twice and returned to her pre–soda complexion.

"Freefallin' hell," cried Dougie. "D'yall see that? "

"Dougie, we were right here in the back seat." I said. "Of course we saw it."

"Marty Jo are you alright?" Maggie asked, putting her hand on Marty Jo's shoulder.

"Yes, but I would like to return to the lodge," Marty Jo replied. She took a deep breath and let it out slowly.

"What've I done?" Dougie bleated, "I'm sorry – are you sure you're OK – I didn't know you were allergic to that stuff or else I never would have given it to you –you got to believe me – I'll take you to the hospital if you want – we can go right now – you OK? – I'll never touch a soft drink again – you're not going to hate me for this are ya?"

"The preferable course of action is to return to the lodge."

"If you say so," Dougie said, as he started the engine.

It was a quiet ride back to the lodge. When we arrived, Dougie was still visibly shaken up, while Marty Jo seemed none the worse for wear. Maggie Jean took her back to the room while Dougie and I headed to where the golf carts were kept. We parked the truck and took a cart the rest of the way to the mowing shed. It was Dougie's idea. He figured the cart, being electric and all, would be a lot less likely to draw attention while we moved the trailer behind the mowing shed. We maneuvered the trailer behind the shed so we could roll the lander off in the best spot. Its shimmering glow peeking out from underneath the tarp provided just enough light for us to work.

"Should we go get Marty Jo to check it out?" I asked.

"Naw," said Dougie softly, "I don't think she's champin' at the bit to see me 'long about now."

"Come on now," I said, "she don't strike me as the one to hold a grudge."

"Mebbe not, but I'd jus' as soon leave things alone tonight."

"Your decision. What about testin' the lander?"

"I got the remote thing. All's we need to do is roll that lander over till the legs is lined up and see if they will come out right so it's settin' up properly. Nothin' to it."

Dougie and me wrestled the lander around for close to an hour until Dougie was satisfied that we had all the openings for the legs 'equal distant' from the ground, he activated the remote. The lander emitted a soft whirring noise as the legs emerged and slowly raised the lander about 5 feet in the air.

"See, I told ya' nothin' to it," Dougie said, wiping his forehead.

"What about the engines? We gonna test them?" I asked.

"Use your head," Dougie said rapping his knuckles on the back of my head. "You don't want to chance blasting that thing off without Marty Jo in it, do ya'?"

"Well, no. Should we go get her now?"

"Them engines weren't busted – only that one landin' leg. We ain't doin' nothing until tomorrow night like we planned. Marty

Jo can fire it up while the fireworks is goin' off and no one will be the wiser." He sucked in a deep breath. "I'm heading out, I've had enough for one day."

***

The next day was the 4th of July. It was getting on in the evening and we hadn't seen hide nor hair of Dougie all day. The picnic was going full blast. Maggie Jean had told every one who had rented a boat they had to be back by 6:00 pm. That was so we could enjoy some of the picnic and music before the fireworks display and of course, sending Marty Jo off. Maggie Jean, Marty Jo and me were waiting for the last boat when I heard the familiar rumble of Dougie's truck.

"There's Dougie," I said, pointing to the cloud of dust coming down the boat ramp. He pulled up easy and rolled the window down. "Too good to mingle with the riffraff?" I teased.

"Naw, I just wanted to let you know I was here. I'm gonna go check on things behind the shed and make sure everthin's OK."

"Don't you at least want a soda or something?" Maggie Jean asked, "It's awful hot."

"Naw."

"Suit yourself, then."

Marty Jo stepped forward and called out to Dougie. "Would you please provide conveyance to the lodge. I too have some matters to tend to."

Before Dougie could do anything, Maggie Jean said, "Of course you would, wouldn't you Dougie." The tone of her voice and the look in her eyes told Dougie he'd better, if he knew what was good for him. He sat sullenly while we walked Marty Jo over to the truck. She climbed in the passenger side. Before they left, Maggie Jean pecked on the passenger side window and waited as it rolled down. "When do you want us to pick you up?"

"No need, I will find you."

Maggie leaned her head in the window. "How about you?" she said to Dougie.

"I don't know – lots of things to do. Don't worry if you don't see me until it's time for the blast off. Remember, we're gonna do it right at the end when they shoot off all the big stuff."

"Suit yourself," Maggie Jean said. "We'll be under the big catalpa tree if you decide to join us. That goes for you too, Marty Jo."

"That's the one with the big cigar lookin' things on it," I added.

"Yes, species *Catalpa bignonioides,*" Marty Jo said. "The name derives from the Muscogee name for the tree, *kutuhlpa* meaning '*winged head'*. The bean–like seed pod is the origin of the alternative vernacular –"

"Sorry to interrupt, but I was makin' sure Dougie knew where we'd be."

"Can we leave before it gets dark?" Dougie barked.

"See you both in a little while," Maggie said, as the window rolled up. Dougie put the truck in gear and started to back it up the ramp. Maggie and I watched until the truck reached the top and disappeared down the road.

After the last boat putted up to the dock, Maggie Jean and me grabbed the picnic basket she had fixed and made our way to the picnic. The catalpa tree was perched on the far side of a large shallow swale filled with half of Perry County. They were all dancing and singing to the music coming from the bandstand on the other side. We laid out our blanket and settled in to enjoy some fried chicken and the joyful noise.

***

Neither Dougie or Marty Jo showed up. Maggie Jean and I enjoyed being by ourselves for a bit after the commotion of the previous two days. Dusk was descending and the Roswells sang their last song. The Chief of the Buckhorn VFD was introducing the County Judge which meant the fireworks were about to commence. I said to Maggie Jean, "Much as I would like to spend the rest of this fine evening alone with you on this blanket, if we don't head out now, we won't make it to the shed by the finale."

We packed up our stuff and set off for the shed. Fireworks started popping in the darkening sky behind our backs as we approached the shed. As soon as Dougie saw us, he started running toward us yelling, "Where y'all been?"

"Under the catalpa tree," I said, a little peeved. "Like we told you we'd be. Where have you been?"

"Where's Marty Jo?" Maggie Jean asked.

Dougie unused to running, took a moment to catch his breath. "She's around back taking care of last minute business. Come on, we ain't got much time," he said, tugging my arm.

"What's wrong, Dougie?" Maggie Jean asked.

"Nothin's wrong."

Maggie Jean looked Dougie in the eye. "You sure?"

"Sure, I'm sure."

Maggie Jean looked at me. "You go with Dougie, I'll go check on Marty Jo." She trotted off to the shed, leaving me with the still panting Dougie.

"What's that all about?" Dougie asked.

"Don't ask me, you're the one come running and shouting like the seat of your pants was on fire."

Dougie got a real serious look on his face. "I got something to tell you."

"I knew it! Wadda ya' done now?"

"I ain't done nothin' – well, I mean I have been doin' somethin' – but it was nothin' – I mean nothin' like what you're thinkin'."

"That alone is enough to make me think you've done somethin' I don't want really want to know about. So whadda ya' done?"

"It's like this – it wasn't the Ale 8 One that set her off," Dougie said breathlessly. "She said she got some of my DNA when she took a swig – and that flickerin' thing come over her because we was perfectly matched at the molarchetectrual level – an accordin' to Marty Jo, that don't happen too often – an' –" he stopped, jaw twitching like a large mouth bass.

"Go on."

"An' –"

"Dougie!"

"An'… an' that means I am the only one she can ever love."

"I hate to tell ya' Dougie boy, that's gonna make for an awful short romance."

"No, that's what I been tryin' to tell ya'. I love her too, an' I'm goin' with her."

22

"Whoa, big fella. You given any thought to what it might be like when she changes back?"

"That's jus' the thing, she don't want to change back. We even tried out the boy girl thing a little, an' she lit up like a Christmas tree. An' I might've changed a color or two myself. Besides, that space ship's got a jim–dandy owner's manual and Marty Jo can use a good mechanic. Here's the registration and keys to my truck," he said, holding out a slip of paper and a set of keys. "Consider it a wedding present."

"Thanks, but I ain't the one getting married."

"Don't matter. We don't need it where we're headed."

"If you're dead set on doin' this, we better get a move on, the fireworks are almost finished."

We found Maggie Jean and Marty Jo hugging and giggling when we turned the back corner of the shed. The tarp had been removed and the clearing was bathed in the soft iridescent glow of the sphere.

"You'll never believe what's happened," I said to Maggie Jean.

"Yes I will. Marty Jo filled me in while you two were dawdling around front."

"We weren't dawdling. Dougie was baring his soul – what little there is of it."

Marty Jo brought the ramp down as we said our goodbyes and exchanged hugs.

"Dougie," I asked, just as they started up the ramp, "what'll we tell folks? I mean about you?"

Dougie tugged at his beard for a moment then smiled. "Tell 'em the truth. Tell 'em I took off with that cute little gal from up North." He put his arm around Mary Jo, pulling her close as they walked up the ramp and through the shimmering opening. It closed behind them as the sphere began to hum. It got deeper and deeper as the legs retracted leaving it hovering above the ground. It gently rose, until it was floating just at the treetops, bathing them in a dreamy glow. When the fireworks reached their crescendo, the sphere shot straight up, joining the blazing display before disappearing from sight.

Maggie Jean threw her arms around me, hugging me tightly and giving me an unusually long and passionate kiss. I swear just before she closed her eyes, I saw a glimmer of fuchsia.

The End?

Your Blue-Read manuscript comes with additional material not appearing in the official text. Please continue reading on the next page for Typos and Outreads

----

Typos

......Our conversation was interrupted by the growl of Dougie's F650 hauling down the gravel boat ramp, kicking up a mighty dust storm. His custom horn blasted the UK fight song as he locked up his brakes and slid right into the lake......

Narrator: "What the hell?"

Author: "Dougie, you're supposed to stop before you hit the water. Alright, let's pull that truck out and try it again."

......"You might be right," Dougie said. At that moment, a soft whir emanated from the sphere as a ramp glided to the ground from an opening portal. Dougie dropped the cable, turning to look. "I told you it was aliens. I think we're about to meet the most advanced beings in the universe." We watched in silence until the ramp was fully extended and firmly resting on the ground. To our utter amazement, Liz Taylor walked out wearing Daisy Dukes......

Dougie: "That's way better than a cow!"

Author: "Marty Jo, you're supposed to be a cow."

Marty Jo: "Oh, I forgot. Sorry."

......"I got the remote thing. All's we need to do is roll that lander over till the legs is lined up and see if they will come out right so it's settin' up properly. Nothin' to it."......

Dougie and me wrestled the lander around for close to an hour until we accidently rolled it over the bank and it smashed to pieces on the rocks below.

Narrator: "Oops! Sorry boss."

Dougie: "You're gonna need a bigger roll of duct tape."

Author: "You two clean that mess up."

......We found Maggie Jean and Marty Jo hugging and giggling when we turned the back corner of the shed. The tarp had been removed and the clearing was bathed in the soft iridescent glow of the sphere.

"You'll never believe what's happened," I said to Maggie Jean.

"Yes I will. Marty Jo filled me in while you two were dawdling around front."

"We weren't dawdling. Dougie was baring his soul – what little there is of it."

Marty Jo searched frantically for the remote. "Sorry, I don't know where I put it. Has anybody seen the remote?"......

Narrator: "Marty Jo, we have to find the remote before the fireworks are done so you two can take off and we can finish the story."

Marty Jo: "Oh, I see. Sorry."

Narrator: 'Never mind, it'll be quicker if I just rewrite it."

Outreads

......"Little green men ain't green and ain't necessarily men."......

Narrator: "So what's this story about?"

Author: "I guess you could say it's a redneck alien romance."

Maggie Jean: "Won't the people in Kentucky be upset if you say 'redneck'?"

Author: "I suppose they could. How about I say 'down home'?

Maggie Jean: "I think that's much better."

......"Shut up Dougie, before I knock you into the middle of next week," I shouted. Then, I looked at Maggie Jean. "You mean to tell me the two of you were in here huggin' buck naked." I was devastated at the thought of it. "How could you do that, Maggie Jean? I thought you loved me."

"I do love you, and it's not at all what you think."

"What am I supposed to think? I come to find out –"......

Narrator: Hold on, how come my name is never mentioned? Maggie's got a name, Dougie's got a name, and Marty Jo has so many names, I can't remember them all. I'd like to know what my name is. Don't you think the readers would like to know?"

Author: "Well, I didn't think it was important to the storyline and that's why I chose not to give you a name. By the way, you didn't mention your name one time just now so it must not be too important to you either.

Narrator: "I didn't because you write everything!"

Author: OK. If you want to get technical about it. But if having a name is really that important, you can be Ashley like Ashley Wilkes in *Gone With The Wind.*"

Narrator: "Alright smart ass, I give up."

......"Well, there's LuAnn who works the front desk. She's real nice."

"Maggie Jean! Doesn't she have a kid in 3rd grade?"

"Of course not, he's not even in preschool."

"I don't think that's gonna work. There's got to be someone else," I pleaded.......

Dougie: "How old is she?"

Narrator: "Come on Dougie, it's Maggie's line next."

Author: "Dougie, you aren't in this passage."

Dougie: "I still want to know how old LuAnn is. I'm not into older women."

Author: "Dougie, What does it matter? You don't go out with her. Now, if you don't shut up, I swear I'm hitting the delete button and finding a new character."

Dougie: "OK, OK. I'll be quiet."

  ......"I asked Marty Jo if she could change her eye
  and hair color to match the lady in the photo. In no
  time at all, I was looking at Liz except with freckles.
  I decided the freckles had to go, so I told Marty Jo to
  make her face look like my derrière."

    "What's a dairy air?" asked Dougie......

Maggie Jean: "Say, I'm not gonna have to show my butt am I? I told you I don't do nudity."

Dougie: "What a shame, I'd like to see that."

Maggie Jean: "Shut up Dougie, it'll be a cold day in hell before you see any part of me where the sun don't shine."

Author: "Put a cork in it Dougie. Maggie, no, you won't have to show your butt. However, I can't be responsible for our readers' imaginations."

Marty Jo: "Young or old Liz?"

Author: "What?"

Marty Jo: "Is it the young Liz or the old Liz in the ad? I don't want to look like the old Liz."

Author: "It's only for the eye and hair color, so her age doesn't matter."

Marty Jo: "Oh, I see. sorry."

  ......Maggie Jean threw her arms around me,
  hugging me tightly and giving me an unusually long
  and passionate kiss. I swear just before she closed her
  eyes, I saw a glimmer of fuchsia......

Maggie Jean: "What does that mean?"

Author: "That means it's the end of the story. Technically, since it's over 8,000 words, it can be classified as a novelette."

Narrator: "I think she means what is the implication of 'a glimmer of fuchsia?'"

Author: "I don't have to spell everything out in minute detail for the reader, do I? As the author, I like to leave somethings to the readers' imaginations."

Maggie Jean: "Yeah, but what does it mean for you?"

Author: "Well, perhaps this: things may not always be what they seem, but sometimes, they can be what you dream."

THE SCROLL AND THE SILVER KAZOO[2]

I was there.

Along with my fellow writers that is, for WACKY day—the annual reading day sponsored by the Writers Alliance of Central KY. We hold it every April in a field in front of a little country store, located at the end of a dusty gravel road deep in the rolling hills of our namesake state. The sun was shining somewhere up above the clouds of the overcast sky. A lady from a little place with a compound name whose claim to fame was that it was near some other place had been reading for twenty minutes. The temperature was typical—somewhere between heatstroke and frostbite—which meant you started with a winter coat in the morning and ended up in a tee shirt by 4 in the afternoon. She was about 1/3 of the way through a fistfull of loose bound manuscript—something about the crops grown in Kentucky during the War of 1812 and their impact on 20th Century geopolitics Upon finishing a page, she would pause, scanning it to make sure she had left nothing out, then carefully move it to the bottom of the stack. She was in that process, when one of those mild spring zephyrs we had grown so accustomed to rolled over the grass toward the podium. It ripped the manuscript from her hand, sending the loose pages flying down the gravel road. The reading tent, meant to shelter the readers from the intense shade of the clouds overhead, rose up from its foundations, looking much like Dorothy's house in the tornado. It tumbled almost all the way over to the creek before landing in the thick vegetation along the banks.

The dogs and some of us from the audience chased the wily sheets of paper as they danced along the ground. I don't know about anyone else, but I had in mind to stealthily stash as many in my pocket as I could in the event the lady decided to return to the mic.

---

[2] "The Scroll And The Silver Kazoo" appeared in the print anthology *Down The Rabbit Hole* published by the Writer's Coop 10/1/2018.

Meanwhile, Chad our Emcee, announced that while the papers were being retrieved, it might be a good time to open the mic up to anyone (else?) who wanted to read.

But the last syllable of the invite was drowned out leaving his lips. High above us, the scrim of cloud brightened, and a sound— something between a whoosh and a roar, but not entirely unlike a howl— filled the sultry air. I turned, hands full of soon-to-be-stashed pages. The crowd gave a collective gasp as the clouds split open, and a blinding shaft of sunlight broke. Some sort of craft, its patchwork metallic skin reflecting a rainbow of colors, slid down the beaming light, wheezing and churning all the way. It came to rest on the dewy lawn, standing like some fantastic galactic rat rod, encrusted with antennae and dishes and protuberances of all manner.

Like a crowd of extras from a Steven Spielberg movie, we all stood motionless, mouths agape, as a figure, covered from head to toe in purple, emerged from the craft. It had one eye situated in the center of its forehead, directly below a white horn that curlicued like a corkscrew. Bright pink gills lined its stubby neck. While it glided just above the wet grass toward Chad and the podium, the spindly hands on each of its six arms gave us the Queen Elizabeth parade wave.

To Chad's credit, he held his ground—surely the sign of a great emcee. Those of us gathering the papers gave up the chase and made it back to our seats just as the alien reached the podium. Ever the trooper, Chad asked the alien if it had anything to share. It responded in a peculiar voice that sounded like Alvin the Chipmunk burping while throat singing a Tibetan chant. Chad adjusted the mic and stepped back. The alien produced a scroll from a pocket and unfurled it with two of its six hands. By now the dogs, who had been steadily making their way toward the alien, were nosing our newfound friend's grey flipper feet tails wagging. Apparently, one of the good things about having six arms is that you can pet three dogs while holding a scroll and still have one hand with which to gesture in dramatic fashion.

Our purple reader began, voice now a deep baritone. We couldn't understand the language, nonetheless, we were enthralled. Its voice moved from a rumbling bass to a quivering tenor in a single phrase. Its free hand made sweeping gestures, while its eye looked into our souls. Then to our utter astonishment, the alien reached into another pocket and produced what looked like a silver kazoo, which it held to one of its gills. While continuing to read, the alien produced a mellifluous sound which Could have only been surpassed by the sweet warble of Gabriel's trumpet. It floated out over the fields and rolled up the hillsides. We basked in its beauty, swayed in its rhythm. It was so grand, so wondrous, the birds flew down from the treetops, alighting in silent reverence on the podium.

The Alien read and played on until it reached the end of the scroll and the last sweet note from the silver kazoo echoed across the fields. Then there was silence, utter silence. Silence from the birds, silence from the dogs, silence from the crickets, silence from us. A silence of wonder, a silence of respect. We let the moment linger in our collective consciousness as long as we could before erupting in applause and shouts and whistles. The birds flew off like doves released at the Olympics. The dogs barked in joy.

Our alien friend waved its Queen Elizabeth parade wave and floated back to the galactic rat rod. As soon as its door closed, the contraption whirred and hummed, rising back up through the hole in the clouds, then whooshed off, clouds snapping shut behind it. We rose to our feet, pumping our fists, slapping our thighs and "whoo hooing" at the top of our lungs. We hadn't comprehended a single word, but we celebrated all the same. Because we understood. We understood the courage it took, to travel down unfamiliar roads and stand before strangers. We understood the courage it took to speak our words and play our music. We understood the courage it took to believe in ourselves. We understood.

THE STARSHINE SPECIAL

Bingo watched the glow of the embers under the cooking pot. He wondered what his grandfather would say.

"Don't get mixed up in moonshine, ain't no good come of it," the old man had said, squeezing the keys to his '40 Ford moonshine tanker into his grandson's hand. "I come too close to jail or even worse, the graveyard, too many times. It may look like easy money but ain't nothin' easy 'bout it. Anyway, mebbe you can fix it up and make it into that racer you been dreamin' about. A lot of boys would haul shine during the week and race on Saturday."

He was just about to wake his snoring companion when Bingo heard a loud whoosh above the treetops, followed by the sound of cracking branches trailing away down the holler. Leaves and shattered branches sifted down through the trees. He jumped to his feet, eyes looking upward, for a clue as to the source of such a sudden and unusual sound. It was a clear night. The moon floated high in a black sky dotted by stars. The disturbance brought the usual nighttime forest noise to a dead silence. That is, except for his companion's snoring.

"Git up Paintball," Bingo said, poking his buddy's butt with his foot. I swear, you could sleep through a cyclone!"

"What's up?" came a groggy voice from the sleeping bag at his feet.

"It ain't what's up, it's what's down or least what's come down outta the sky. Don't tell me you didn't hear all that ruckus."

"Naw, all I hear is your big fat mouth. I thought you said we was supposed to be quiet and not go stompin' round and yellin' at the top of our lungs. Wasn't it you said that the sheriff might be out on the lookout for stills?" Paintball complained, pulling the sleeping bag back from his face.

"I 'spect this poor excuse for a still would be the last thing on his mind about right now if he was anywhere abouts and heard what I just heard."

"What's that?" asked Paintball.

"What I'm tryin' to tell you, knucklehead. Somethin' just came whooshin' over top of us and crashed down in the holler!"

"What was it?"

"Well how am I supposed to know that?" growled Bingo.

"You were the one on lookout weren't you? Apparently, you ain't much of a lookout if some big ol' thing come whooshin' by and crashed and you didn't see nothin!"

"Git up, Paintball, we ain't got time to argue 'bout this. Was probably a plane or somethin' like that. There could be people hurt down there. We might be the only ones for miles around that could help 'em out." Just then, they heard a loud crack from above. Both men looked up to see a large branch tumbling down from the treetops. It collided with other branches, bumping and flipping until it landed on top of their still, sending a swirl of angry sparks into the air. Paintball, still nestled in his sleeping bag, rolled to the edge of the clearing in an effort to get clear. Bingo grabbed the mason jar under the condenser tap in an effort to rescue the meager output of their night's distilling. Boiling mash poured out of the ruptured cooking pot, drowning the embers with a snake-like hiss.

Paintball wiggled out of his sleeping bag, rubbing the sleep out of his eyes. "How'n the world d'ya let that happen?" he asked, pointing to the demolished still.

"What d'ya mean how'd I let that happen? You think I got any control of things fallin' outta the sky, you idjut?"

"Well whadda we do now?" asked Paintball.

Bingo eyed the remains of their ill-fated still under the branch. "Nothin' with this mess. I guess we better git down to where whatever it was that did this crashed." He opened the cooler they had brought and gently placed the mason jar inside. "You ready?"

Paintball jammed his feet into his sneakers. "I'm always ready. Which way?"

Bingo switched on his flashlight. "Bring your flashlight. Sounded like it went this way," he said, pointing off to his right. They pushed through the woods and undergrowth, moving steadily down into the holler. They hadn't gone far when the forest floor began to fill with broken branches. Soon, splintered treetops were plainly visible in the moonlight. The farther they went, the shorter the remnants of sheared tree trunks got until they came upon a crumpled mass of metal on the forest floor. Haze drifted up from the leaves and pine needles under the wreckage.

"Looks jus' like the still, 'cept a little bigger," whispered Paintball.

"Not much. Ain't got no still pot or thump keg or no wormbox that I can see. Looks more like someone flipped a minivan," said Bingo, shining the beam of his flashlight all around. "You see anythin?"

"Well, yeah, I see that hunk 'a junk," Paintball said, shining his flashlight at the wreckage.

"Hell, that's obvious. I mean do you see anything else?"

"Like?"

"Like survivors, bodies, bits and pieces, knucklehead," Bingo hissed.

"Oh. Well that thing don't look big enough to have more'n one or two inside," Paintball continued. The two approached the wreckage, picking their way through the debris. "Damn," shouted Paintball, as his foot came down awkwardly on a limb, flinging him headlong to the ground. His flashlight twirled in the air, tracing a wild light spiral against the dark forest.

"You OK?" asked Bingo.

"Bingooooooo," Paintball's shaky voice replied from the forest floor.

"What?" said Bingo, shining the flashlight on the ground, tracing Paintball's body from his feet to his head.

"Bingoooooo, I think I found somepin."

"Where?"

Paintball's hand appeared in the light, finger pointing ahead to where his flashlight had landed, illuminating a pair of feet sheathed in silvery boots. "Hot Damn!" exclaimed Bingo. "Would you look at that. Told ya there might be survivors. Let me help you up, twinkle toes," he said, grabbing Paintball's collar and pulling him to his knees. Then, he shined his flashlight in the direction of the feet. Its beam fell on a slight figure, dressed in a shiny red jumpsuit, head topped with a silver skull cap. Two bulbous eyes, separated by a narrow hooked nose, peered at them from within.

"Hell, that must be the pilot," said Paintball.

"No doubt about it," agreed Bingo.

"I kaa aeui kvaod Emsrekr," the pilot said.

"What the hell kind of language is that?" asked Paintball.

"Don't know, I ain't heard nothin like that ever," said Bingo.

"He must be a Ruski! Look at that red suit and all that. I knew we should 'a brought a shotgun with us. What ya think? Is he one of them cosmicnauts? Maybe he's a spy."

The pilot cleared his voice then said, "I apologize for using my native tongue. Given the circumstances, you can see how I might forget to use your language. I said, 'I see you speak English.'"

"Well, that shows how much you know," growled Paintball. "We don't speak English, we speak American. No wonder y'all lost the cold war!"

"I don't think he's Russian," said Bingo. "He ain't hardly bigger than a jockey and his skin looks just a bit bluish. And Russians are big fellers and I don't think they's blue."

"Mebbe he's a Blue Fugate from down in Hazard," ventured Paintball.

"Naw, ain't been no Blue Fugates for years. No, I don't think he's from around this neck of the woods."

The pilot held up a hand. "Gentlemen, if you will, I can explain. My name is Gezmusraoream… "

"Giz-what?" asked Paintball, turning toward Bingo. "Sure sounds like a Ruski name to me."

"Gezmusraoream. If you will please let me explain, I can clear all this up," the pilot pleaded.

"Pipe down," Bingo said, putting his hand on Paintball's shoulder in an effort to settle him. "Let Gizmo here have his say before we go jumpin' to collusions." He looked at the pilot. "I don't think we can handle that name of yours. Is it OK if we just call you Gizmo?"

"By all means. Now to continue. My planet of origin is Kavrar which is about 490 of your light year units from this planet. . ." continued Gizmo.

"So, how far is that?" asked Paintball.

"It's a helluva long way. Now hush up and let him finish," said Bingo.

Gizmo continued, "Our star, Raddvork, is what your scientists would call a Red Dwarf, not at all like your yellow star. I was sent here because our scientists believed your planet to be within the circumstellar habitable zone." He paused, looking at Paintball, "Meaning it would have sufficient atmospheric pressure and liquid water to support life. It seems they were right. My mission is to make observations and report back."

"Sounds like a lot of bullcrap to me!" Paintball growled. "You mean to tell me that you flew a spaceship all the way here from that Kevlar planet and then you couldn't keep it out of the damn trees? I ain't buyin' it. I still think you're a spy up to no good."

"We had no way of knowing about all the debris orbiting this planet. Very messy. How you keep your satellites up I will never know. As I was entering orbit, something hit my ship and it was all I could do to make a landing."

"If you call that a landing," Paintball chortled, pointing to the wreckage behind Gizmo, "Then I sure would hate to see what you call a crash. I don't think you are headed anywhere, much less back home, in that."

Gizmo sighed, "Point well taken, Mister … ah… I am afraid I did not catch your names."

Bingo smiled. "I'm Bingo and this here is Paintball." Gizmo stared at them but didn't say a word. "I know Paintball is a kinda strange name. He got it from the time he got caught by Ellie Compton's daddy, sneakin out of her bedroom window one night. Now, his real name is Hector Gooch. Anyway, Ol' man Compton let loose on him with a paintball gun, peltin' him all over, including a couple of times in the head. If you've ever been hit by a paint ball, you knows it hurts like hell and could easily be mistook for a gunshot. When Hector, here," said Bingo patting Paintball on the head, "rubbed his head and felt that wet paint, he thought it was blood and jumped in his truck and sped over to the hospital. When he got there, he busted into the 'mergency room screamin' bloody murder. The nurses had a good laugh when they seen him come in all covered in green paint. Didn't take long for that story to get around town and he's been Paintball ever since."

"Well as long as we're relatin' information about names and such," Paintball snipped, "they call Bingo, 'Bingo', because his Memaw…"

"Memaw?" Gizmo interrupted, "I am unfamiliar with the noun Memaw."

"Grandmother," Paintball continued. "Anyway, she used to take him to the Bingo hall – that's where they play Bingo, that's a game where they have all these numbers in a little cage. . ."

"We ain't got all night," groused Bingo, "come on, lets git goin."

"Whoa, whoa, whoa, we had time for you to tell all how I got my nickname. Now, it's your turn. What goes around, comes around. Anyway, to git back to what I was sayin, when he was a toddler, his Memaw would take him to the Bingo hall where he'd run up and down the aisles saying 'Bingo, Bingo, Bingo.' And he's been Bingo Claunch ever since.

"Are you done flappin your gums?" asked Bingo.

"Lemme see," said Paintball, tugging the scraggly beard at the tip of his chin. Bingo glared at him. "Yeah, I guess that's all. But, as far as I'm concerned the jury is still out on him bein' a spy."

Bingo turned to Gizmo. "You ain't hurt or nothin, are ya?"

"No."

"Good, cause I don't rightly know what we'd a done if you was. We need to git you somewheres you can rest a bit before we figure out jus' what to do with you."

"We are leaving this place?" asked Gizmo.

"I figure we'll head back to our cookin' spot, git the truck and head back to the garage."

"You takin' him there? Ain't nobody supposed to know 'bout that," said Paintball.

"Well, it's either that or walk back to the garage. You can walk if you like, but me, I'm ridin," countered Bingo.

Before Paintball could respond, Gizmo held up his spindly arms, waving his spidery hands. "Wait!" he demanded. "Before I can go anywhere, I must find the Soekrix."

"The what?" asked Paintball.

"The Soekrix," said Gizmo.

"We can't be spendin' all night hunting a soap dish. We need to be getting' back before daylight," said Paintball.

Bingo gave Paintball a sharp jab in the ribs. "I'm not rightly sure what he is talkin' 'bout, but it ain't no soap dish, knucklehead. Let's find this thing he's so hot after and git outta here!" He looked at Gizmo. "What's this thing you're huntin' look like?"

"It is an orb."

"You mean like that ball thingy from *Phantasm?*" asked Paintball excitedly. "Cool."

"Shut up, Paintball," said Bingo, "and git lookin, I don't think he's huntin' some movie prop."

"Well, he's the one that said it!"

"I said, shut up and start lookin!"

"OK, don't git your panties in a knot. I'll look around here and you go look over behind the ship-thing."

They had searched quite a while when Bingo called out, "Hey, I think I found it. Over here." Paintball and Gizmo tromped through the debris to the edge of the crash site where Bingo was standing. His flashlight beam reflected off a shimmering blob, free floating, about 4 feet in the air. Its undulating surface iridesced with the colors of the spectrum. It was constantly changing its appearance. One moment it looked like a bumpy sycamore seedpod, then it quickly morphed onto a shiny cue ball. Gizmo stepped forward. The quivering orb elongated into a thin silver rod, stretching out in his direction, then returned to its spherical shape above his outstretched hand. With his free hand, he pulled open a large side pocket in his jump suit. Immediately, the sphere poured out from his open hand into the pocket. He closed the pocket and said nonchalantly, "Ready."

"D'ya ever see the like?" gasped Paintball.

"Never," replied Bingo.

"I'm startin' to come around to thinkin' he really is from Kevlar."

Bingo pulled off his ball cap, scratching his balding head. "Gizmo," he asked, "what is that thing?"

"The Soekrix is like a liquid computer, but infinitely more complex and powerful. Among its many useful purposes is the ability to make interstellar travel possible. The Soekrix has determined my ship is damaged beyond repair."

"I could 'a told you that after one look," said Paintball.

The wreckage began to vibrate and crackle. Arcing electricity crawled over the remains of the spacecraft. "The Soekrix has initiated automatic disintegration," Gizmo said. "We should leave."

"Come on, then. Let's get movin," said Bingo. "It's been one long night and there's a lot left to do before we git home."

They retraced their steps to the remains of their still with Gizmo in tow, while the hiss and pop of disintegration faded behind them. They arrived at the distilling camp to find their smashed equipment was now cool, thanks to the spilled mash, which had flooded the furnace and doused the fire. "Come on Paintball, we better not leave this stuff for someone to find. Since we ain't got no automatic disintegratin' equipment like somebody we know, we'll have to toss it in the back of the truck." He looked at Gizmo. "You ain't the only one that had something get all busted up tonight. One of them big ol' branches you knocked off while you was landin' tore the hell our of our brand new still. We had jus' barely got a pint of shine before it went bust."

"Shine?"

"Shine, you know, shine like in moonshine," Paintball said, shaking his head. "It was gonna be the best shine since Bingo's granddaddy, 'Big Haul' Claunch, was makin' and haulin' shine. They called him 'Big Haul' cause he made his runs in a '40 Ford Coupe fitted out with a flathead V8 and a huge tank in the trunk. He could haul over 100 gallons of shine like he was drivin' uptown for a soda."

"Yeah, we was makin' some shine to sell," Bingo began to explain in a tired voice. "Then we was gonna use the money to finish our race car, the 'Moonshine Special'. Then we was gonna make it big on the race circuit." He sighed. "But that's gonna have to wait now. We put everythin' we had into that still and now it's about as useless as your spaceship." He pointed to the cooler. "Got what little we could save in here." He grabbed the mason jar and held it out to Gizmo. "Check it out."

Gizmo took the jar and held it in front of the lantern Paintball had just lit.

"Hey, be careful," shouted Paintball backing away, "That stuff will blow sky high if you get it too close to fire." He watched Gizmo pull the jar under his long nose, take a deep breath and smile. "Told you it's the best stuff around."

Before Paintball could say anything else, Gizmo poured some of the clear liquid into his pocket. "The Soekrix will conduct a molecular analysis," he said.

"I don't care if it's gonna sing karaoke. If all you are gonna do is pour it in your pocket, hand it over," winced Paintball.

The Soekrix emerged from Gizmo's pocket as he held the jar out to Paintball. It flew around the smashed still, then stopped in front of Gizmo, flattening into a rectangle about the size of a cafeteria tray. It floated there for a moment before melting back into its resting place. "Yes, it is as you say, however the Soekrix has determined that its potency could be increased. Of course, we will have to make some adjustments to your production equipment and processes."

"If you think you and that flying hitch ball can make better shine than we can, you got another thing comin," barked Paintball, balling up his fist, "and it's called a knuckle sandwich."

"Chill out," Bingo said, stepping between the two. "I don't think he meant any harm. After what I've seen this night, might be he could do what he claims. But I can tell you this, I'm way too tired to referee a fight tonight. Besides, who knows, he might have a ray gun or some other crazy thing in his pocket. So, if it's alright with you, we'll take him back with us and sort it out in the mornin'."

"Where we gonna put him?" asked Paintball.

"He can sleep on the cot in the back room of the garage. Now let's load up the truck."

***

Early the next morning, Bingo swung by Paintball's trailer, laying on the horn until he poked his head out of the door. "Come on," Bingo yelled, "I got you a cup of coffee and a couple 'a doughnuts from the Grub Mart. Put your stuff on and let's git goin. I don't want to leave our guest alone for too long." The head disappeared back into the trailer. A couple of minutes later, Paintball stumbled out of the door, tucking his shirttail into his jeans.

"Why?" he asked, climbing into the cab and grabbing the coffee from Bingo.

"Why what?"

"Why don't you want to leave our guest alone for too long?"

"Hell, I don't know," said Bingo, "mebbe it's cause we don't want him to go wanderin' around where someone might see 'im."

"Did ya put a shot of French Vanilla and sprinkle some cinnamon in my coffee?"

"No, since when do you like that crap?"

"I don't. I jus' didn't want to take a sip if you had. Is this my doughnut?" he said, reaching for the Grub Mart bag on the seat between them.

"Be careful, there's another cup of coffee and a long john I picked up for Gizmo 'sides your doughnuts in there. Don't spill nothin."

"What if I want a long john?" asked Paintball

"I didn't think you liked long johns."

"I don't."

"Then why're you whinin about it?"

"A fella likes to be asked," chuckled Paintball.

"Eat your doughnut, drink your coffee, and don't say another word till we get there," ordered Bingo, gunning the engine and pulling onto the pavement. Paintball happily munched on his doughnut, running the search feature on the radio until they reached the garage.

43

"Kinda sounds like that Gizmo feller 'fore he started speakin' American," mumbled Paintball through a mouthful of doughnut. Bingo parked the truck under the old oval Standard Oil sign, hanging from a rusty bracket. Except for the red flame protruding from the top, it had been painted over with: **Bingo's Garage and Speed Shop**. Bingo grabbed the Grub Mart bag and scrambled out of the truck. Paintball swigged the last of his coffee, set the cup on the dash and followed. Bingo had already gone inside the office by the time Paintball reached the door. He flipped the lights on just as Bingo came rushing through the door at the back of the cluttered office. "See I told you," Bingo huffed, "he ain't there! He must'a left."

"D'ya check the crapper?'

"Yes."

"Wasn't the entrance door locked?" asked Paintball.

"Yes."

"Then he couldn't 'a got out that way."

"Mebbe he got out through the garage somehow, looked like the lights was on when we pulled up." Bingo rushed to the side door of the office, pulling it open and peering into the work bays that housed the garage portion of the enterprise. The grimy, cluttered garage had been transformed into a clean and organized shop, worthy of a Popular Mechanics centerfold. In the middle of the speed shop bay, Gizmo had lifted the hood of a tattered AMC Pacer. Paintball, having retrieved the Grub Mart bag from the office desk, squeezed by the motionless Bingo, saying, "Hey, brung you some coffee and a long john." As soon as he saw Gizmo, he hollered, "Hey git away from there! That ain't none of your bizness!"

"Steady," said Bingo, snapping out of his trance.

Gizmo let the tarp fall back in place. "Soekrix has optimized the work area to initiate field operations."

"What'd he say?" asked Paintball.

"We cleaned and organized the work area," Gizmo continued. "Where so indicated, we effected repair and refurbishment of tools for optimum utilization. In other words, we tidied up a bit and got everything ready to start working."

"Working on what?' asked Bingo.

"Reconfiguration and reconstruction of the still to produce the organic solution or shine, as you call it, with increased potency and, of course, construction a suitable replacement for my ship. Soekrix has determined that there are sufficient resources here to accomplish both."

"Well, la-de-da," scoffed Paintball. "We're so glad you find it all acceptable and such. The shop looked jus' fine before you and the ball hitch got out the scrubbin' bubbles. And we'll be the judge of whether or not you do anythin' around here."

"Wait a minute," Bingo interjected, "from what I see, we could learn a little from Gizmo here. Jus' look how he's set up the work benches and rerouted the 'lectric and air, not to mention how the tools's laid out. This is what a real speed shop should look like. And there's nothin' on the floor to trip over. I'd say he's done a right smart job here."

"Your Mom can tidy things all up, but can she set up a still or build a race car? We shouldn't let him loose on nothin' till we see he knows his stuff about mechanics."

"Fair enough. How 'bout we let him try fixin' that worthless piece of junk?" Bingo said, pointing to the dilapidated Pacer. "Neither one of us's been able to get it runnin' right. If he can fix that, I reckon he can fix 'bout anythin'."

"OK, but I wouldn't hold your breath. The motor's shot and the carburetor's wore out, not to mention everthin' else that ain't working. If he can get that thing runnin' right, I guess he can work on anything he wants." He looked at Gizmo, holding out the Grub Mart bag. "Here, you might want to eat a little somethin' before you get started. You're gonna be awhile."

Gizmo took the bag and opened it. He drew it under his long nose, drawing in a deep breath. He retrieved the long john with spindly fingers, holding it up to the light. He turned it, examining golden crust and dark brown icing. "440 earth nutritional energy units," he said, shoving the whole thing in his mouth. His cheeks quivered, followed by a noticeable lump descending down his thin neck. He licked his fingertips, then reached into the bag again lifting out the coffee cup. He pulled off the plastic lid and slid his finger into the brown liquid. "Ah, French vanilla with a hint of cinnamon. The vehicle referred to as AMC Pacer has been repaired and is ready for inspection." He drained the cup with a single gulp.

"You mean you already fixed it?" asked Bingo.

"Yes."

"We'll be the judge of that," said Paintball, walking over and jerking the Pacer's door open. He climbed in and turned the ignition key. Much to his surprise and chagrin, the engine roared to life. He revved it several times in a fruitless attempt to stall it out. He let it settle back to idle speed. Leaning his head out of the window he said, "The tranny was messed up too."

Gizmo nodded, "Yes the motive transfer device has been repaired."

"No way," countered Paintball, "You can't get parts for this tranny. We've been trying to find a substitute for two months. You may have got the motor runnin, but this heap ain't goin nowhere."

"See if it'll go in gear," said Bingo. Paintball pulled the gear selector to 'D' and the car lurched forward. He jammed his foot on the brake, scowling. Bingo reached over and hit the button to open the garage door. It began to roll up. "Take it out and see what it'll do."

"What if I git stranded out on the road?"

"Don't think you will," answered Bingo. Paintball glared at him for a moment, then hit the gas, shooting the Pacer out of the garage like a drag racer. He pulled onto the highway and wound it out. As the roar of the engine faded, Bingo turned to Gizmo, asking, "So what do you suggest we do next?"

"Reconfigure and reconstruct the distilling apparatus and commence production of shine."

"Works for me. I'll pull the truck around back. The Speed Shop's back there. We can work there in private, if you know what I mean. That's where we keeps our shine making stuff anyway. You can head out that door," said Bingo, pointing to the rear of the bays, "and I'll meet you there."

They had most of the remains of the still unloaded by the time they heard the roar of the Pacer approaching. The sound grew steadily louder, then fell silent. A few minutes later, Paintball poked his head in the door. "I figured you might be back here when I didn't see your truck out front. So you went ahead and made a decision?"

"I take it the Pacer ran OK," said Bingo.

"No, it didn't run OK. Hell, it run like a top! Drove all the way to Ruckville and back and didn't miss a beat. Let it all out on a half mile stretch and was still acceleratin when I had to hit the brakes to make the curve. Even the radio works."

"Then, I take it you'd be willing to agree Gizmo here is a right fair mechanic."

"Well, yeah," Paintball grumbled.

"And that we ought to give him a chance?" continued Bingo.

"Yeah."

"Ok," Bingo said, clapping his hands together, "now that's settled, since you've been out joy ridin' all mornin, Gizmo and me are gonna take a break while you finish unloadin' the truck. After that, you and me will take the Pacer back to Mrs. Bigler while Gizmo gets started on the still."

It was mid-morning before Bingo and Paintball returned from delivering the Pacer. While they were out, they stopped for supplies and food at the Allmart. Bingo pulled the truck into his usual spot under the old Standard sign. "You take the food and I'll git the other stuff out of the back," Bingo said, sliding out of the driver's seat. Paintball lifted the Grub Hub sack from between his legs and followed him. Once inside, Bingo said, "Put the food in the fridge while I put this stuff in the back room. After you done that, go fetch Gizmo."

"Anythin' else, your Highness?" asked Paintball.

"Take him some water, he might be thirsty."

After shoving the food into the refrigerator, Paintball grabbed a bottle of water and headed out back. He pulled aside the big sliding door, hand painted with large block letters saying 'Speed Shop'. There, he found Gizmo standing in the midst of a neatly stacked pile of empty corn sacks and some 55 gallon drums. To the side there was a large assortment of paraphernalia. Some things Paintball recognized, some things he had no idea about. "Ain't you been a busy bee since we been gone. Here, thought you might be a bit thirsty," he said, holding out the bottle of water.

Gizmo looked up from his work long enough to eye the bottle. "Thank you," he said, extending a hand and taking the bottle, which he promptly put in his pocket. He returned to his activity.

"Well, what've we got here?" Paintball asked. "I don't know if you're building a moonshine still or a nuclear reactor. Where'd you get all this stuff?"

Gizmo stood up. "Soekrix retrieved the necessary components from the spare equipment storage location. Some fabrication will be required."

"You mean you got all this outta the junk pile?" asked Paintball, tugging at his beard. "What's in the barrels?"

"I believe your term for it is mash. We will commence production of the organic liquid you call shine. Soekrix has determined that its potency will be enhanced approximately 100 fold."

He looked closer at the contraption. "Really! Do you even know what mash is, much less how to make it?"

"A cursory review of your primitive digitized data base revealed the basic information required to prepare the concoction.

Soekrix was able to analyze the organic compounds in the immediate vicinity and determined the necessary ingredients were stored in the hidden compartment at the rear of this building."

"You found our stash?" gasped Paintball.

"Yes, along with the containers necessary to prepare it."

"Sneaky bastard! Well, you ain't even got your mashed cooked and aged. That'll take a couple of weeks."

"Soekrix has genetically enhanced the biological agent used for the conversion of sugar to alcohol. The result is significantly enhanced molecular matrices of carbon, hydrogen and oxygen. . ."

"Whoa, whoa, whoa, talk in plain American," said Paintball.

"The mixture should be ready for conversion tomorrow afternoon."

"You ain't pulling my leg are you?" asked Paintball.

"I am unfamiliar with the concatenation 'pulling my leg'."

"Well, I ain't familiar with whatever the hell it is you said," Paintball shot back, glaring at Gizmo. "What I want to know is, are you are telling me the truth."

"I have calculated a 99.96% probability of success. Within that parameter I can say with confidence: yes, my statement is truthful."

"I better go git Bingo," said Paintball, "You stay here and don't go nowhere." He rushed to the door, shoving it so hard, it slammed open against the corrugated siding, emitting a loud 'whump'. He shot across the gravel drive that separated the two buildings in a couple of strides. Just as he reached the garage, the door flew open. Bingo popped out of the opening. "What was that? I was just comin' to see what was takin' you so long."

"You gotta come with me and see what Gizmo's been up to,' huffed Paintball. "You ain't gonna believe it."

"Believe what?"

"Well, he's done been in the junk pile and done found our stash room and, well, you jus' gotta see what all he's been up to."

"You ain't makin much sense. Lead the way," said Bingo, turning him around. Paintball headed back to the storage building, shaking his head. Once inside, Bingo steered Paintball to an old chair. "Now you sit here and be quiet while I go talk with Gizmo." Paintball nodded and slumped down. He watched as Bingo walked over to Gizmo. The two talked for several minutes before Bingo came back.

"Gizmo explained it all. He sure can work for a little fella, can't he," said Bingo. "I don't see what you was so confused about. Made sense to me. He's got it all worked out. So if you finished with your siesta, let's help him finish up." The Soekrix wrapped itself around the base of the barrels one by one, heating the water, before they added the corn. They let it all cook for a while, making sure to stir the mix every so often. It was almost dark by the time the Soekrix cooled the mash and they added the enhanced yeast.

"The conversion will take approximately ½ planetary rotation."

"So, how long is that?" asked Paintball.

"Till morning, knucklehead," said Bingo. "Let's get somethin' to eat." He started toward the door.

"Works for me," said Paintball. He looked at Gizmo. "You like pizza?"

"Does it taste like long john?"

"Yeah, about the opposite," called Bingo over his shoulder, "We'll bring you some long johns in the morning. Let's wash up while we wait for the pizza," he said, pulling his phone from his hip pocket. They quickly fell in behind him as he stepped outside. "Don't forget to close the door," he said, without looking back. Paintball shoved the door closed, just as the Soekrix darted out. It circled his head a couple of times like an angry bee before zipping out of reach as he tried to bat it down.

Bingo was standing out by his truck, ready to meet the pizza driver. He didn't want to answer any questions in the event the driver came to the door and caught sight of Gizmo. Paintball joined him. "I gave gizmo the clothes you picked up for him. He's tryin' 'em on. You think he's really got a chance of making shine with all that junk back there?"

"Hell, I don't know. Probably not. I just didn't want to say nothing in front of him. I mean I think he's well-meaning and all, but I don't think no spaceman, if that's what he really is, can make moonshine. It's just that after the still got all busted up, mebbe I was hoping against hope that somehow he could make shine and somehow we could still build the Moonshine Special."

Their conversation was cut short by the arrival of the Pizza Fest delivery car. Bingo paid the delivery man and gave him a ticket for a free carwash as a tip. "I'll take the grub and get Gizmo. You bring some chairs and meet us in the speed shop," Bingo said.

"Why do I have to get the chairs?" asked Paintball.

"Cause I got the grub."

Once Paintball arrived with the chairs, they arranged them around something covered with a dusty tarp that Bingo had put the pizza on. Paintball opened a pizza box and held it out to Gizmo. "This here's my favorite," he said, "anchovies and ghost peppers - on a whole wheat crust mind you. Got to eat healthy I always say."

Despite Bingo vigorously shaking his head 'NO', Gizmo took a fat wedge. Holding it up to the light, he examined the gooey accretion on the limp crust. "529 earth nutritional energy units," he said, before folding it in half, then sucking the whole thing into his mouth. Once again, his cheeks quivered. Once again, a lump worked its way down his neck. He followed that by turning up one of the 2 liter bottles of crème soda they had ordered with the pizza, draining it in a single gulp. He burped, "170 earth nutritional energy units," then reached for another slice of pizza.

"Whoa, big fella, ain't you ever heard about sharing?" exclaimed Paintball, drawing the box back from Gizmo's outstretched fingers. He handed him a different box. "Here, try a breadstick." Gizmo opened the box and eyed its contents. He pulled out one of the foot long rolls of baked pizza dough. "270 earth nutritional energy units." Tipping his head upright like a baby bird, he dropped it straight down into his waiting mouth. It disappeared as if it had been dropped in a well. After the breadsticks were exhausted, Gizmo looked at the pizza box again. "Man, that boy can eat," mused Paintball. He looked at Bingo. "Your turn."

Bingo offered his box to Gizmo. "Hope you don't mind, this don't contain no thermonuculer peppers or nothing weird like that – just mushrooms and pepperoni and we don't care about the calories." They continued eating in silence until the pizza was finished. He stood up. "This is what it was all about," he said. carefully rolling back the tarp from the race car chassis. This is why me and Paintball was even fooling with moonshine. We been dreaming 'bout building this car ever since we was kids. All we needed was a little luck and some money. . ."

"And an engine," interrupted Paintball.

"Making shine," continued Bingo, sitting down and leaning back in his chair, "was our ticket out. Sell it down in Hazard and use the money to finish up the Moonshine Special – that's what we was gonna call it - and take it on the circuit. I was gonna be the driver and Paintball was gonna the chief mechanic. We coulda done it too."

"Yeah, we coulda," echoed Paintball.

"You really think your contraption can make shine?" Bingo asked Gizmo.

"I have calculated a 99.96% probability of success."

"That's more of a chance than most folks around here got. I guess we can wait till tomorrow before we throw in the towel. Gizmo, there's something else I want to show you," he said. walking to the back corner of the Speed Shop to another dusty tarp covered vehicle. "Paintball, help me pull this back," he said. grabbing one corner of the tarp. As the rolled the tarp back, a chrome grill, followed by fenders, painted in black lacquer appeared. "This here is my

Granddaddy's '40 Ford Coupe that Paintball was telling you about. Purdy ain't it. I've kept it in tip top running condition all these years. He run a lot of shine in this old tanker. I bet it could still outrun anything the sheriff's got on the road today. Come take a look at this," he said, leading Gizmo around to the trunk. He reached under the fender and pulled a lever. The trunk lid popped open. That," he said, pointing inside, "is a stainless tank he took out of the milking house. Holds about a hundred gallons. Even full, this car will take you anywhere you want to go." He closed the trunk lid. "Alright, Paintball, let's put the tarp back and clean up our pizza boxes. Wouldn't want Gizmo to stay up all night cleanin'. Then, we better be goin' before we meet ourselves coming back," said Bingo.

"A common problem when traveling through wormholes," said Gizmo, "but, I doubt it would be a problem here. You will acquire more long johns for consumption?"

"He'll bring ya some, don't worry," assured Paintball.

"And more crème soda?"

"Sure, anything you want," said Bingo. "Sleep tight, Gizmo, see ya tomorrow."

***

The next morning, Bingo was surprised to see Paintball sitting on the concrete block steps in front of his trailer. He hopped up at the sight of Bingo's truck and scampered around to the passenger side, tugging the door open before the truck had a chance to come to a full stop. "Where you been?" he asked.

"Getting coffee and a couple 'a doughnuts from the Grub Mart. Like I do every day before I come here and honk my horn while you are still getting outta bed."

"What took ya so long?"

Bingo checked his watch. "It's 7:50 AM – the same time ever morning I get here. The only difference is this morning I didn't have to wake up all creation to get you outta bed."

"You get long johns?"

"Yes."

"You get some coffee with French Vanilla and cinnamon sprinkles?"

"What's this sudden interest in food about?" asked Bingo.

"Nothing, I just want to make sure Gizmo's happy, that's all. What are you dawdling for? You act like you could care less about whether or not that crazy thing of Gizmo's is gonna spit out some shine."

Bingo turned the volume down on the radio as he pulled onto the pavement. "Don't you think it's a little strange that Gizmo don't seem too concerned that his ship is kaput and he ain't got no way home?"

"Mebbe he phoned home."

"That's funny, knucklehead."

"Well, mebbe he sent out a distress signal before he crashed. Mebbe a rescue ship is on the way. Mebbe he figures the best way to make it till they get here is to make the locals happy so they don't raise a ruckus."

"Paintball," said Bingo, "Dammed if ever once in a while you come up with something that makes some sense."

"Glad to be of assistance."

"OK, don't spoil the moment, eat your doughnut, drink your coffee, and don't say another word till we get to the garage," said Bingo.

"If you need any more mysteries solved, just feel free to ask,." Paintball added, as he cranked up the volume on the radio and punched the search feature.

When they arrived, they found Gizmo siphoning the liquid from a barrel into a large gleaming container. It was connected to a number of other contrivances by a complicated network of tubing. A thick electrical cord ran along the floor, disappearing into the fuse panel. Bingo studied the setup. "Looks like they made some changes since yesterday,' he said.

"Don't look like no still I ever seen," said Paintball. "I guess that's the still pot he's filling, but that thing it's connected to ain't big enough to be a thump keg," he continued, tugging at his beard, "then he's got all them other thingamajigs that I ain't got no idea what they're for." He walked along the array of equipment until he reached the end. "This here must be the worm box, at least I hope that's what it is. "See," he said, pointing to a spout protruding from another gleaming canister over a large copper vat, "this must be the tap. If this is a still, they sure got a funny way to make shine on Kevlar."

"Kavrar," corrected Gizmo.

"OK, Caviar! Mr. Nitpicky."

Gizmo shot him a sidewise glance as he pulled the siphon hose from the container. The Soekrix flowed over the surfaces of the equipment, glowing like St. Elmo's fire, before returning to its spherical shape. He looked at Bingo. "Did you bring long johns?"

"Uh, yeah, but what about that?" he asked, pointing to the equipment which had begun to emit a soft hum.

"It will commence initial output by the time consumption of long johns is completed."

"OK, I can take a hint,' said Bingo, holding out a fat Grub Mart bag. "Got you half a dozen long johns and a couple of bottles of crème soda. If that ain't enough, you're outta luck. That's all the long johns they had."

Gizmo took the bag and quickly stuffed a long john in his mouth. It was followed by one after another, interrupted only by long gulps of crème soda, until the sack was empty.

"That boy must have a hollow leg!" exclaimed Paintball, as Gizmo downed the last long john. "Damn lucky for us he don't eat people."

While Gizmo had been finishing the long johns and draining the last drops of crème soda, a clear liquid had begun to flow from the spout, spilling into the waiting copper vat. Bingo and Paintball were so busy watching Gizmo eat, that they did not notice until he pointed it out. "Hot damn!" cried Paintball. "Do you think he's really made some shine?"

"Well, there's only one way to find out, let's have a taste," responded Bingo, walking down to the vat. He was just about to stick a finger in the liquid when Gizmo grabbed his arm. "What?" he asked.

"Output is not suitable for consumption in this state," Gizmo said. The Soekrix fluttered under the stream like a bird in a puddle, then flattened out in front of Gizmo. "The Soekrix has calculated potency increased by a factor of 99.2

"Hell, that'd make it almost 200 proof. That's damn near pure grain alcohol," exclaimed Paintball.

"Assumption incorrect. Shine calculated to be approximately 10,000 proof – not suitable for consumption."

"Bullcrap!" cried Paintball. "Ain't nothing could be 10,000 proof."

Gizmo held up the unopened half liter bottle of water Bingo had given him the night before. He twisted off the cap and held it under the stream of liquid. Then, he poured one drop into the bottle. Putting the cap back on, he gave it a shake and handed it to Paintball.

"I'm supposed to drink this?"

"Output now suitable for consumption," said Gizmo.

"Bullcrap, you drink it."

"Give it here," said Bingo, reaching out for the bottle.

"Don't do it," pleaded Paintball. "You ain't got no idea what's in that stuff. You could end up blind or even dead."

"Where was all this concern a minute ago when I was gonna take a taste full strength?"

"Well, I've had time to think about it."

"Hell, it's just one drop in a bottle of water," said Bingo. "Besides, I think if Gizmo was gonna do something to harm us, he would've done it by now." Before Paintball could object further, he put the bottle to his lips and took a sip.

"Aw no!' cried Paintball. "Spit it out before it's too late."

Bingo shook his head no, holding the liquid between his teeth and lips. Then, he let the liquid fill his mouth. The sweet flavor of shine rolled over his tongue. He let it slide down his throat, feeling its prickly burn as it made its way to his stomach. He looked at Gizmo, then Paintball. Finally, he said. 'Well, if it don't kill me, it's the best shine I ever had. I'd say about 100 proof."

"Can you see me?" Paintball asked, looking hard into Bingo's eyes.

"Yes."

"How you feelin'?"

"Fine. You want to try some?" Bingo said, holding out the bottle. "Go on, it ain't gonna hurt ya."

Paintball stared at the bottle, then he looked at Gizmo. "You sure?"

"Output now suitable for consumption."

"If I die," warned Paintball, "I'm gonna beat the crap outta you." He took the bottle from Bingo and took a swig. His eyes widened as he let the shine slip down his throat. Then he shook his head.

"Confirm output suitable for consumption?" asked Gizmo

Paintball looked at him for a moment then said, "Hot Damn, this stuff ain't your run of the mill moonshine. It's Starshine! Let's get some jugs and start bottling."

"Wait a minute," said Bingo. "We ain't gonna bottle this stuff."

"Wadda ya mean," asked Paintball, "We ain't gonna bottle this stuff?"

"I mean we ain't gonna bottle this stuff. We got a bona fide moonshine tanker right here, ready to roll. Why make ten trips when we can make one? Why should we go to the expense and trouble of mixing up and hauling all them bottles when we can make one haul and let 'em fool with it on their end? Don't you see, one big haul, one big payoff, and we're home free."

"Sounds like a plan to me," chortled Paintball, rubbing his hands together. "So wadda we do now?"

"I'll get the Ford. You and Gizmo fill it straight out of the wormbox. While that's goin on, I'll make a phone call or two and set things up." Bingo headed for the door, while Paintball prepared to take another swig. "Wait until we're done before you start celebrating," Bingo said over his shoulder. "We got a lot to do. Wait until I get back here before you roll the door up."

Paintball waited until he heard the soft growl of the Ford's flathead V8 before sliding the door open. Bingo pulled the sleek black coupe inside, parking it alongside Gizmo's contraption. He cut the engine and got out. 'It's all yours," he said to Gizmo. "Take good care of it. The keys are in the ignition. Now if you don't mind, I got some phone calls to make. How long before the tank in that thing," he said pointing to the Ford, "is full?"

"Approximately one half planetary rotation."

Bingo checked his watch. "That'll be around 10. I'll tell 'em we leave out around midnight." He walked out into the morning sunshine, motioning for Paintball to slide the door shut behind him. As soon as the door was shut, Gizmo climbed into the driver's seat.

"Don't touch nothin!" hollered Paintball. "All we need is for you to screw this whole thing up." Gizmo shoved the key into the ignition and started the engine. Its throaty rumble filled the storage building. "I told you not to touch nothin," Paintball whined. "Now cut that thing off before Bingo gets back. He'll be mad as hell if he finds you fooling around with that car. It was his Granddaddy's, you know." Leaving the engine running, Gizmo got out and walked around to the front. He opened the hood, peering into the engine compartment. The Soekrix whirled around over the engine, occasionally touching down like a bee on a cupcake. Then it flattened out in front of Gizmo.

"Soekrix has determined that operational efficiency and output is at 15% of potential," Gizmo said.

"No way in hell!" said Paintball. "That's the best runnin' engine I ever seen. Bingo rebuilt it hisself. That ain't no worn out Pacer you got there." He reached past Gizmo and slammed the hood shut. "What you need to be doin' is figurin' out an easy way to get the juice into the tank."

"Soekrix will begin immediately."

By the time Bingo came back, they were working on the second drum of mash. "That's a right smart set up," he said to Gizmo, eyeing the small pump that had been added to the wormbox and the tubing that now carried the shine right into the tanker. "Sure saved Paintball a lot of dipping and funneling."

"I'll have you know it was my idea," said Paintball, "he and the flyin' horse apple just did the heavy liftin."

"I guess that means thanks is due all around," Bingo said, tipping his ball cap.

"How'd you make out"?

"We're set."

They spent the rest of the day sitting around while Gizmo's contraption pumped a steady flow of shine into the tanker. After it converted the contents of one barrel, Gizmo would siphon the mash liquid from another into the still tank and the process would begin again. They were sitting around the Moonshine Special, the afternoon winding down, when Bingo said, "I say we take turns keepin' watch on things while the others get some sleep."

"No need for unnecessary expenditure of energy," interjected Gizmo. "The conversion equipment will need little in the way of effort to maintain production. The Soekrix and I are well capable and willing to undertake the necessary activities. You should return to your habitation modules to engage in your naturally recurring state of mind characterized by altered consciousness, relatively inhibited sensory activity, inhibition of nearly all voluntary muscles, and reduced interactions with surroundings."

"Come again?" stammered Paintball.

"Go home and get some sleep."

"You sure?" asked Bingo. "We're happy to stay."

"Yes," said Gizmo, "What little there is left to do I am capable of accomplishing."

"I say never pass up a chance to hit the rack," added Paintball.

"Well as long as you're sure," Bingo said to Gizmo, "Then I could use the rest for tonight. I'll need to have my wits about me if I'm gonna make a run to Hazard."

"Then it's settled. Let's git," said Paintball. He turned to Gizmo. "Don't forget, there's grub in the icebox up front if you get hungry."

Bingo was at Paintball's just before midnight. He had to lay on the horn until Paintball poked his head out of the bedroom window, yelling for him to hold on while he washed his face and brushed his teeth. "I see nothin's changed," quipped Bingo, as Paintball hopped into the cab.

"Cleanliness is next to Godliness," said Paintball, punching the search button on the radio.

"Shut that thing off for a minute," said Bingo in a somber tone.

"What?"

"I said shut it off."

Paintball turned the radio off. "Hey, I sorry I was late," he apologized.

"This ain't about you bein' late."

"Then what?"

"What if we don't make the run tonight?" asked Bingo

"I 'spect the folks in Hazard will understand. You not feeling well?" asked Paintball.

"I feel OK. It's just that Granddaddy told me not to get mixed up with moonshine when he gave me his tanker. Somehow, I feel like I'm lettin' him down."

"Well, didn't he run shine to provide for his family?" asked Paintball

"Yeah."

"Well, ain't that kinda what you're doing? Tryin' to provide a way to get outta here and make somethin' of yourself. It ain't like you have chosen to pursue a life of crime. It's just this one time, you said so yourself."

"It don't sound so bad when you put it that way, I guess you're right. It's just I got this naggin' feelin' about it, that's all," said Bingo.

"Look, if you don't want to, don't do it. I guess we'll figure out somethin' else. I'm with you whatever you decide."

They drove on in silence. The moon had climbed high in the sky by the time they pulled up in front of the Speed Shop. Bingo opened the big sliding door. Inside, they found Gizmo Standing by the Ford, the Soekrix hovering above his head. The driver's side door was open. There was no sign of the equipment that had filled the area just hours before.

"Look it there, Bingo," said Paintball, "he's got his red PJs and his little cap thing back on."

Bingo looked at Gizmo, "Did you get enough to fill the tank?" he asked.

"Sufficient quantity produced to match the capacity of the containment vessel," replied Gizmo.

"What does that mean?" asked Paintball.

"I believe it means its full and ready to go," said Bingo. "Am I right?"

"Assumption correct," answered Gizmo. "In addition, energy conversion unit and motive transfer device have been reconfigured to insure optimum output in anticipation of imminent departure."

Bingo was silent for a moment before he said, "Paintball, I ain't takin' this vehicle to Hazard tonight." He looked at Gizmo. "But, I think you already knew that."

"Affirmative," said Gizmo, sliding behind the wheel. He pull the driver's door shut. The Soekrix hovered over the Ford for an instant before sending tendrils of electricity crawling over its surface. The car rose a few inches before gliding through the door. Bingo and Paintball followed it outside. They watched as it continued to rise above the roof, then above the treetops. Then, the soft blue glow of electricity was replaced by the brilliant white arc of energy as the Ford shot straight up into the sky. Bingo and Paintball watched until it became a tiny speck of light, indistinguishable from the myriad of stars in the night sky.

Finally, Paintball asked in a hushed voice, "What the hell, just happened?"

"I guess you could say Gizmo's gone home."

"Hell yeah, in our Ford! Sorry, I mean your Ford. Well, slip and fall in a cow pie if that don't beat all. He had us fooled from the beginnin."

"Mebbe we was just foolin' ourselves. Mebbe Granddaddy was right. Mebbe there weren't no good to be had from getting mixed up with moonshine. Ain't nothin' we can do 'bout it now. Ain't much left to do here but go on home."

'You just gonna leave it like that?" asked Paintball.

"Whadda ya suggest?" barked Bingo, "Call the Sheriff. Tell him some alien was helpin' us make moonshine, but he double crossed us and drove my Granddaddy's '40 Ford Coupe off into outer space?"

"Well, no."

"I didn't think so. Now if you're finished, I'd like to go home. Let's close up." He was reaching for the lights when his text message alert buzzed. "What now?" he said, looking at the message on the screen. "Well I'll be damned!"

"What's it say?" asked Paintball.

"It's from Gizmo,"

"Get outta here, he don't even know your number. What's it say?"

"It says to look under the tarp."

"Look under what tarp?"

"Well there's only one I can see," said Bingo, walking over to the Moonshine Special. He pulled back the tarp. "Git over here, quick," he called out. Paintball trotted over and joined him beside the now-finished race car. "Everythin' looks perfect," he said, opening the engine compartment. A gleaming Flathead V8 sat in the previously gaping hole. He studied the engine, checking the production numbers. "Paintball!" he exclaimed, "This here is Granddaddy's Flathead. Gizmo must've done his magic on it and stuck it in here." He dropped to the floor and looked under the racer. "He must've got the tranny too. I'll be damned." He pulled himself back to his feet and closed the engine compartment. "I think Granddaddy would be OK with the way all this has turned out."

"Yeah, he'll be watching proudly when you hit the track for the first time in the Moonshine Special."

"'Cept I won't be in the Moonshine Special."

"What?" exclaimed Paintball.

"I said I won't be in the Moonshine Special, 'cause we're renaming it the Starshine Special."

VISITORS

Walter gazed out across the parking lot of the Grover Mill. It was summer shutdown for plant maintenance and all but a skeleton crew and some administrative employees were off on a two week 'vacation.' The main parking lot, designed to accommodate 200 cars, had been freshly sealed and the black asphalt coating seemed to suck in the bright summer sunlight. It just sat there, a large black square in the middle of the green landscaping; no lines, no cars to mar its perfect blackness. Walter imagined that from high above it looked like the light was pouring over its edges like water into a bottomless drain. His attention moved from the black hole below his office window to the cloudless sky above. A brilliant blue vista stretched before him from horizon to horizon, interrupted only by a small round cloud directly above.

A turbulence roiled down from its center. Walter watched it spreading out as the cloud descended. A bright flame burst through the billowing white as a low rumble rattled the building. Three large round pods attached to long appendages drifted out from the now visible cigar shaped, silver cylinder from which the violent thrust emanated. The fresh black coating of the parking lot boiled under the rocket engine's heat as it gently touched down. A whoosh of vapor plummeted down from the engine compartment, quickly cooling the smoking pavement. As the smoke cleared, Walter could see a towering spaceship glistening in the sunlight. Fully the width of ten parked cars at its base, its top seemed to disappear like the tip of a needle into the sky above.

Before he had a chance to catch his breath, a portal opened and a long ramp emerged, dipping down to the black pavement. A large being dressed in a fuchsia jumpsuit appeared at the portal. Large black eyes set deep in an iridescent green skull peered up at him. A long thin arm raised, offering him a golden scroll.

"Mr. Binnell, here are the files you asked for," Shelley chirped, breezing through the door holding a manila folder. The sound of her voice abruptly pulled him back from his daydream. Whirling around from the window, he bolted upright in his chair.

"Uh," he stammered, eyes focusing on the file clerk. "Just put them there," he gestured toward the inbox on the corner of his desk.

"Alright, anything else?" she asked.

"No, I'll call if I need anything," he replied, trying not to let the adrenaline make his voice shake. He watched her leave, high heels tap tapping on the tile floor. She was very attractive, tall and leggy, and he wished he had engaged her with some witty conversation. He pursed his lips and then looked back to the empty parking lot and sighed.

It could happen, he thought.

The drive home that evening felt as uneventful as usual. He had just reached the County Park and traffic had come to a stop at the entrance to the little league ball fields. The evening rush of parents and players arriving for the evening games brought everything to a grinding halt. The stands were already filling. It was then he heard a loud humming that throbbed in his eardrums. The radio spewed static and the engine died. From his car, he could see the people in the stands pointing toward the sky. He craned his neck and gazed up through his windshield just in time to see the spinning cerulean disk as it slowly circled the three diamonds. Dust and debris blew about as the gyrating spacecraft hovered over center field. The coaches, players and spectators ran in disarray as the great saucer softly touched down. As soon as the rotation ceased, a large section of the ship's hull dissolved into a large opening. A dark figure emerged from the gaping maw as the civil defense sirens blared.

"Hey, buddy, want to move it on!" the irate driver behind him bellowed as he honked repeatedly. "If you want to watch the ball game buy a ticket and sit in the bleachers!"

The sound of the car's horn angrily bleating snapped Walter back to the here and now. He sat upright in his car. looking in his rearview mirror to see the driver furiously pointing forward. Forgetting he had stopped in third gear, he quickly hit the gas and let out the clutch. His car lurched forward and died. More exasperated honks filled his ears. Finally, he started the engine and took off. Anger welled up inside. *Should'a stopped and taught that idiot a thing or two about common courtesy.* Furtively, he looked in the mirror as the irate driver turned off and the ball fields faded in the distance.

It could happen. he thought.

He turned down the narrow lane that drifted over the hill to his home. It was the perfect place. Away from the city and perched on a hill with a softly sloping pasture running to the creek below, he had an unobstructed view of the sky. There was nothing on his side of the hill to interfere with his view of the heavens. Far from the glare of town, the sky was free from annoying nuisance light leaking from streetlamps and convenience store parking lots. On clear moonless nights, stars blazed in the inky blackness and the Milky Way drifted across the nocturnal universe. He would scamper up the ladder and lie on the porch roof gazing into a crystal night sky.

"Walter, there's a made-for-TV movie on tonight," offered Aline as she gathered the dishes from the table. "Want to watch?"

"Honey, no moon tonight," he responded with a 'don't you know' inflection.

"There's no moon many nights."

"Forecast says that the sky will be clear, it's a perfect night."

"It's always a perfect night to you unless it's raining or snowing," she sniffed, turning toward the sink fighting back tears. "Walter, this obsession of yours with spaceships and visitors from other planets is just not healthy. You can't spend the rest of your life on top of the roof looking for little green men. It's not normal."

"Don't I have a good job, bring home a good paycheck? I go to church every Sunday and only drink a beer on the Fourth of July and Super Bowl Sunday. I think most folks would think I'm pretty normal!"

"Walter, normal people don't spend every night on their roof looking up into the sky. Normal people don't believe everything written by UFO nuts. Normal people can have a conversation without mentioning Project Blue Book!" She turned and glared at Walter. "I can't go on like this. I love you. I need you. I want to have a family. I want kids and I want those kids to have a father, a real father, who will read them bedtime stories. A father who will help them with their homework and not drag them up on the roof looking for space monsters. I want to go on vacation somewhere other than Roswell, New Mexico. I want to have a husband who has room to share some of my dreams, too."

Walter looked at her sheepishly from the table. "Aline, ever since I was a kid, I have known there were others out there," he plaintively explained, pointing to the darkening sky that was visible through the kitchen window above the sink. "I don't know how, but I know. And I don't know why, but I know that somehow I'm destined to be a part of it. I just can't miss out on it. I don't know how to explain it any better, but I just can't."

"Walter, you've built this up in your head to the point where it can never live up to your expectations. Believe me, the spaceships aren't coming. Sure, they may find some life on distant planets, but that's not going to happen in our lifetime. You can't go on living in a fantasy world. Can't you just appreciate what you have? If you just look around the world you live in, there are enough wonders to fill a lifetime. I hate to burst your bubble, but I am worried about you. If you won't do something about this, I will."

"I never thought. . ."

"No!" she protested, cutting him off mid-sentence. "The problem is, you spend too much time in thought! Too much time daydreaming. I'm too tired to argue with you. Go on, lie up there on the roof, you'll find some reason to end up there anyway." Fighting back her tears, she slumped in the chair by the telephone stand across the room.

He watched her for a moment not knowing what to do. Then, furtively, he got up and took his dishes to the sink. He looked out the window. It was a perfect night, the stars were just discernable in the clear, dark blue sky. As he slipped out the door, he wished he could take her hand and the two of them just flop on the couch to watch that silly movie.

It could happen, he thought.

He watched the sky turn from sapphire to obsidian. The stars blazed like diamonds on black velvet. The panorama spread out before him. He quickly surveyed the constellations - Hercules, Draco, Cassiopeia, and the rest. Jupiter's brilliant presence dominated the moonless sky. They were his friends; he had known them since he was a boy. As he lay peering into the inky depths of the sky, leftover warmth from the roof floated up around him, drawing away the tension of the day. The stars moved ever so slowly on their inexorable journey across the sky. To the casual observer they would appear motionless; but Walter, after a lifetime of patient observation, could follow their nocturnal journeys as they glided through his field of vision. A soothing, dreamy, calmness wrapped him like a warm blanket.

He bolted upright as a shimmering fuchsia orb seemed to split apart from Jupiter and dance about the sky. His heart raced. This was no airplane or weather balloon! It floated down toward him turning an iridescent green, the intensity of its glow throbbing as it approached. Finally, looking like a quivering blob of mercury the size of a hen's egg, it came to rest, hovering at eye level a few inches from his face.

"Pretty isn't it?"

Wild panic gripped Walter's chest. Blood pounded in his head. The words seemed to come from right next to him. Adrenaline coursed through his body urging him to flee. He sat motionless though, too terrified to even turn his head and see who or what had just spoken to him.

"Oh, I apologize. Please forgive me. I surely must have startled you. It's not often I have occasion to arrange a first encounter of the fourth kind on a roof. "

Walter began to breathe again. The voice didn't sound menacing and he reasoned that if it's owner had intended harm, it would have already happened. He stared intently at the silver blob still floating in front of him and ventured a weak, "Yes."

"Yes? Oh, the gimcrack. Quite useless of course for anything other than what you see. Let me introduce myself. My name is Martin - Martin Landin."

Walter, having calmed somewhat, screwed up enough courage to turn his head stiffly in the direction of the voice. Sitting beside him on the roof was a small man. The gimcrack had begun to give of a soft white glow, shedding enough light for Walter to see that the man was dressed in a grey suit. His white hair was tucked neatly under a fedora with a deep rose-colored feather tucked in the band. He had an amicable smile and his eyes reflected bright flecks of starlight. He extended a steady, welcoming hand to Walter who, after a hesitant moment, accepted it.

"Nice home you have here," Martin quipped, still gripping Walter's trembling hand in a long, firm embrace. "Far away from the hubbub of the city. Just perfect for…" he paused, turning his eyes toward the evening sky, then gesturing with a wide sweep of his arm, "keeping watch?" Walter's eyes followed, tracing a wide arc. "Which really brings me to the purpose of our meeting."

"I don't understand," stammered Walter.

"Am I not correct that you have been waiting and watching a very long time for 'THEM' to appear?"

"Who?"

"Us, of course! Visitors from out there," Martin said, pointing to the sky. "Aliens from the heavens!" The gimcrack rolled itself into a fat, silver cigar and flew around in lazy figure eights above Walter's head before landing in front of his eyes. "Well here I am, at your service," he said, removing the fedora and gracefully bowing his head.

Walter's lips quivered and his ears burned just as they had the time his mother confronted him with the dog-eared, pin-up magazines she found hidden under his mattress. The gimcrack took on a shapely female figure, striking a provocative pose. A quick grimace from Walter started it spinning until it flattened into a bright blue disk. He turned his attention back to the small man in the business suit holding his fedora. Walter felt drained, as if his perfect night had been ruined by a sudden downpour.

"I suspect you are feeling very confused about now," said Martin, placing the fedora back on his head. "Let me explain as best I can. The easy part is that we have been here for a very long time. The not so easy part is why and how we came. Let it suffice to say we were an adventurous lot. It started with our discovery of a celestial canali bridging the vast distance between our planet and your Earth. Think of it as an instant, but unpredictable connection of two points of the universe over immeasurable distances. Through the looking glass so to speak." The gimcrack vanished, then reappeared a few feet away, only to blink out of sight once again and pop up inches from Walter's nose. " Well our celestial canali led us here. We traveled back and forth until one day it disappeared. Those of us left stranded here had no choice but to quietly assimilate.

"As you see, we are quite homologous to homo sapiens although we have certain characteristics and abilities that set us apart. Until we learned to keep these to ourselves we were often persecuted as witches, demons or heretics. But, through trial and error, we learned and now we are quite unrecognizable among the population, although you have seen our contributions. Are you familiar with the work of da Vinci? Newton? And don't forget our poor misunderstood Tesla."

"Now you are making fun of me!" sputtered Walter indignantly. "First you try to get me to believe this yarn about instant space travel, then you want me to believe some of the greatest accomplishments of mankind come as a result of some alien mad hatters falling down a cosmic rabbit hole."

"Would you have us come blasting down in some tin can? Would that make any more sense? Are you saying it can't be true if it isn't scripted like a Spielberg movie? I am sorry to tell you but spaceships simply can't overcome the time and distances involved in traveling through the vastness of our universe."

"That's not it at all," Walter whispered, looking up in the sky. "I... I just wanted to experience the wonder."

"Walter, you are surrounded by wonders! You just have to recognize them. If I were to suddenly fly about your back yard, I bet you would gaze upon me in wonder; but, you take for granted the robin that flies through it every day." The gimcrack sprouted wings and a beak and fluttered about. "If I took a bit of protoplasm and fashioned a creature from it, I bet you would consider that a wonder. And it would be no less a wonder than the child Aline carries in her womb."

"What did you say?"

"Five weeks along I would say, but I'm sure you can pinpoint the exact date. But enough of that, I really have to go and I think the only thing I can do is give you a practical demonstration which will convince you that what I have told you is true. I don't often make a concession like this, but in the interest of time, I am forced to take exceptional measures." With that, he reached over and gently touched Walter's arm.

Even though they had been in earnest conversation, the unexpected physical contact unsettled Walter. Before he had time to protest, he felt the cool night air rushing over his body.

"Steady, we're only going on a quick spin around the yard," came Martin's calming voice.

Walter looked down to see the roof gliding away from under him. Then, he saw the patio, garden and the shed pass underneath him. They floated in a tight arc as his house came back in view. The Gimcrack promptly divided into parallel points of light marking a makeshift runway as they softly landed on the roof.

"Do you believe me now?"

"I… don't know what to say."

"Say nothing. You don't have to look to the sky to find the wonders in your life. Just believe." Then Martin winked. "And remember, no one will buy a story of meeting a small, grey haired man on the roof who flew you around on his arm." He held out a hand and the gimcrack softly nestled in his palm. "This is for you, Walter, a memento of our meeting," he said, placing it in Walter's hand. Its light lingered for a moment before going out. "Sorry, I forgot. The ability to animate a gimcrack is in the DNA. Keep it anyway - to remember." And then he was gone.

Walter looked about his empty roof-top observatory blinking his eyes. Jupiter beamed down on him from the night sky. The constellations drifted along their ceaseless journeys. Time to go in, he thought and scooted down the ladder.

It could happen, he thought.

Aline heard Walter's footsteps on deck outside. She turned to meet him as he came in through the door. "Forget something?" she asked.

"A lot of things," he said, sitting down at the table. "Has the movie started?"

"Not yet."

"What station?"

"Channel 6. Go turn on the TV while I finish up in here." Walter got up from the table. 'What's that?" she asked.

Walter stood in silence for a moment, pondering the dark lump he clutched tightly in his hand. "Nothing I suppose, just something I found outside." He gently set it on the table before he slipped through the door. Then, he turned back and popped his head inside the kitchen. "Anything you want to tell me?"

"Yes and no. After the movie. Now shoo." She watched as he disappeared down the hall. Walking over to the table, she picked up the gimcrack. She smiled as it formed a pair of blue booties.

SOME COMPANY ON THE JOURNEY[3]

As the plasma barrier of his stasis locker evaporated, Eldon shuddered, sucking in a deep draught of oxygen and atomized stimulants. *God, I hate animating from jump stasis!* Lying prone in stasis for long space journeys had its drawbacks. He struggled to keep his eyes open in the glare of the programmed dim-light. He took another breath, lungs tingling, as the analeptics transferred into his blood and coursed throughout his body. His heart nearly stopped when a face appeared in his field of vision. It appeared to be a man's face, albeit upside down in relation to Eldon. He strained to make out the facial features in the dim-light.

"Didn't mean to startle you so," the man said. "But I thought I would go ahead and get you up."

Eldon struggled to say something, but nothing would come out of his dry mouth and throat. *Holy hell, wake-up deliriums. They said this might happen.* He blinked his eyes. The face was still hovering over him.

"I fancy a cup of tea, care to join me in the commissary?" the man invited, just before his face slid from sight.

The locker began steadily repositioning. When Eldon reached a seated position, it paused to give the fluid in his inner ear time to settle and his brain time to adjust. He shut his eyes to fight the stasis induced vertigo. Once the spinning in his head stopped, he engaged the controls at his fingertips, gradually bringing the locker into a position where he could stand upright. Satisfied that his legs would hold his weight, he unfastened his restraints, stepping away from the locker.

---

[3] "Some Company On The Journey" appeared online in *Spank The Carp* 4/1/2017.

"SysOp, lights up," he called out, surveying the remaining lockers in the stasis hold. There was no activity he could discern. *What the hell? Has something gone wrong?* "Status report."

"Holoscreen activated," SysOp replied. "Manual activation of stasis locker number 106, assigned to crew member Lieutenant Senior Grade, Eldon Welk, detected. Bioscan indicates metrics within acceptable animation limits. All other systems within normal operating parameters."

"Duration of stasis before animation?"

"97.3 Earth years." The data on the holoscreen confirmed the operating system's report.

Manual activation? Something's not right. "Identify individual responsible for manual activation," he said.

"Insufficient data."

"Is anyone else up and moving about this ship?" Eldon barked.

"All other crew members remain in stasis."

This ain't good, something is definitely out of whack. "Run complete systems diagnostics and forensic analysis to determine how locker number 106 was activated. What is the estimated time until completion of directive?"

"Time remaining 17 Earth minutes."

"Open the commissary." Eldon ordered.

"Commissary already activated."

"Well then, who the hell is in there if the rest of the crew is in stasis?"

"Insufficient data."

Damn stupid computer! "I guess I will have to figure this out on my own. Reduce artificial gravity by 15% for ten minutes, then increase to normal Earth level over the period of 1 Earth hour."

"Artificial gravity adjusted as directed."

Eldon left the stasis hold on shaky legs. He worked his way through the maze of bulkheads and corridors, bracing himself against the walls with rubbery arms, until he arrived at the commissary. *God, I hate animating from jump stasis! Wake up deliriums, systems activating for no apparent reason.* The door slid open as he approached. Before entering, he scanned the room. Seeing no one, he proceeded past the empty tables and chairs to one of the food kiosks lining the wall to his left. He faced the screen order icon and said, "Coffee with extra sugar." The screen display read: **Not indicated for animation replenishment.** *The sneaky bastard knows everything!* "What do you suggest?" he asked, knowing the answer. The screen displayed: **Animation Nutrition Replenishment Ration indicated.** "OK," he grumbled.

The kiosk made a soft thumping sound as a tray appeared. Eldon looked down at its contents with disgust. *God, I hate animating from jump stasis!* He took the tray and plopped down in the nearest chair. He peeled the lid from a container simply labeled: macronutrients.

"Is this seat taken?" asked a voice, startling Eldon to the extent he dropped the container, splashing macronutrients all over himself and the table. He turned to the direction of the voice so fast, he lost his recently regained balance, tumbling to the floor. He rolled on his back, waiting for the room to stop spinning. When it did, a face appeared in his field of vision. It appeared to be a man's face, albeit upside down in relation to Eldon. "Oh, it seems I've surprised you again," the man said, extending a hand. "Sorry about that. Seems we've gotten off on the wrong foot, or at the very least you have. Let me help you up."

This can't be a wake-up delirium. Maybe it's a full blown breakdown. Eldon hesitated a moment before taking the man's outstretched hand. Once firmly in its grasp, he easily returned to his feet. He remained tense as he examined the man, whose grey clothes, resembling the scrubs worn by the med crew, hung loosely on his diminutive frame. *Surprising strength for such a small man.* Piercing steel eyes looked out from the man's smooth, finely featured face.

His skin was the color of beach sand. Curly brown hair tightly circled his balding pate. *Maybe this is real!*

"I don't recognize you. Are you a member of the crew?" asked Eldon warily.

"No."

"How the hell d'ya get in here?" Eldon demanded.

"I would think the more important question would be why am I here?" the man countered.

"Don't parse words with me. What I want to know is how you got on this vessel."

"Well it's not like you have a bolt on the front door. I wanted some company on my journey, so I just came in. That may sound simplistic, but it's true."

"You just 'came' in?"

"If you had just completed a long excursion," the man continued, "across the universe and arrived at a distant planet, wouldn't you say something like 'Greetings, I have come from Earth on my spaceship,' without explaining all the politics and technology of how you got there. So, other than the fact I didn't come from Earth on a spaceship, my response is much the same as yours would be. Beyond that, I don't have the time or inclination to go into the details."

An enviro servo appeared from behind the kiosks and began to whir about the spilled macronutrients. It scooped up the container from the floor, depositing it in a cart it pulled behind. After it mopped the floor, it began to twitter about until Eldon said, "It wants to wipe off the table."

"Of course," said the man, "shall we move to another?"

Eldon stared at the man while the servo continued to twitter. "SysOp, identify unauthorized individual in the commissary," he barked.

"Insufficient data."

"Explain insufficient data," Eldon directed.

"Bioscan of commissary indicates presence of a single authorized crew member, Lieutenant Senior Grade, Eldon Welk. Mechscan of commissary indicates presence of enviro servo 403927. No other bio or mech entities identified."

"That's impossible. I'm looking at him right now. How do you explain that?"

"Insufficient Data."

"How much time remains until systems diagnostics and forensic analysis requested is complete?" Eldon asked.

"Time remaining 6 Earth minutes."

"Belay that and run SysOp diagnostics for algorithm malfunctions which might explain apparent failure to identify unauthorized presence in commissary."

The man smiled, "I am afraid that will yield no better result than you have already experienced."

"Did you have anything to do with my animation?" Eldon asked.

"Yes, Eldon. No offense, but it was purely a random selection. I was hoping for some company on my journey. As it happens, we share the same destination, so I decided to tag along, so to speak."

The enviro servo continued to twitter as Eldon and the man conversed. "How would you know what our destination is? That is classified information. Besides, we have been in jump stasis for 100 Earth years. You could not have survived the stress of jump travel as a stow away over that period time and there were no extra stasis lockers to use."

"Shall we see to it you get a clean pullover and find a place to continue this conversation that will satisfy this contraption?" the man said, gesturing to the enviro servo.

Eldon eyed him for a moment. "What do you suggest?"

"Let's move to the helm. You can sit in the captain's chair. Fine view from there."

Bastard! "Now I've heard everything. First you compromise our ship, then you would have me engage in insubordination? I don't care about the view! I want to know who you are and why you are here." The man held out a clean pullover. *What the hell?* "Where'd you get that?"

"From the laundry if you must know. Now can we be on our way, I fear this poor machine will burn up its circuits if we don't let it get on with its business."

Eldon eyed the pullover, then glared at the man. *If he wanted to harm us, we'd be dead already.* He peeled off his macronutrient soaked pullover and tossed it over to the enviro servo. The machine snatched it from midair, dumping it into the cart. Then, he reached hesitantly out and took the pullover from the man, who smiled, but otherwise remained motionless. He slipped the fresh garment over his head, keeping his eyes on the man as best he could. Once Elden finished tucking it into his trousers, the man said, "Shall we go?"

"You first," Eldon said, pointing toward the door. *Let's see if you know your way around the ship.*

The man set off at a brisk pace negotiating the ship's passageways with flawless precision. As they reached the helm, Eldon prepared to hold up his palm for a bio scan authorization. Before he could, however, the man made a slight sweeping gesture and the door slid open. Eldon stopped dead in his tracks. *What the hell just happened? He shouldn't be able to open anything on this ship.* The door shut before Eldon could regain his composure. He stepped forward and held up his palm. The door opened again.

The man was already seated as Eldon entered. He made his way forward to the control console chairs. He gazed in wonder at the universe, freckled with a billion points of starlight stretching out on the other side of the plasma window. He had been placed in stasis before the launch and had never seen space from any vantage other than Earth. He jumped when the man spoke, "Astonishing." Eldon nodded, unable to find his voice. "Sit down," said the man, "and we will talk until we reach our destination."

"I don't think so, this mission called for a 273 Earth year jump. You woke me up just a little early. By my reckoning that leaves about 170 years before we get there. Unless I go back into stasis, I'll be long gone before this ship rests. I don't know what you'll do."

The man smiled, "SysOp, some music please. I've always been fond of Russian composers from the Earth's late 19th to mid-20th centuries. Start with Nikolai Rimsky-Korsakov. Scheherazade, if you will and not too loud." The grim bass motif of the first movement began. "The Sea and Sinbad's Ship. Please sit," said the man, motioning to the captain's chair.

Eldon, sensing he had no choice, sat down. He paused for a moment, then said, "The least you could do is tell me your name."

"I have no name that I call myself," the man began, "however, others have called me by many. Jesus, Krishna, Allah, Osiris, Zeus, Yahweh to name a few from your lexicon."

Oh God, he's psycho! We're all doomed. "So you're God?"

"Not in the sense of a capital 'G'. That is your concept. To be sure, I exist beyond your corporeal limits. Am I the feathered serpent god, Quetzalcoatl, that came down to the Aztecs? No. Am I a burning bush on the mountain side? No. However, I will claim responsibility for dropping a few bits of amino acids on a wet rock and the occasional suggestion whispered into a waiting ear. Beyond that, I had mostly a wait and watch role. The concept of a power greater than… is probably closest."

"Prove it," Eldon demanded.

"Parlor tricks?" questioned the man. "Is every human from Missouri?"

Before Eldon could respond, the music faded, replaced by the electronic voice of the ship's operating system. "Holoscreen activated, SysOp diagnostics for algorithm malfunctions completed as requested. Complete systems diagnostics and forensic analysis completed as requested,"

"Report," Eldon said anxiously.

"No algorithmic malfunctions detected," the electronic voice continued. "All systems operating within normal parameters. Forensic analysis confirms unexplained animation of crew member, Lieutenant Senior Grade, Eldon Welk and activation of enviro servo 403927. Ancillary systems activated as per Lieutenant Senior Grade, Eldon Welk. No other bio or mech entities identified."

"Is the ship on course?"

"Ship remains on course to Galaxy GN-z11."

Maybe I can throw him off balance. "So, what is your interest in GN-z11?" Eldon asked the man.

"We will not reach GN-z11 before we reach our destination. You see we are headed to the center of the Universe."

"You just heard SysOp's report!" *Idiot thinks I am a fool.* "We are on course for GN-z11, not the center of the Universe."

"No, I do not think you are a fool. SysOp is correct. It is just that we will arrive at the center of the Universe before we would arrive at GN-z11. You see, the Universe is swiftly collapsing. This ship is like a minnow swimming in your planet's Niagara River. Within the minnow's frame of reference, it is merrily swimming upstream toward its destination. In reality, our poor minnow and the water surrounding it are being inexorably pulled along toward the falls. It doesn't know and won't until it reaches the event horizon - that being when it tumbles over the edge into the chaos that awaits. In the case of this ship, it continues to advance relative to stars and galaxies surrounding it while in reality all are rushing toward the center of the universe." The man raised his hand, making a circular motion with his finger. The points of starlight swirled beyond the plasma window.

"Orientation of ship altered," reported SysOp.

"Explain!" panted Eldon.

"Position of ship now oblique to jump vector."

"Let me guess," he whispered, "the helm is now orientated toward the center of the Universe."

"Affirmative," responded SysOp.

The man waved his arm in an arc from left to right. The hull dissolved, leaving an unobstructed view. Eldon gasped, bracing for the blast of flesh-shattering cold and blood-boiling vacuum that never came. "Easy, my boy," assured the man, "just wanted a better view. I can close it up again if you prefer." Eldon opened one shuttered eye then the other. The atmosphere remained warm on his face.

He tentatively drew in a breath which flowed smoothly into his lungs. "Why this ship? Why me?"

"I just wanted some company on this final journey. Surely, that is not too hard to believe. I have always had a special fondness for humans despite all their foibles. This ship just happened to be farthest away. And as for you, it was mere chance, although I am quite happy with the choice. Besides, how do you know I'm not having this very conversation with all the other crew members?"

"How long," asked Eldon, "before we get there?"

"Time enough, as Mr. Carrol's Walrus would say: 'To talk of many things: Of shoes—and ships—and sealing-wax— Of cabbages—and kings— And why the sea is boiling hot—And whether pigs have wings.'"

Eldon laughed, "I haven't heard that since I was a child." He paused. "What's there? I mean at the center of the Universe."

"Our fate," said the man. "Technically, it is the mother of all black holes. Philosophically, it is the graveyard of gods and galaxies."

"Can't you stop it?"

"Even I have a power greater than myself. I, like you, am but a minnow swimming against the current."

"And that's it?" Eldon said, pointing out toward the stars. "Everything – all this beauty, all this undiscovered wonder, the entire Universe just collapses in on itself and is gone."

"Not quite. I believe everything will pass through this black hole and emerge as a new Universe. There, all things will be possible."

"Could I be like you in this new Universe?" asked Eldon.

"Anything would be possible," said the man.

Eldon pondered the man's words for a moment then said, "This Russian music is pretty good, have you ever listened to Bluegrass?"

DOING TIME ON A PEBBLE[4]

Guy strode up the hill away from the city with his trainee in tow, the bus stop just visible in the intense light of the streetlamps. "This is Pickup where we pick up pickups," he said, once again to his trainee.

"Uh-huh," came the same response.

Their feet made soft scrunching sounds as they plodded along the gravel path. Guy studied the ground at his feet. "I don't know why Top didn't bother to pave the way up here. Almost everything else is paved. But it is not for us to question. Top's motives are mysterious and not necessarily meant to be understood by us." They arrived at the edge of a parking lot under a cluster of streetlamps glaring down on the flaking concrete parking lot and some peeling benches. Guy's white Panama suit reflected the light, which filtered down, so it seemed almost to glow. A spindly green creature with a bulbous head was perched on the nearest bench. "That's Pete," Guy said, pointing toward the bench. "He's a Pathfinder like me. He looks like a Pedathian because he picks up Pedathians. I call him Pete for your sake. No one but Pathfinders can understand Pathfinder-speak. And no one but Pathfinders can comprehend Pathfinder names. So, we don't even try to tell Pickups our names. Besides, Pete speaks only Pedathian while on duty and since Pathfinders are always on duty, that is all you would hear from him. For the most part, the Pedathian language is unintelligible to humans; not to mention quite harsh on the ears, so don't bother to try to strike up a conversation. Just nod and go on about your business. Like I said, he's here for Pickups like we are." The trainee nodded to the creature, who acknowledged with a circular dip of its head.

---

[4] Doing Time On A Pebble appeared online and in print in *Abstract Jam Issue 2*, 3/2016.

Just outside the arc of light, an impenetrable barrier of black loomed. Guy tilted his head slightly, turning an ear toward the black. "Here comes the bus now," he said matter-of-factly, as the growl of an old engine drifted into the light. On cue, an old Bluebird school bus emerged from the misty darkness and ground to a halt, brakes squealing in pain, dragging a storm of blue exhaust. The perfume of partially oxidized hydrocarbons soaked the atmosphere. The bus was painted like a Mexican flag: red on top, a white swath from front to back across its midsection, and green, fading into dust, along the bottom. As the door creaked open, amber-hued interior lights flickered on, leaking through grimy windows wet with the perspiration of the passengers.

A Pedathian driver, resplendent with a tattered generalissimo cap, reminiscent of a South American dictator, hopped out of the door with a fistful of papers, and let out a terrible screak that sounded like the hull of a sinking ship tearing apart.

"Hold fast," Guy muttered, putting his hand on the trainee's arm, "Pete was here before us, so he goes first. Let's hope he's only got one." He had explained this protocol to the trainee time after time during pick ups, but trainees required constant instruction so one more was in order.

Pete tumbled off the bench and ambled up to the driver who stuffed the papers into his outstretched hand. Pete perused the documents and let out his own rendition of a sinking ship. When Pete finished, the driver snapped his spidery fingers. A bulbous green head appeared at the bus door, followed by a gawky set of arms and legs all connected at the center by what resembled a spoonful of green school lunch jello. Pete took his Pedathian Pickup by the hand and set off down the gravel path toward town, his voice tearing metal in a low tone while they walked.

The driver jumped back on the bus. He had barely cleared the door when a Human driver appeared, donning the same grimy dictator cap, and jumped out of the opening. "Got two," he yelled, holding up some more papers and looking about as if he was hailing a transport client at a busy airport.

"Come on," Guy said, grabbing the trainee's arm and moving toward the driver with outstretched hand, "unless you intend to wait for the next bus." He took the papers from the driver and examined them closely. He handed half the documents to his trainee. "These are Transit Authorizations," he said. The trainee furrowed his brow and peered at the papers. "And these are Pickup Assignments," he added shoving the remaining documents into the trainee's hand. "Can't pick 'em up without these papers. Number one of many number one rules passed down from Top. If you forget any rule, don't forget this one." Guy waited as always while the trainee read through the information. "Any questions?"

"Uh-uh," came the usual reply.

"It's highly unusual to have two pick ups."

"Uh-huh."

"Yes, really. You sure you don't have any questions?"

"Uh-uh."

"I'm finished examining the papers. Are you?"

"Uh-huh."

Guy proclaimed at the top of his voice, "Pickups may now depart!" He raised his eyebrow and gave a look at the driver who snapped his fingers. A bewildered looking man with thinning grey hair stepped out from the bus. He looked around, blinking his eyes as they adjusted to the bright streetlamps. After he quit blinking, Guy beckoned to the Pickup. "Welcome to Petrogehenna, Pickup. We will take you to your assignment momentarily. Please stand over here by me until the other Pickup disembarks." While the Pickup took up his position, Guy spoke to the trainee. "Got to say the welcome part just like that every time or else Top gets irritated. And you don't want Top to get irritated." He had told this to the trainee every time they welcomed a Pickup, but trainee Penitents had to be constantly trained - it was their assignment.

The driver snapped his fingers once again. Another head, with flowing red hair, popped out of the door. This head, perched on top of a slender female torso, climbed down the steps and stood in front of the others. Guy took a quick look at the papers in his hand and announced, "Welcome to Petrogehenna, Pickup. Says here you are assigned to the task of bus driver. You may now put on the driver's hat." The bus driver handed over the generalissimo hat to the Pickup, who promptly placed it on her own head. A tug on the bill nestled it firmly around its new owner's temples. She hopped up the bus steps, disappearing into its recesses. The door slapped shut, the engine growled, followed by the sound of well-worn gears grinding. The bus lurched once, then lumbered off in a cloud of blue exhaust.

"Well, another Penitent begins her tour of duty," Guy said, producing a quill from his shirt pocket and making a notation on one of the papers. "Pay attention," he said to his trainee, "documentation is one of Top's pet peeves. As I said before, number one rule of many number one rules passed down from Top. If you forget any rule, don't forget this one. Comprende?"

"Uh-huh."

"I bet," Guy muttered as he turned his attention to the former driver. "Greetings Parolee, we will take you to Parcels and as soon as your package arrives, you will go to Purge and then to Port." Guy leaned in close his trainee. "Top has a thing about alliteration. Don't ask me why, Top's motives are often mysterious and never to be questioned – in public anyway. Just ask the Bright One. As for Pickups, as soon as they arrive, they already know everything they need to know with regard to how to perform their assigned task. You, as a trainee, know everything there is to know about knowing nothing about the job for which you are training. It's what distinguishes you as a trainee. Make sense?"

"Uh-huh."

"Of course, it does. Anyway, like any other trainee, you must be constantly trained by your trainer - that being me - in your immediate activity regarding the job for which I am training you. Unfortunately, you retain nothing as trainees are wont to do, and because you will never be anything other than a trainee during your stay here on Petrogehenna, you require constant retraining."

"Uh-huh."

"Alright then, first stop will be Pizzeria so our Penitent may begin his duties. Then on to Parcels and so on and so on. Follow me." Guy started off down the gravel path which led to Petropolis. The group passed from the glaring lights of Pickup onto the dimmer path. Fewer lights lined the path. Ahead, the buildings of Petropolis looked like stacks of glowing sugar cubes on a black velvet carpet. After they walked a bit further, Guy raised his hand to halt the procession. He looked up to the jet black sky, filled with stars. "Mind you, it's not nighttime here on Petrogehenna. This lonely little rock meanderers through the cosmos without the benefit of a sun to tug it around and shower it with warm radiance. The light here is artificial, courtesy of Top. Breathing gasses are also kindly provided by the Big Guy. No need to thank him, it's all included in the fare. Once in Petropolis, you won't be able to see the stars, so take a look while you can."

He started off once again down the path. The procession continued in its descent until the gravel morphed into a concrete sidewalk which was soon paralleled by a paved street. As they continued toward the city, the road leveled and the distance between the streetlamps decreased. They began to pass the sugar cube buildings they had seen from Pickup. All had rows of windows pouring out light. Whatever the height of a building, its attenuate streetlamp, festooned with clusters of lights, stretched up to its summit. The group came to an intersection. Guy stopped, raised his hand again, letting out a loud whistle. A dingy, grey cab immediately pulled up, tires screeching as it came to a stop. The cabbie, resplendent with a garish Hawaiian shirt, jumped out, trotted around to the curb and opened the rear door. A woman slid out and stepped aside, raising her hand to hail a cab. "Alright everyone, get in," Guy said, gesturing to the open door, "Next stop, Pizzeria." His trainee, the Parolee and the Penitent climbed into the back seat. Once the Penitent's backside disappeared into the opening, the cabbie slammed the door shut, pirouetted to the front door, opening it with a grand flourish. "Thank you," Guy said, as he took his seat. The cabbie trotted back around, slipped into the driver's seat and sped off. Guy looked over his shoulder at his trainee. "As I have told you before, no need to tell him the destination – cab driver Penitents always know where to go."

The cab dashed through the streets as they journeyed deeper into the heart of the city. The sidewalks grew crowded with pedestrians of all sizes and shapes. Guy named each species they passed for his trainee. "Pay attention, now, there will be a quiz later. The ones with very long ears that look like wings are Gerenukids and the ones that look like hairballs are Teludrians. Then there are the Miglizaks, recognizable by their prominent scarlet dorsal crest, the Cormorunes, with the bright blue facial spots, not to mention the Belgizoids with their purple gills and of course you recognize the Humans. All are Penitents, everyone one of them, except for Pathfinders, like me, of course." The cab maneuvered through the crowded streets, dodging service vehicles, and other cabs. "No personal conveyances here," he added, "only working vehicles permitted. You getting all this?"

"Uh-huh."

"Oh good. For a minute, I thought I lost you. Well, it looks like we have arrived." The cab rolled to a stop in front of a Miglizak with her arm raised. The cabbie hurried around to the curb and pulled the door open for Guy to exit. Then, he did the same for his other passengers. The Miglizak got in, careful not to bump her dorsal crest.

The cabbie flipped the door shut, hurriedly got back in his cab and sped off.

Guy pulled his trainee close by the shirt collar. "Make a note. That was a cab fare Penitent. They do nothing but ride in cabs. Keeps the cab driver Penitents busy when they aren't transporting Pathfinders." He turned loose of the trainee's shirt. "Here we are at Pizzeria," he said, pointing to the bright green neon sign. "All you can eat all the time, provided of course you are an eating Penitent, in which case, all you do is eat all the time. The place is packed with 'em. But please, no special orders. Just plain cheese on plain dough. The pizza cooking Penitents are pizza cooking all the time." He unfolded the Pickup Assignment he had pulled from his pocket. "Hmmm, just double checking. Nope, not an eating assignment or cooking assignment for you, my friend," he smirked. "Did you pinch a nun or something?" He looked at his trainee. "That's a rhetorical question of course." At that moment, a Human Penitent wearing grease soaked coveralls emerged from Pizzeria. The odor of rancid animal fat rolled over the sidewalk like a sandstorm. Guy turned to the Penitent. "Says here you are assigned to the task of grease pit cleaner. You may now put on the coveralls." The grease trap Penitent pulled the sticky hood from his head, and shimmied out of the gooey, stinking coveralls and handed them over to the Penitent who tugged them on and walked straight through Pizzeria's door, disappearing into its recesses. "Well another Penitent begins his tour of duty." Guy produced a fountain pen from his shirt pocket and made a notation on the Pickup Assignment. "Allow me to iterate once more," he said to the trainee, "documentation is absolutely imperative."

Guy addressed the former grease trap cleaner, "Greetings Parolee, we will take you to Parcels and as soon as your package arrives, you will go to Purge and then to Port." Raising his arm, he whistled. Another dingy cab pulled up. The Belgizoid cabbie, like all the other cabbies, scampered around with his Hawaiian shirt tails flapping, and opened the door to exchange passengers. Once accomplished, he slid behind the wheel and took off, leaving its former occupant at the curb hailing another cab.

The cab raced along the crowded streets between intersections, never failing to stop at each for a red light or stop sign. "Part of the charm of cab rides is the stop and go," Guy chortled. "No express lanes for the masses." The congestion lessened as they moved toward the outskirts of the city. The sugar cube buildings grew smaller and vacant lots intervened along the streets. The choke of sidewalk inhabitants gave way to the occasional pedestrian. Fewer streetlamps illuminated the pavement. The cab veered to the right and abruptly stopped in front of a furry Teludrian female with arm raised. "We're here," announced Guy. "Or at least this is where we get out of the cab and start walking. Don't dawdle. I'm sure our well-meant Penitent has places to go, as do we."

The change out of passengers was accomplished in the usual speedy fashion and the cab sped back toward the bright light of Petropolis. Guy ushered the group along the street until the pavement faded into a patch of weeds. Just beyond, the concrete sidewalk dissolved into a gravel foot path. "As if I haven't pointed this out to you before," he said to his trainee, "this is the way to Parcel. That's where Parolees pick up their packages. They can't go to Purge or Port until their packages arrive. Savvy?"

"Uh-huh."

"Well, don't forget it," Guy cautioned, rolling his eyes. They followed the path in the sparse light of a few streetlamps until a large grey metal building could be seen ahead. The gravel led right up to a large overhead door. To the left was a bench. To the right was a pneumatic tube station. A canister waited in the opening at the bottom of the vacuum tube. Guy pulled some papers from his vest pocket. "Got to put the paperwork in the thing-a-ma-bob," he said, fumbling with the top of the canister, "and…" he paused while his fingers tugged at the canister. Finally, the carrier lid swung open and he stuffed the papers inside. ". . make sure everything is buttoned up tight and send it along." He shoved the canister into the opening, pushing the red button next to station. The door began to ascend, accompanied by the wail of gnashing gears.

Light poured out from the building, empty except for a large section of square sheet metal ductwork dropping down from the ceiling just beyond the raised door. Guy pulled the trainee close, "Never, I repeat - which I have done too many times to count - never go inside until the package comes down." The ductwork shuddered, followed by a "Fshhhhhhhhhhhhhhhhup," then belched out a backpack the size of a refrigerator. It slammed to the floor, kicking up a cloud of dust. Guy held his arm out as a blockade to his trainee. "Wait, remember, we got two Parolees looking for packages." Another shudder shook the building. A small red tag fell, drifting like an autumn leaf wafting in a cool breeze, from the opening. "OK, all safe now. Let's see what we got," Guy called out as he approached the backpack. Guy examined its packing slip tucked inside a clear plastic sleeve. "This is yours," he said, pointing to the former grease trap cleaner Parolee. "Come on and get it." He looked at the former bus driver while pointing to the red tag, "and that's got to be yours." He picked up the red tag and handed it to the Parolee. "It's still searching for your package. Might be a good omen. Sometimes, the smaller ones are hard to find. Take a seat on the bench till it gets here. We'll catch up with you at Purge."

The former grease trap cleaner hefted the backpack up on his shoulders and set off down the gravel path as Guy took his trainee by the arm and walked back to the pneumatic tube station. The moment they cleared the door, it rolled back down, thumping the concrete. "Remember, you got to wait for the paperwork before you leave. If you leave without the paperwork the whole system gets messed up. The whole system gets messed up; Top gets really upset. You don't want that. Number one of many number one rules - et cetera, et cetera, et cetera, as the king would say. Are we clear on that?"

"Uh-huh."

"I bet you say that to all the Pathfinders."

"Huh?"

"Never mind."

A puff of air escaped from the opening of the tube followed by a "Schwiiiiiiiiiiiiiz - pop." A canister appeared. Guy retrieved it and wrestled the lid open. He pulled the paper out and examined it before returning the canister to its cubby hole. He took a ballpoint from his hip pocket and made a notation on the Purge Authorization. "Paperwork, paperwork, can't say it too many times. Right?"

"Uh-huh."

"Right. Let's get back and hail a cab. Got to get to Purge post haste." He led his trainee down the gravel path. As they reached the pavement, Guy raised his arm, and whistled. A cab pulled up. They traded places with its Cormorune Penitent who promptly raised her hand to hail another cab. Their cab driver made a U-turn, barely avoiding the cab that was barreling down the road to pick her up. They passed the backpack toting Parolee just as they got up to speed. "We've got to get to the other side of town, and we don't have time for city traffic. Let's take the express," Guy said to the cabbie, who swerved off the pavement and nosed the cab into the sudsy tunnel of an automated car wash.

They emerged as the last soap bubbles were sloughed away by the gentle spray of the spring rain rinse nozzles. The cabbie, who had not let off the gas while they were in the foamy tunnel, pulled back on the pavement and let the cab roll to a stop just in front of the orange and white barricade at the end of the road. There, a Pathfinder and a Gerenukid were waiting. Guy pulled a pocket watch from his vest and eyed the dial. "Only two minutes and a clean cab to boot. Not bad eh?"

"Uh-huh."

"How you doing, Gertie?" Guy said as they traded places in the cab. The Pathfinder wiggled her long ears. "That's how

Gerenukids greet others," he said, as the cab whisked away. "They're off to Port."

Just to the side of the barricade a gravel path led up the small hill in front of them. They followed it to the crest. From its vantage, they could see the path dipping down before rising again and terminating at a gate in the center of an imposing grey wall. They spied the backpack toting Parolee trudging along about midway along the path. "Very good," Guy said, nudging his trainee forward, "we should catch up with him at the gate. Come on, while we walk, we'll spend some time talking about time, which on Petrogehenna is not really time. I mean not time as one would expect. Time here is like an insurance sales pitch; it expands and contracts to fit the confines of the space in which it finds itself. Not bound by the unified field theory or Microsoft operating systems, time is free to ebb and flow or otherwise do what it damn well wants. Why? I suspect Top finds it useful.

"Now, in the case of our erstwhile grease trap cleaner, a journey that took two minutes in Pathfinder time, albeit we took the express, may have taken him a year in Parolee time. None the less, we all end up here together. And, I am confident we will find our former bus driver, who we left at Parcel, waiting for us when we reach the gate. That's just the way it works on this pebble. Think of the pizza eating Penitents sitting back there in Pizzeria eating their plain cheese pizzas constantly for hundreds if not thousands of years in Penitent time for what, to us, was a brief stop. What about the Belgizoid cab rider Penitent sitting in a cab at a stop light for a millennium, listening to a Pedathian cabbie Penitent sink the Titanic while we, in the next cab over, have barely enough time to check our watch before the light changes? Training you seems endless to me; I can't imagine how long it is for you. Well, there's time for me to answer any questions you may have. Anything you want to ask?"

"Uh-uh."

"Time to move on then," Guy said, as they caught up with the backpack toting Parolee. It was not long before the three were standing before a large door. The former bus driver Parolee was sitting on a bench with a small box in his lap. "Told 'ya," Guy quipped, pointing to the package wrapped in Kraft paper, "the small ones always take longer." A pneumatic tube station reached down from the blackness above alongside the bench. It jittered as a canister appeared, accompanied by a "Schwiiiiiiiiiiiiiiz - foop." Guy retrieved the paper and pencil contained within and placed the canister back in the tube. Making a notation on the Purge Authorization he reminded his trainee, "Paperwork, paperwork, can't say it too many times. Number one of many number one rules."

"Uh-huh."

"What we've got here is failure to communicate," Guy grumbled, lifting the knocker and rapping it three times against the gate. The door swung inward, revealing a vast courtyard. In the center was small man sitting at a bench. Guy beckoned the Parolees and his trainee to follow him as he entered. When they reached the man at the bench, Guy handed him the Purge Authorizations saying, "Greetings, Purger." He examined each and nodded to Guy, who announced at the top of his voice, "The Purge will begin." He motioned to the Parolee holding the small package to approach the bench. As he did, the Purger snapped his fingers. A Teludrian appeared from the dark recesses of the courtyard. He produced a mortar and pestle from a burlap sack, which he placed on the bench. "That's the Assistant Purger," Guy whispered to his trainee.

"Uh-huh."

The Purger selected a Purge authorization, tore it into shreds and placed them in the mortar. Then he nodded to the Parolee with the small package who placed it on the bench and opened it. From within, the Parolee extracted a brown wafer which he held to his forehead before handing it to the Purger, who in turn dropped it into the mortar, then hefted the pestle and began to grind. The Parolee retrieved another wafer, holding it to his forehead before handing it over. Like the one before it, the wafer was placed in the mortar while the grinding continued. Another wafer was produced. It too went into the mixture. While the process continued, Guy pulled his trainee aside. "The wafers are the distillation of all that comprised the Parolee's life before he got here: the good, the bad and everything between. All that was processed into those wafers while he performed his Penitent task. The more there is to purge, the longer the task and in like fashion, the larger the load. Now, the Parolee acknowledges his life by placing the wafers to his forehead, then divests himself of his past by giving them up to the Purger. Voilà, he becomes ready for Passage." The Parolee handed the last wafer to the Purger who tossed it in the mortar. After a few grinds, he placed the pestle on the table and held out his hand. The Teludrian Assistant retrieved a slender tube from the sack and handed it over. The Purger filled it with the contents of the mortar, holding it out for the Assistant, who took it and backed off into the shadows.

The Purger nodded to the other Parolee who stepped forward, placed his backpack on the bench and opened it, beginning the process again. The Parolee retrieved wafer after wafer from the backpack, holding each in turn to his forehead before handing it over. Just as the Parolee presented his last wafer, the Assistant Purger returned from the shadows, producing another slender tube. As before, the Assistant took the filled tube and disappeared.

"Only one thing left to be done," Guy said to his trainee. "By now he has installed all the necessary pyrotechnic accouterments. Three, two one..." A fat streak of fine sparks shot skyward accompanied by a soft "Phtsssssssssssssssssssssssssssss," followed immediately by a twin. The initial trail sparks blinked out, soon followed by the other. "Wait on it, wait on it," Guy advised. A brilliant flash, followed by a loud bang, broke the silence. High above, petals of glowing embers shot out, filling the sky with a fiery chrysanthemum. A second report, louder than the first, splayed another burning flower above their heads. "Now it's stardust."

By the time the last glowing fragments of the sky flowers had faded, the Assistant Purger had returned to collect the empty box and backpack as well as the contents of his burlap sack. Guy continued to look skyward until two papers drifted down through the night sky. He caught each before they reached the ground. "Always remember to get the Letters of Transit," he said to his trainee, "or it is all for naught." He examined the documents before handing them over to the Purger. "If you don't mind, you fill in the names. That'll make it even more official." The man pulled an inkwell and dip pen from under the bench and proceeded to sign the papers. He handed them back to Guy, who folded them carefully, tucking them into his pocket. "All in order," he said to his trainee, "documentation, number one rule, yada, yada, yada." Then he addressed the two Parolees, "Greetings Passengers, we will take you to Port. Now we really need to get moving, we just have time enough to make the next cab." He nodded to the Purger and led the entourage out of the courtyard and onto the gravel path. Along the way back to the pavement, they met a Miglizak pulling an oxcart heaped full of wafers.

Just as they arrived at the barricade, a cab pulled up, all bright and shiny. A Miglizak Pathfinder hopped out. Just before the cabbie closed the door, Guy put his hands together over his head simulating the Miglizak's crest and called out to the Pathfinder, "He's on the path. Remind me to ask you when I see you next time what he did to deserve an oxcart. Got to run, T-T-F-N." Guy settled in his seat as the cabbie turned onto a wide boulevard. "This is the bypass," he said to the Passengers. "No more city traffic for you. Non-stop to Port it is." No sooner had he said it than the cab pulled up in front of a brightly lit pier.

A Pedathian Pathfinder was waiting. He jumped in the cab as soon as Guy and his group were clear, and the cab sped off. Guy pulled the Letters of Transit from his pocket and handed them to the Passengers. "Passengers, this way please, The Livingston is about to dock." He led them down a long, sparsely lit wooden pier. They reached its end just as a small boat, powered by a huffing steam engine, glided into view from the black that surrounded them. It nudged gently into the bumpers that lined the pier. Guy reached into his pocket and handed each Passenger a gold coin. "Give this to Charlie. He'll take good care of you." He turned to his trainee. "Don't forget the coins. Charlie gets crabby if he doesn't get his coins. When Charlie gets crabby, Top gets upset. You get the picture."

"Uh-huh."

Guy held the bow line while the Passengers boarded. "Next stop, Paradise," he called out, shoving the boat away from the dock with his foot. The boat surged forward, its boiler spewing out a cloud of steam and disappeared into the black. "They don't all come through here, ya' know. No matter what their planet of origin, the Dearly Departed have only three ways to move on. Some fly non-stop to Paradise. The majority, though, have to take the bus, with a layover here for adjustment. Then, there are a few deserving miscreants who ride a dung cart, but it ain't to Paradise. Come on," he said, tugging his trainee's arm, "we're due at Pickup."

"Uh-huh."

BIG AL

"Ohhhhhhhhhhhhhh!" Iris shouted, piercing the still morning with her crackling voice. There's something in the living room." The sound was accompanied by the rapid thump, thump, thump of her feet as she ran down the hallway toward her son and daughter-in-law's bedroom. Her grandson, Tommy, awakened by the commotion as his grandmother passed his room, sat up in his bed. He listened as she continued up the hall. Rubbing the sleep from his eyes, he peeked into the hall, just in time to see his grandmother stop outside his parents' bedroom. Her white hair was drawn back in a ponytail. She was wearing her favorite tie-dyed Grateful Dead t-shirt. Pink bunny slippers kept her baggy sweatpants from spilling onto the floor.

"Ohhhhhhhhhhhhhh," she repeated, looking inside, "wake up, there's a big ol' man in the living room and he doesn't have any clothes on," Iris bleated, reaching the end of the hall.

"What's that, Mom?" her daughter-in-law, Vera, asked groggily, rising up from her pillow. "Who doesn't have any clothes on?"

"Vera," asked her husband, Sam, pulling the covers up over his head, "what's all the commotion about? What time is it? Can't a guy get to sleep just a little late on a Saturday morning?"

"It's a big ol' man and he doesn't have any clothes on," Iris said. "It's just terrible. Just terrible. I was going to watch the Stooges when I remembered that there weren't nothing in the livin' room but the new carpet, that's when I saw him in all his glory."

While Iris continued, Tommy tugged on a pair of jeans, and slipped a Seattle Warriors jersey over his head. He laced up his Nikes, then crept into the hall, pausing in front of his sister Monica's room to see if she had heard the commotion. He placed his ear against the door to listen for any sign of activity. Detecting none, he figured she had finally gone deaf from the ear pods which remained in her ears twenty-four/seven.

"It's 6:30 and Iris says someone is in our living room," Vera said, pulling back the covers and shaking Sam's shoulder. "Do you think it's the carpet installers? I thought they finished up yesterday afternoon. Maybe they forgot their tools or something."

"Whoa there," said Iris, "you're barking up the wrong tree. That ain't one of them rug cutters."

"I'm with Mom," said Sam. "I doubt that any of those fellas would be up at 6:30 on any morning, much less a Saturday morning. They seemed to be a well-meaning bunch, but they didn't even start until after lunch yesterday. And as for tools, I think the only thing they brought with them was a cigarette lighter. Before they had finished, they had borrowed half my stuff."

"Sam, don't you think we better find out what is going on?" Vera asked. "Come in, Mom, and tell us what's got you so upset."

Tommy continued along the hall until he reached his parents' bedroom, tentatively poking his head through the door.

"What's going on? Did Gramma say someone's in the living room?" he asked.

"Tommy, not you, too?" groaned Sam.

"Oh no, Dad, Gramma woke me up too," he said. "You want me to go see what's up?"

"Good idea," said Sam, rolling over.

Vera jabbed her husband in the ribs. "Sam! You're not going to let Tommy go in there. You have no idea what's going on. Now get up and find out what's got your mother so upset."

"She doesn't look upset to me."

"Well she *sounds* upset! Now are you going, or do I have to get ugly on you?"

"Alright, alright," Sam mumbled, as he threw his legs over the edge of the bed and stretched his arms above his head. He stood up, hiking his faded red gym shorts to meet a tattered white t-shirt. He jammed his feet into his old sandals and made his way to the door.

Vera rolled out of the bed, stepping into her slippers while pulling a pink terrycloth bathrobe over her pajamas.

Sam stopped in front of Tommy, who now stood squarely in the doorway. "Do you mind?"

"What?" asked Tommy, forgetting that he was blocking the way. Sam wiggled his right forefinger, signaling him to move. "Oh, sorry Dad," Tommy said, stepping back into the hall.

"Got your bat in your room?" asked Sam.

"Sure."

"Well, don't just stand there. Get it." Tommy scooted down the hall, disappearing into his room.

"What are you going to do with Tommy's bat?" asked Vera.

"Work on my golf swing. What do you think I'm going to do? I'm going to see what's up."

"Sam, don't be foolish. What if it's a burglar?"

"Oh, I don't think it's a bugler," said Iris. "He didn't have a horn, at least I didn't see a horn. If he had a horn, it would be a big horn and I think I would have noticed a big horn. No, I don't think he is a bugler."

Sam marched down the hall, until he reached Tommy's room. Iris and Vera followed. "What in the world is that?" he asked, eyeing the contents of Tommy's hand.

"My wiffle bat."

"I can see that. I was thinking maybe your real bat."

"It's not here, Dad."

"Should I dare ask where it is?"

"I let Pudgy borrow it."

"Why on earth would you let that Pudgy borrow your bat?" asked Vera. "Isn't he the one who rode your bike through the broken glass and flattened your tires?"

"No, Mom, that was Buzzy."

"The issue at hand is not about a flat tire," Sam said, holding his hand up. "Everyone please be quiet. Now Mom, are you sure you saw a man in the living room? It wasn't a shadow or something like that?"

"As sure as eggs is eggs," said Iris. "He wasn't hard to miss what with all the furniture missing and the like."

"The furniture is not missing," said Sam. "It's all out in the garage."

"Lot of good it's doing out there," said Iris. "What was I going to sit on to watch the Stooges?"

"See, I'm not the only one who thinks we should have paid the installers to move the furniture back in," Vera added. "I could've had the living room put all together last night, if you hadn't been so cheap."

"I'm sure we will have the time," said Sam, "to discuss the finer points of feng shui later, dear. Do you still want me to find out what's going on in the living room?"

"Actually, in the historical sense," said Tommy, "feng shui was widely used to orient buildings…"

"Precisely," said Sam, taking the wiffle bat from Tommy's hand. "Now, if we are in agreement, all of you wait in Tommy's room. If I don't return, call 911."

"Sure, you don't need any help, Dad?" Tommy asked.

"I'm sure, son, but thanks for asking," Sam said, without looking around.

* * *

"I don't know why your father couldn't have put that furniture back last night," said Vera.

"What's that got to do with this?" asked Tommy.

"Well, if the furniture was there, maybe this person or whatever it is, wouldn't have been so ready to take up residence on my new carpet."

"So, what you're trying to tell me is an empty room is more attractive than one with a nice soft couch?"

"Oh, I give up, you sound just like your father," said Vera. "Just once in my life, I wish something could turn out as planned. All I ever wanted was to lead a normal life, to have a husband with a normal job, have a normal family, in a normal neighborhood, with normal neighbors."

"We're not normal?" asked Tommy.

"You're missing the point," huffed Vera. "Having a stranger in the living room is not normal. Why does this always happen to me? Is anything happening out there?"

Tommy peeked out the door into the hallway. "Nothing."

"That's just what I was talking about," said Vera. "What do you mean, nothing? Something has to be happening. Don't you see anything?"

Tommy looked again. "No, Dad must still be in the living room. Want me to go take a look?" He started out the door, but Vera grabbed him.

"Oh no, young man, you stay right here."

"I'll go," said Iris. "He's mine, anyway. I found him. Finders keepers."

"Mom, you stay here, too. Sam will handle things… I hope. You see anything now?"

"No. You won't let me out in the hallway," said Iris.

"Not you. I meant Tommy."

"Here he comes," said Tommy, stepping into the hallway.

Iris and Vera joined Tommy, waiting in silent anticipation as Sam ambled toward them. He quickly shooed them back into Tommy's room and took a measured breath. "Mom's right. There's something big in there," he croaked. "And it sure looks kinda like a big man." He looked at Vera, eyes wide and mouth agape. "And for sure, he doesn't have any clothes on."

"Well, what did you do?" Vera asked.

"He's really big, Vera," Sam said very slowly, "with no clothes on, and just sitting on the floor. And he's all grey looking."

"On my new carpet!" gasped Vera, "We'll probably have to get it cleaned before we even get one day's enjoyment out of it. I knew we should have moved the furniture back in last night. We could have paid the installers to move it, but no, you had to save a few bucks."

"Vera, what's that got to do with this situation?"

"Well, there would have been something to sit on. Sam, what are you going to do about this?"

Sam put a finger to his lips. "Shhhhhhh. Stay calm. Everyone use their 'I'm in church' voice. Vera, let me explain the essentials as I see them. There's something that looks like a really big man, bare ass naked, sitting on your brand new carpet in our living room. His head is almost touching the ceiling. If he stood up, he'd be standing in the middle of the attic. I'm willing to concede that at this moment in time this may look like a big thing, no pun intended. However, in the grand scheme of things, I think it's a perfectly manageable situation."

"Well, I am quite capable of grasping the situation," Vera huffed. "Don't you think you are exaggerating things just a bit? We have a nine foot ceiling in the living room. Besides, anything will look big in an empty room. If the furniture was in there, I'm sure things would look a lot smaller. Regardless, you have to do something."

Sam nodded in agreement. "I realize the status of our furniture is gaining significance in your estimation. Can we agree to discuss that later? Right now, I suggest we have bigger fish to fry - again, no pun intended. As I see it there is a really big situation in our living room and I think our first priority is to address that."

"Vera, you can bet your bottom dollar, he's really big," said Iris. "If you remember, I was the first one there. Can I keep him?"

"No, you can't keep him," said Vera.

"Finders, keepers."

"You already said that, Mom," said Vera,

"As tantalizing as that proposition sounds," said Sam, "I agree with Vera. I'm afraid the answer is no."

"See what you've done, Sam? Now you have your mother all upset and confused," Vera said, shaking her head.

"What do you mean I have confused Mom? She's the one who started all this."

"I found him, he's mine and I want to keep him," whined Iris.

"That'd be way cool," said Tommy. "I'll help Gramma take care of him."

"Stop, stop, stop," fumed Vera. "This isn't a puppy you can keep in a garage. I want it, or him, out of there right now, Sam. What are you going to do?"

"Everyone listen," said Sam. "First thing, I think we've got to get out of here as quietly and quickly as we can. I don't think he saw me. At least, he didn't move the slightest bit when I went into the living room. If we all are very quiet, maybe we can sneak out the front door without disturbing him. Once we get outside, we'll hash out what to do next."

"Oh, I could do with some hash, I'm hungry," said Iris.

"Not now, Mom," Sam said, holding up a hand.

"There's no hashing to it," said Vera. "He's got to go. That's it."

"Dad, where's my wiffle bat?" asked Tommy.

"Sorry, dropped it in the living room. We don't have time to worry about your wiffle bat right now. Let's stick to the plan. If everyone will just work with me a little, I think we'll be okay."

Sam took a deep breath. "We're gonna go quietly down the hall past the living room and out the front door. He's sitting in the corner. I don't think he'll see us. But we've got to be very, very quiet. Come on everybody, move as fast as you can, but be very, very quiet." He looked Iris in the eye. "You got that, Mom?" She nodded. Sam then said, "Now, everyone follow me." Taking his mother's hand, he led her down the hallway. Vera followed. She looked back over her shoulder for Tommy. He hadn't moved.

"Tommy!" she hissed.

"But…"

"Don't 'but' me! Get over here, pronto." If her eyes had been lasers, they would have burned two holes straight through him. Tommy squeezed past his mother and quickly got in step with Sam and Iris.

When they reached the opening to the living room, Sam stopped, eyes open wide. He craned his head around and peeked inside. He turned to Iris and the others, slowly raising his hand. Placing his finger to his lips, he whispered, "Wait until I open the door before you follow me any further. Walk straight ahead and don't stop to look." Sam then tiptoed through the foyer and gently unlocked the front door. He pulled it open, then gingerly pushed the storm door as he stepped out onto the porch, hoping the pneumatic return would not squeak.

Vera herded Iris and Tommy toward Sam. When Tommy passed the opening into the living room, he craned his head through the opening before Vera could catch him. He saw it was as empty as they had left it the evening before, but with one exception. Sitting on the floor, in the corner, was something that looked like a man. He was very big, naked as a jay bird and leaning against the wall for support. A sheath of pallid grey skin hung on his immense frame in soft folds like an ill-fitting slipcover on a lumpy couch. His knees were drawn up to a plump belly. Elbows rested on top, right arm folded across his chest, the other cradled the chin of his large bald head. Black, almond shaped eyes stared out from under heavy eye lids.

Suddenly, Tommy was yanked back into the hallway coming face to face with his scowling mother.

"Mom, you won't believe…"

"Go," she said, pointing to the front door.

"But Mom," Tommy insisted, "it's an alien."

"Hush, now you sound as silly as your father," she said, turning him toward the front door and giving him a soft nudge. After Tommy joined Iris at the front door, Vera took a deep breath and stepped into the living room. She took one look at Tommy's alien before rocking back and forth then crumpling to the soft shag.

Sam watched Iris and Tommy appear from the gloom of the foyer. He waited for a moment for Vera to follow. "Where's Vera?" he asked.

"She was right behind us," said Iris.

"Well, she's not there now."

Tommy turned and called out, "Mom, where are you?"

"Shhhhhhhh! Don't yell," said Sam. "You don't want to disturb you-know-who."

"Mom?" asked Tommy.

"No. Who do you think? You-know-who in the living room."

"You mean the alien," said Tommy.

"The what?" asked Sam.

"He's a grey alien," said Tommy. "Let's call him Big Al."

"Tommy, I don't have time for this. Besides, aren't grey aliens little fellas? Didn't you see E.T.? I thought you had that on DVD. Now, you two stay put and don't say a word. I'll go find your Mom. Okay?"

Sam walked back into the foyer, letting his eyes adjust to the shadows before tiptoeing inside the living room. There, he could see Vera crumpled on the floor. Kneeling down, he gently shook her head in an attempt to wake her up. Having no success, he rejoined Iris and Tommy the porch.

Sam looked at Tommy. "Your Mom has fainted in the living room. I need your help. Now, listen carefully. All I'm going to do is go back in and pick her up and bring her out. I need you to get the doors, Tommy. That's all, nothing more or less. Got it?"

"But Dad... "

"We don't have time for 'buts' right now, just do what I say, okay?"

"Okay Dad, but… "

"Shhhhhh, what did I tell you? Don't answer that. Just do what I told you."

Tommy nodded. He followed his father back into the house, stopping just inside the foyer while Sam continued to the living room. Tommy patiently watched him tiptoe over to his mother and attempt to scoop her up from the floor. She was so completely limp, no matter what part his father grabbed, he could not get her off the floor. Tommy watched his mother's head bang dully on the carpet a couple of times before his father sat her up, wrapping his arms around her chest. He then proceeded to drag her out, heels leaving two ruts in the new carpet.

Tommy held the screen door until his mother was safely on the porch.

"Each of you get a foot," Sam panted. "We'll put her on the lawn until she wakes up." Iris and Tom each grabbed a foot and Sam began to back down the concrete steps. Vera's backside bumped down each step and then scraped across the walk until they reached the dewy grass.

"Tommy, make sure the doors are shut tight," said Sam.

"But Dad…"

"Tommy, I'm sorry about your bat, we'll get it later."

"That's not it, Dad."

"Then what?"

"Monica."

Sam stood up, allowing Vera's head to fall with a soft 'thud' on the wet grass, then looked around as if he had lost something. He put his hand to his forehead, then pulled it down across his face and along his throat until it rested on his chest.

"Monica?"

"What about Monica?" Vera mumbled, as she rolled to her side, gingerly rubbing her behind.

"That's what I've been trying to tell you," Tommy said. "Monica is still in her room."

"How in the world did you let that happen?" Sam asked Vera.

"I'm all wet and my butt hurts. What happened?" she mumbled.

"You conked out and we brought you out here to rest." Iris piped in.

Regaining her senses, Vera snarled, "This is all your fault, Sam Wecco." She struggled to her knees and then stiffly stood up, rubbing her backside all the while. "If you weren't so tight with a buck, we could've had the installers put the furniture back in and we wouldn't have that... that... thing sitting... on... the...fl... "Her eyes rolled back in her head just before she slumped to the wet grass.

"Mom," Tommy shouted.

"Leave her be. She'll be OK," Sam said, "It's Monica we've got to worry about.   How're we going to get your sister out of the house?"

"Sam, maybe we should call for some help," said Iris.

"Good idea. Tommy, call the cops while I figure out what to do about Monica."

"Dad, you think that is a good idea? We don't want to hurt him or anything."

"I don't think it would come to that," said Sam. "What else are we going to do?"

"Okay, I'll call them. Give me your phone,"

Sam pursed his lips as he patted his threadbare tee shirt and raggedy gym shorts. "Gee, Tommy, does it look like I have my phone on me? Mom, do you have your phone on you?"

Iris patted her clothes. "I don't think I have any foam on me. Do you see some?"

"Is it too much to ask that one of you would have your phone handy?"

"Whoa, Dad, take a chill pill," said Tommy. "I'm not the one who forgot to bring his cell phone."

"Well I'm not the one who was running all over the house waking me from a sound sleep, whining about some big man in the living room." Sam said.

"Alien, Dad," reminded Tommy.

Iris knelt down and pulled one of Vera's eyelids open. "Conked out again," she said. "I would think with all this excitement she'd be able to stay awake."

"Leave her alone," said Sam. "She'll wake up in a bit. Let's enjoy the quiet while we can."

"Sam, I'm hungry," said Iris. "What about that hash? You know what happens if I don't eat regular."

"Listen, Mom, I'm a little busy right now, but, as soon as I get this straightened out, I'll take us all to Huge Harold's for pancakes. How about that?"

"I don't like pancakes. You know I get constipated if I eat pancakes."

"Well, Mom, you can have something else. They've got a breakfast buffet with everything on it. I'm sure you can find something you'll like."

"I bet they don't have breakfast burritos," said Tommy.

"I don't like burnt toast, neither," Iris whined.

"Whoa, whoa, whoa, everybody! We'll worry about the menu later. Right now, I need some quiet so I can think about what to do next. Look at me." Sam put two fingers to his eyes then pointed them at Tommy and Iris. The three stood motionless in a Mexican standoff.

The momentary silence was shattered by a shout of "Oh gross!" blasting out from the house. Sam, Tommy and Iris wheeled around just in time to see Monica come stomping out onto the porch.

"Has anybody looked in the living room?" she asked, pointing back into the house. "Who or what the hell is that?"

"Language," warned Sam.

"Monica," said Iris, "your father wants to feed me pancakes. You know what that does to my system."

"I agree with you Gramma, I remember the last time Dad fixed pancakes. Besides, didn't you see what's in the living room?" Monica giggled. "How can you think about food after seeing that?"

"He's an alien," said Tommy. "Probably one of those greys they talk about on the History Channel. I named him Big Al."

"Big Al belongs to me," said Iris. "I found him."

"It could be any number of things," said Sam. "the least of which is an alien. Monica, get down here."

"Hold on Dad," Monica said, retrieving a cell phone from the waistband of her low rise short shorts. She held it to her ear. "Hey, Daphne... Nothing... Maybe later... Oh, you gotta see what's in our living room... Dad says it's an alien... "Monica stepped back into the house.

"Monica, no." Sam yelled to an empty doorway.

Monica reappeared at the door, fingers nimbly poking the display screen. Returning the phone to her ear, she said, "Isn't that the grossest thing you've ever seen... not the carpet. The big alien man... the big alien man sitting on the floor, you can't miss him... what do you mean there's nothing? I just took his picture... "

"Monica," pleaded Sam.

"Not now, Dad. Can't you see I'm on the phone? Sorry Daph. Didn't my photo come through? Just the carpet? Well, I wouldn't have chosen olive green, but if you like that sort of thing, I guess it's OK... Mocha or Charcoal, but then you'd have to paint the walls , and definitely not shag... Oh, Dad was too cheap to pay the installers to put the furniture back... "

"Monica, please," yelped Sam.

Monica held her hand up, palm facing her father. A look of exasperation filled her face. "And you don't see the big alien man? He's absolutely gross. We're calling him Big Al. He looks all grey and wrinkly, like he's got elephant skin or something. And his junk is hanging out and everything, but he may just look that way cause he's sitting on that green carpet. Green has a tendency to make things look funny and without any furniture...... wait a minute..."

She drew the phone down from her ear and stared at the display. There was the photo of the living room, complete with olive shag carpet, but no Big Al. Stepping back into the house, she looked into the living room. Big Al was sitting in the corner, big as life. Looking at the display, she shook her head, then peered back into the living room. Bringing the phone up to eye level, she clicked another photo. The display blinked and another picture of the empty living room appeared. She hit the back button, and the previous photo of the empty living room popped up. Stepping in closer, she took another photo. The same image of the empty room appeared on the screen. Carefully backing out onto the porch, she said in a hushed voice, "Daph, I'll have to call you back... no, no, everything is OK... no, don't come over. I'll call."

"Monica, get off the porch," Sam barked, motioning for her to join them on the lawn. "Hurry, we got to call for help. Give me the phone."

"No way," Monica protested, tucking her into her hot pink bandeau top.

"Monica." Sam glared at his daughter. She stared back with all her defiant might. The two stood motionless like gunfighters in a B western. Finally, Sam gave in. "When you have a moment, would you mind calling the cops?"

"Of course, Daddy, why didn't you just ask in the first place?" Monica started to enter the number when they heard the faint sound of a siren.

"Wow, that was fast. How much is that thing costing me a month?" asked Sam.

* * *

A bright blue Jeep Wrangler, with a City of Bunyan Police decal on the hood, finally appeared. The siren bleated once before the cruiser screeched to a halt in front of the house. A young officer hopped out, wearing khaki slacks and a forest green shirt with BPD embroidered over the pocket. He pulled a matching green ball cap over his wavy brown hair and trotted up the front walk, keeping his eyes on the small group standing in the dewy grass. Surveying the scene, his eyes eventually settled on Monica. She struck her best swimsuit edition pose, shaking her long auburn hair.

"Can we help you, officer?" Sam asked, positioning himself between Monica and the officer in an attempt to block his view.

The officer diverted his eyes to Sam. "Well sir, you see, we got a report here that some wacko and a woman identified as *very* wacko, accompanied by some other wackos, are terrorizing the neighborhood in their jammies. Apparently, the *very* female was observed sleeping in the grass. It seems at first glance, ya'll match that description."

"Oh, officer, I think there's been a bit of a mistake," Sam said meekly, inching forward. "However, we're really glad you showed up. You see we're the Weccos."

The officer immediately lowered his right hand to the vicinity of his holstered pistol. "So, you admit you're the wackos that the lady called about. Don't any of you move," the officer commanded. He unclipped his radio, bringing it to his lips. He keyed the mic. "This is Bunyan 54, do you copy, this is Bunyan 54, I need backup. I found the wackos. Come at once to 324 Grandhomme. Repeat, I need backup."

"No, no, we're not wackos. My name is Sam Wecco, W - E - C - C - O, and this is my wife Vera, Vera Wecco. Those are our kids, Tommy, Monica and my mother, Iris. We live here."

"Sir, do you have any ID?"

"Sam, what's' going on?" Vera asked, sitting up. Wet grass clippings clung to her face and hair, giving her the appearance of a used lint roller. She tugged at her dew-soaked bathrobe, which clung to her like a wet beach towel.

"Not now, Vera, I'm trying to explain things to the policeman."

"What policeman?" asked Vera, rubbing her eyes.

"Stay where you are ma'am," said the officer, tensing.

"Oh, don't shoot her, she's harmless." Iris said, as Vera slumped back to the wet grass.

Sam looked at Vera then to Iris, "Well, she's harmless for the time being," Sam said. "Now hush, Iris, while I explain things to the nice policeman." Sam looked at the officer. "You see officer," he said plaintively, "it's like this. We kinda left the house in a hurry and really didn't think too much about bringing any ID."

"That's them, officer," rang out a shrill voice from the yard next door. "I'm the one who called."

The officer whirled around to find a diminutive grey haired woman standing defiantly in the driveway between the two houses. Arms folded; she was wearing a teal camo hoodie. Her face scowled from underneath a crown of pink curlers.

"And who might you be?" the officer asked.

"Emma Medler."

"Exactly," puffed Sam.

"Emma, I should have known you be sticking your nose in where it doesn't belong," said Iris, frowning.

"I'm the one who called," Emma snapped, glaring at Iris over her thick glasses. She turned her attention to the officer. "What took you so long? Is this what I pay my taxes for? To have the police dawdle around while crime runs rampant in our neighborhoods?"

"Are you telling me you're the person who called about the wackos?"

"That's Weccos." Sam said.

"That's right," Emma responded smugly. "Nothing happens in this neighborhood what I don't know about it. When you can't depend on the police, you have to take measures into your own hands."

"Ms. Medler, do you know these folks? Do they live here?"

"Sure, they've lived there for fifteen years, and I've endured every one of them."

"Now, I'm confused. The wackos are your neighbors and they've lived here fifteen years?"

"That's Weccos," Sam repeated.

"Of course, I know them, don't mean I like them," Emma said matter-of-factly.

"Why then, did you call the police?"

"Well, nobody in their right mind would dance around their lawn in their pajamas at 6:00 in the morning. It's just outrageous that a body can't look into the yard next door without seeing a display like that. What has this town come too? Just wait, I'll take this up with the Mayor."

"6:30," corrected Tommy.

"I'm afraid he's right Ms. Medler, the call came in at 6:33 am," the officer confirmed.

"Well, I guess the word of an upstanding, law abiding citizen doesn't account for much anymore," Emma hissed. "If you don't have anything else for me, that's all I got to say." She drew her lips into a tight sneer.

"Gosh folks," the officer said sheepishly, "I guess you can go on about your business. Sorry for the mix up. I'll just fill out my report and be on my way." He brought the radio to his lips. "This is Bunyan 54, do you copy, this is Bunyan 54, cancel backup. The wackos turned out to be the legal residents. Repeat, cancel backup." He reached his hand out to Sam. "Hubie Strange."

"What?" exclaimed Sam.

"Officer Hubert Strange. Most folks call me Hubie. Pleased to make your acquaintance, Mr. Wacko."

"That's Wacko, Uhh, I mean Wecco, I mean…"

"Right, sorry 'bout that, *Mr. Wecco.*"

"Anyway, thanks," Sam said, breathing a sigh of relief. "Come back anytime."

"Wait a minute," Tommy shouted. "What about the alien?"

"Alien?" asked Hubie. "You mean like illegal alien? Like a homeland security alien?"

"Oh yes… I mean no. I mean," said Sam, wagging his head, "we were just about to call you before you showed up. It seems we have a big situation in our living room…"

"I found him first, all by myself," said Iris. "His name is Big Al."

"Officer, that's what we call him. He's a grey alien from outer space and he's really, really, really big." Tommy added.

"Tommy," said Sam. "I'm still not convinced he's an alien."

"And don't forget the part about him being totally naked. Gross!" Monica shivered.

"I was going to tell Officer Strange all that," said Sam, "if you all hadn't so rudely interrupted."

"Let me get this straight," said Hubie. "You have an illegal alien named Big Al in your house?"

"Well we don't exactly know. All I can tell you is that we have something inside that looks like a big grey man and I don't think he's from around this neck of the woods. That's why we're all out here."

"Well, it all makes perfect sense now," mumbled Hubie, shaking his head. "Why don't you start from the beginning? Better yet, let's not." He pulled a notebook from his pocket and flipped it open to a blank page. "Can you describe this illegal alien?"

"He's big and grey looking, although Monica says that may be because of the green carpet," said Iris. "Like I said, I was the first one to discover him. Did you write that down? Oh, and he ain't got no clothes on."

"Officer, I don't think he's an illegal alien," said Sam. "I mean I don't think he is from South America or something like that."

"Okay, is he armed?" asked Hubie.

"I don't think so, not unless he's got Tommy's bat," said Sam.

"Is it a wooden bat or aluminum?" Hubie asked.

"Wiffle," said Tommy.

"How'd he get the bat?"

"Dad gave it to him."

Hubie looked at Sam. "You gave him the bat, sir?"

"Of course not," huffed Sam. "It was like this officer, my mother found him in our living room. I went in to investigate and took it for protection. I guess I sort of dropped it in there when I left."

"So, let me get this straight," said Hubie. "You thought there may be a big illegal alien in your living room…"

"A real alien," said Tommy.

"With no clothes on," said Iris. "Don't forget that. Did you write that down?"

"Alright, let me get this straight. You thought there may be a big illegal alien in your living room *with no clothes on* and you decided to take a wiffle bat with you for protection."

"I would have taken a real bat if Pudgy didn't have it," said Sam.

"Who's Pudgy?"

"He's a friend of mine," said Tommy. "I lent him my real bat."

"Alright, let's get back to this case," said Hubie. "I don't know if a wiffle bat meets the definition of being armed. Was he engaged in any suspicious activity?"

"Other than sitting buck naked in our living room?" asked Sam. "I think you would understand everything if you just took a peek inside."

"Well, I prefer to collect all the eyewitness accounts before examining the scene. So what else can you tell me?" asked Hubie. No one answered. "Okay then, everyone stay here." He tucked the notebook back in his pocket and unsnapped the cover on his holster. Glancing at Monica, he cocked an eyebrow. "I've got everything under control."

"Oh, wait a sec," she said, stepping in close to him. She snapped a selfie, then cooed, "Oh, do be careful, officer."

"Don't worry Monica," he said. Crouching down, he pulled his gun, spun around, bounded up the steps and disappeared into the house.

* * *

Vera blinked her eyes, picking wilted blades of grass from her mouth. She attempted to pat down her hair which resembled the crown of rays that encircles the head of the Statue of Liberty.

"What's going on?" she asked in a wobbly voice. "Can someone help me up?" Sam pulled her to her feet.

"Do try to stay awake, Vera," he chided. "We've managed to get Strange in the living room."

"I know something strange is in the living room, you don't have to explain that to me. The question is, what are you doing about it?"

"Hubie Strange, Vera."

"I'm not strange. What in the world do you mean, saying something like that?"

"What are you talking about, Vera? I'm talking about Officer Hubert Strange. He's the policeman who is here. He's inside right now taking care of our little situation. If you hadn't slept through all this, you would know what is going on. Anyway, I'm sure he'll have everything under control in short order."

"Vera, my son, your husband, wants to feed me pancakes", Iris interjected. "You know what they do to my system."

"Sam, you know your mother can't eat things like that," said Vera. "Why would you try to feed her something you know will make her sick?"

"It wasn't like that at all. I…" started Sam.

Before he could finish, Vera noticed Monica leaning against the porch rail and barked, "Young lady, what in the world are you doing parading around outside in that outfit? Go put some clothes on this minute, before…"

She was interrupted mid-sentence by the appearance of Hubie, holding Tommy's bat. He slowly moved to the edge of the porch and drooped to the steps. His face was pale, and his eyes looked as if they were focused on something very far away. Monica immediately sat down beside him.

"That's Strange," Sam said.

"What's strange?" asked Vera.

"Not 'what', 'who'. That's Officer Strange."

"Well, Officer Strange, what have you done?" Vera demanded.

Hubie leaned forward, placed his elbows on his knees and took a deep breath. "You were right," he stammered. "Big Al is really, really big and I don't know if it is the green carpet or not, but he does look grey. And I agree with you Mr. Wecco. I don't think he's an illegal alien."

"Don't forget, he's sittin' on the floor an' he ain't got any clothes on,' reminded Iris.

"Speaking of clothes," Vera said, eying Monica, "Young lady, march inside right now and get some clothes on."

"Oh, I don't think she should go inside under the circumstances," cautioned Hubie, looking at Monica. "By the way, looks nice, ma'am."

"What?"

"The carpet, ma'am," said Hubie, "The carpet Big Al is sitting on."

"Who is this Big Al everyone is talking about?" asked Vera.

"He's my alien," said Iris.

Hubie keyed his radio with a shaking hand. "This is Bunyan 54, do you copy, this is Bunyan 54, uncancel the cancel backup call at 324 Grandhomme. Better send Fire and Rescue while you're at it. Repeat, uncancel the cancel backup. We've got a really big situation here."

"Thank you," said Vera, "I trust you wiped your feet before you tracked any dirt in."

"Ma'am, did you know there's no furniture in there?" asked Hubie.

"Don't ask me, that's Sam's deal," said Vera. "Personally, I think if there had been furniture in there, that big thing wouldn't be sitting on the floor."

"Ma'am, I don't think there's any furniture made that's big enough for Big Al to sit on," said Hubie.

"My point exactly," Sam offered, flashing a smug smile at Vera.

"Well, what do we do now, Officer Strange?" asked Vera.

"He seems quiet now, let's wait for backup."

"Can I take a look at your Jeep while we wait?" asked Tommy.

"Sure," said Hubie, standing up, "come on. You want to sit behind the wheel?"

"You betcha," said Tommy

"Can I come, too?" asked Monica.

Hubie grinned. "Most certainly. You can check out my equipment, if you like."

"Really, that sounds like fun," giggled Monica. Hubie's cheeks turned crimson.

"Does that equipment include a taser gun?" asked Iris.

"Yes."

"Can I use it on Emma?"

"No ma'am, it's for emergency situations only."

"Shucks," said Iris. "One could only hope."

"You coming, Mr. and Mrs. Wecco?" asked Hubie.

"No, I'm going to sit on something other than my front lawn," said Vera, plopping down on a porch step.

"You kids go on, I'll stay with Mom," said Sam. He waited until they were out of earshot to ask, "Well, this sure has been an interesting Saturday morning, hasn't it?"

"No, it hasn't," said Vera. "It's a complete disaster. Why can't you ever see things like they really are?"

"I don't understand. What are you talking about?"

"Sam, waking up to find that thing in the living room is not interesting. Having our neighbor call the police on us is not interesting. Sitting out here in my nightclothes on a Saturday morning is not interesting. Anyone else would see that, but not you."

"Well, honey, I know you're upset about Big Al," said Sam, "but aren't you making things out to be a lot worse than they really are?"

"Now you are on a first name basis with it. That's so like you, Sam. You just don't get it. You have no concept about what's been happening this morning. To you it's just something that came up - no big deal. You just go along."

"Sure, I guess. What's wrong with that?"

"Nothing, if you're content to just let life happen to you. I'm not. I just thought things would be better than the way they've turned out. Don't you have goals and aspirations? You just take things as they come along. Like your job for instance."

"What's wrong with my job? I own my own business. Not everyone can claim that distinction."

"Sam, you own a septic tank pumping truck which you inherited from your father. I don't think that exactly qualifies you as a businessman. You have a college degree in Philosophy and you spend all day pumping out septic tanks. Don't you see a disconnect?"

"It's a valuable service and people appreciate it."

"Sam, I get so tired of people asking me if I'm married to the septic tank guy. I'd like to drive a car that doesn't have *Wecco Waste - You Stink Therefore I Am!* painted on the door."

"But you have to advertise."

"You're missing the point. Don't you ever wish for a new car, a car without an advertisement painted on the side? Don't you ever think about buying a new house? Not moving in with your Mother, not buying a *new* fixer upper? We've been fixing up this dump for ten years and no matter how much paint you put on it, it's still a dump, in a dumpy neighborhood. Don't you want something better for us, not to just settle for whatever?"

"I just thought it was *who* lived in a house that's important."

"I just want Monica to be able to go to the University, not have to commute to night school at the community college in Littleton. Would it be too much to dream of joining the country club, so Tommy doesn't have to swim in that petri dish they call the public pool? Would it be too much to go to the Bahamas for vacation instead of spending a week in your buddy Frank's hunting cabin at Weasel Lake, serving as the buffet line for mosquitos?"

"Honey, I just thought one should focus on the *who* not the *what* they have in life. If you do that, you don't have to ask for much."

"Why can't things work out the right way just one time," asked Vera, "just for one moment? If that could happen, I would be happy. I don't want much, but I do want that. Tell me, is that too much to ask?"

* * *

Quite some time passed before the faint wail of another siren drifted down the street. The Weccos and Hubie huddled around the porch at 324 Grandhomme as the blare of the siren swelled. They watched as Bunyan's other law enforcement vehicle, an old silver Crown Victoria, whizzed past and came to a screeching stop six houses down. Amidst the grinding of gears, it lurched into reverse and waggled backward until it stopped alongside Hubie's vehicle. a few moments passed before the driver's side door swung open with a grinding scritch. A short, chubby policeman dressed like Hubie squeezed out, put a Smoky Bear hat on his balding head and tottered up the sidewalk. He was using a grimy towel to dab at a large brown stain which ran down his shirt until it disappeared from sight on the underside of his protruding belly.

"Spilled my coffee," he explained through the doughnut crumbs in his mustache. "Are these the wackos?" he asked, pointing to the group huddled around his fellow officer.

"That's Wecco," said Sam.

"Hey, these folks are okay," Hubie explained. "This is Mr. Wecco, his wife Vera, his mother Iris and their kids, Tommy and Monica. I assume you can tell who is who."

The officer held out his hand. "Well, Mr. Wacko, Hugo Nutts."

"Wait a minute. I've had enough of this. The name is Wecco, W - E - C - C - O, and this is my wife Vera, Vera Wecco," he explained hotly. "Those are our kids," he said, pointing to Tommy, Monica and my mother Iris. "We live here."

"Sorry, Mr. Wecco," said Hubie. "This Officer is Nutts. Hugo, H-U-G-O, Nutts. He didn't mean any disrespect."

"Well, alright, but don't let it happen again," said Sam.

"Hugo, what took you so long?" asked Hubie, "I called for backup over an hour ago."

"Well, after you canceled backup," Hugo began, "I went on break. Drove over to Huge Harold's. There was a group from that new church over in Littleton at the all-you-can-eat breakfast buffet. You know the one where they're always out protesting something. They were lined up for the buffet clean to the cash register. By the time I got to the food line, they were out of most everything. Then you cancelled the cancellation, so I didn't have time to wait until they brought out some fresh fixin's. So... "

"Okay, Hugo. We get the picture," Hubie said, rubbing his forehead. "Just apologize to Mr. Wecco."

"Oh, right you are. Wait a minute. Wecco? Sorry Mr. Wecco, no disrespect intended. I didn't make the connection. Would you be the same Wecco as in Wecco Waste?"

"One in the same," said Sam, breaking into a big smile.

"Love your slogan: *You Stink, Therefore I Am* kinda philosophical sounding. I remember Wecco Waste from when I was a kid. That wasn't you, though."

"That was my Dad. I took over when he retired," said Sam.

"Oh, that makes sense. His name was Hank, wasn't it? They called him Full Tank Hank. But didn't he have a different slogan back then? Oh yeah, *If Your Tank Goes Wacko, Call Wecco.*"

"That's right," said Sam.

"So, what do they call you? Septic Sam?"

"Usually they call me Mr. Wecco."

"What you say we start over?" Hugo said. "Nice to meet you Mr. Wecco. Say, I got a great idea. I stopped at Large Marge's on the way over and picked up some doughnuts. Got 'em down there in the cruiser. Assorted and fresh. Anybody interested?"

"Doughnuts are no better than pancakes," Iris protested. "If I eat them, I get all stove up."

"What kind you got?" asked Tommy, ignoring his grandmother.

"Let's see, in alphabetical order," Hugo mused, ticking off each on a stubby digit, "beignets, Bismarcks, cake, cream-filled, crullers, dunkers, éclairs, fritters, glazed…"

"I hate to break up this coffee klatch," Vera shouted, bringing clenched fists to her temples, "but is anybody going to do anything about that creature sitting in my living room on my brand new mistletoe tint, sculptured, shag carpet?"

"Oh yeah, Hugo. You better check it out." Hubie sheepishly said.

"I thought we were here for the wackos... err Weccos," said Hugo.

"Things change, Hugo. You better go inside and take a look."

"Why me?"

"Cause I've *already* looked."

"Oh," Hugo mumbled, looking into all the faces now trained on him.

"Don't look at us," Monica chided, "been there, done that. I even took a picture," she said, holding up her cell phone.

"Let's see," Hugo asked, holding out his hand.

"No way," Monica protested, tucking her hand behind her back. "You can look, but you can't touch." She tapped the display screen and held the phone out for Hugo.

He studied the display. "Looks nice, ma'am"

"What?" cried Vera.

"Nice carpet, ma'am," he offered, looking at Vera. "Did you say that was mistletoe tint? Looks more like pistachio to me. By the way, I see there's no furniture in the room. Were you aware of that?"

"I have nothing more to say on that matter," Vera snapped.

"Well, I don't see any big man in this photo. No sign of him anywhere. Guess we can wrap this one up," Hugo sighed in relief.

"Oh, I forgot," Monica said, checking the display. "I took his picture, but he isn't in the picture." She held it up for everyone to see. "But, he's there, in the living room just the same, only he isn't here, in the picture, that is. You can ask Daphne; she didn't see him either."

"Where's this Daphne?" Hugo asked.

"She's not here," said Monica.

"Why did you let her leave?" Hugo asked Hubie.

"Oh, she hasn't been here," said Monica. "Well, of course, I mean she *has* been here. Before, that is, just not today. Anyway, I can call her."

"No need to call Daphne," said Hubie. "Hugo, just take a quick look. Please."

"I just looked," Hugo said, pointing to the phone.

"No, I mean the living room," growled Hubie.

Hugo hesitated for a few seconds, then grasped his flashlight in a chubby paw. "Stand aside," he ordered. The group parted and Hugo marched up to the porch. He paused a moment at the door, wiping his forehead with the coffee stained towel. Tossing it aside, he stepped in. An instant later, he backed out, turned and leapt from the edge of the porch, landing in a heap on the lawn.

Emma rushed forward, dropping to her knees beside the limp Hugo. "Officer down, officer down," she cried.

Hugo opened his eyes. "Who are you?" he asked, smiling.

"Apparently the only one around here that gives a hoot about a brave public servant who has placed himself in harm's way," said Emma.

The rest helped her tug Hugo to a sitting position while he stammered, "There's a big man in there. We need backup."

"Sorry, Hugo, you *are* backup," Hubie reminded.

"He doesn't have any clothes on," Hugo puffed.

"I know. We all know."

"Oh. Well, what are you going to do?" asked Hugo.

"Let's think this thing out. First, there's no sign of forced entry. Fact is, I don't even know how he could have gotten through the door. Mr. Wecco, was anything damaged or stolen?"

"No," said Sam

"What about the furniture?" Hugo asked.

"According to Mrs. Wecco, Mr. Wecco took the furniture," Hubie continued.

"Why did he take the furniture?"

"Because he was too cheap to pay the carpet installers," said Vera.

"Penny saved, dollar lost, I always say," said Hugo.

Hubie continued, "If you don't mind. Second, nothing was damaged or stolen."

"Did Mr. Wecco assault or threaten anyone?" asked Hugo.

No," fumed Sam.

"Why would you ask something like that?" asked Hubie.

"Well, he did take the furniture."

Hubie shook his head. "Third, he, *the illegal alien*, didn't assault or threaten anyone. Fourth, he's naked and in an obvious state of mental incapacity, and…" Hubie hesitated in mid-sentence.

"And?" repeated Hugo, hoping the next thing out of Hubie's mouth did not involve him.

"He's a grey alien from outer space," said Tommy.

"Oh, I don't think so," said Hugo, "according to True UFO, greys are very slight in stature compared to humans. Big Al is much too big to be a grey. Could be a reptilian though."

"Told ya," said Sam.

"Well, alien or not," continued Hubie, "he's just too doggone big for us to handle. For the record, Mr. Wecco, does he live with you?"

"Of course not," said Sam.

"That being the case, I am going to declare him a homeless squatter and let Fire and Rescue deal with him. Hugo, call dispatch."

A wide smile spread across Hugo's face. "A grand idea, Strange, simply grand. Help me up. After I call dispatch, would anyone want a doughnut?"

* * *

They waited on the sidewalk, munching doughnuts and sipping water from the garden hose for the longest time before a bleating horn signaled Fire and Rescue's arrival. The old LaSalle pumper lumbered up the street and creaked to a stop in the remaining roadway beside Hugo's cruiser. Six firefighters decked out in soot-stained turnout gear spilled out from every opening in the old truck. Two dragged barricades to the end of the street. The other four grabbed hoses from the compartments under the tank and lugged them across the yard, until they came face to face with Emma.

"Well, thank goodness I was here to tend to Hugo," said Emma, with a scowl on her face. "The whole town could have burned down before this bunch showed up. Even a cat stuck in a tree could have found a way down by now."

The leader pulled off his mask. "Who are you?"

"Emma Medler. I'm the one who called in the first place. So long ago it's old news by now. Is this what I pay my taxes for? No wonder this country is in the shape it's in, what with our neighborhoods burning down around us and the fire department nowhere to be found. Don't think I won't take this up with the Mayor and Commission."

"Who is in charge here?" the leader asked, looking at Hubie.

"That'd be me, Chief," Hubie said, standing up. "What took you so long?"

"Well, we decided to fuel up before we answered the alarm, since it wasn't a fire or some other *real* emergency." He shot a glance at Emma. "Wouldn't want to run out of juice right in the middle of a run. So we stopped at Colossal Carl's Car Care, you know, across from Huge Harold's. There was a church bus pulled up to the pump. It was that new church from over at Littleton. You know the one where they're always out protesting something. But the bus was empty except for the driver. It seems the rest of them were across the street at Huge Harold's for the all-you-can-eat breakfast buffet. Well, we waited until he topped off the tank. He paid Carl and went to start the bus and wouldn't you know, it was dead as a doornail. We sat there for a while trying to figure whether it would be quicker to help him get the bus started or to run over to Fat Phil's Fill'er-Up..."

"Okay, okay, Chief. We get the picture."

"Alright then, what's the story on the homeless wackos?"

"That's Wecco," Sam growled, stomping his foot. He moved in so close to the Chief, their noses almost touched. "W-E-C-C-O, Wecco. And we aren't homeless."

"Hey, hey, everyone settle down," Hubie coaxed. "We're not concerned about wackos any longer. Chief, say hello to Mr. Wecco and his family."

The Chief looked at Sam for a moment, then smiled, holding out his hand. "Mr. Wacko, Yuri Dickelous."

Sam clapped his hands to his head and yelled in frustration, "I can't believe this! I don't have to take this kind of abuse."

"No, no, Mr. Wecco, you got it all wrong," Hubie said, rapidly stepping between Sam and the Chief. "This is Chief Dickelous, Yuri Dickelous, a fine man of Ukrainian decent. Look Chief, we've got a bit of a situation here and we need your assistance."

"Well, what is this situation?" said the Chief, eying Hubie. "Looks more like a picnic than a reason to call out Bunyan's finest. So, what goes? Dispatch said something about a homeless man. Do we need to take someone to the hospital?"

"Yes and no," said Hubie.

"What do you mean, yes and no? Which is it?" asked the Chief.

"Yes, technically… I mean I guess the homeless classification is as good as any… at least for now. We couldn't find any identification… and the subject hasn't said anything. But no, in the sense that I don't think the hospital will end up being the solution."

"Does this homeless man need to be rescued or not?" asked the Chief.

"Not in the true sense of the word 'rescue' but, loosely defined, it could be construed as a rescue," answered Hubie.

"How loose?"

"For the official record," said Hubie, "we will classify it as a homeless situation and a rescue would be in order."

"You're not making any sense," said the Chief.

"Okay, okay. Truth is there is a big, for want of a better term, *man* in the Wecco's living room and we don't know how to get him out. So, you see, you could say it's the Weccos who need to be rescued… from this situation."

"It's a grey alien," said Tommy.

"A what?" asked the Chief.

"Did you tell him he doesn't have any clothes on?" asked Iris.

"According to the witnesses," said Hugo, "His name is Big Al."

"You called us out on a wild goose chase? Come on men," the Chief called over his shoulder, "pack up, we're outta here."

"Just as well," said Hubie. "I didn't think you guys could handle this one, anyway,"

"And just what do you mean by that?" huffed the Chief.

"What I mean is that I don't think you can handle one measly homeless person, big or small."

"Where is this Big Al? We'll have him outta there in sixty seconds," growled the Chief.

Hubie smiled and pointed to the front door. "In the Wecco's living room."

"Just stay out of my way," the Chief said, brushing past Hubie.

"You're not going to walk on my new carpet wearing those filthy boots," Vera said, folding her arms across her chest, while taking up a stance directly in the Chief's path.

"What did you say?" asked the Chief.

"Take those boots off," she demanded.

"But…"

"Don't 'but' me! I've had it with people 'butting' me today. If you're thinking of walking on my new carpet, get those boots off, pronto." She focused her laser eyes on the Chief. He looked at her long enough to gauge her resolve, then pulled his boots off. He squeezed past her and quickly moved up the steps and disappeared into the house.

"Hugo," Hubie called out, "better let dispatch know what's up."

Hugo was barely halfway to his cruiser when the Chief appeared at the door. Cupping his hand to his mouth, he called out, "Guys, take your gear off and get in here. Pee Wee, you stay out here and make sure no one comes in."

The four remaining firefighters quickly shed their gear and filed through the door under Vera's watchful eyes. Everyone else waited anxiously outside. It had not occurred to them that they could see what was going on inside until Iris climbed on the spigot located underneath the living room picture window. The rest quickly lined up along the window on either side of her and peered intently at the scene unfolding inside.

The firefighters were engaged in an animated discussion. They moved around Big Al like ants on a Twinkie. One was taking photos with his phone. Now and then, one would separate from the group, gesturing toward the door or the window. One dropped to the carpet and rolled around, then wiggled like a worm. Another pointed to the ceiling and made a circular motion with his hand, only to have the others shake their heads in a definitive 'No!'. Finally, they huddled in the center of the room before heading out on the porch in single file.

The Chief descended the steps and said, "Pee Wee, better call dispatch and tell them we have a code fourteen."

"A code fourteen?" asked Pee Wee. "Chief, this ain't no code fourteen."

"What would you code it?"

"Maybe an eleven or perhaps a seventeen, but not a fourteen."

"Well, I don't see it as a seventeen. Maybe an eleven, but definitely not a seventeen."

"What about a nine?"

"No, no, not a nine."

"Nine is just as good as eleven."

"Well maybe. Let me think about it while I address the group." The Chief held up his hand, signaling everyone to be quiet. "We've made an assessment of the situation and are ready to make our report. First, we can confirm we have what has been alternately described as a big man or a grey alien in the wacko's living room. I think it's also safe to say he's not just big, but very, *very* big. There is some disagreement as to whether his skin has a grey or green cast to it. Consensus is that this may be as an effect of light reflected off the green carpet. The record will note that he is not clothed. Subject appears to be alive, although nonresponsive to verbal prompts and physical stimuli. Whether the subject is incapacitated or unwilling to communicate is undetermined at this time. We don't think he's a local. For purposes of discussion he will be referred to as Big Al."

"Thank you, Chief Dickless, can you tell us anything we don't already know?" Vera cackled.

"That's Dickelous, ma'am. Are you aware that there's no furniture in there?"

"Chief, I wouldn't go there if I were you," Sam warned.

The Chief looked at Vera. Her eyes were shooting laser bolts at him. "Gotcha. We measured his lower leg to be forty-eight inches. Extrapolating that, we estimate his overall height to be at least fourteen feet. As you may be aware, he is packing on a few extra pounds and we figure if he was buying pants at the Big 'n Tall downtown, he would need a 175-inch waistband - 173 if he got the stretchy ones. We think he would weigh in well over 1000 pounds, give or take a hundred or so. We've made a complete photo record. He's very big..."

"Chief, can we see the photos?" asked Hubie.

"Let me have the phone," said the chief. The fireman who took the pictures pulled his phone from his pocket and handed it over. The Chief stared at the screen intently as he brought up the photos.

He began to drag his finger back and forth across the screen, shaking his head.

"This can't be," he said.

"Let me guess," said Hubie, "plenty of photos of the carpet and nothing else."

"No way."

"Yes, way. Same thing happened with Monica's photos."

"But he's there, we all saw him."

"Of course, he's there," said Hubie. "Apparently he's not photogenic. The question is, what can we do for these folks?"

"Well, we discussed that. First thing, he's awful heavy, and assuming he's not likely to leave on his own, we don't really have a good way to pick him up. Second, we checked the doors and they're all standard thirty-six inch widths. With a 175 inch waste, there ain't no way we can squeeze him through. It would be helpful if you could tell us how y'all got him in there in the first place…"

"We didn't get him in there," said Sam.

"He probably teleported down from the mother ship," said Tommy.

"Like, *Beam Me Up, Scotty*?" asked the Chief, raising an eyebrow. He looked at Hubie. "Have you located the mother ship?"

"Well, we haven't really looked, to tell you the truth."

"Oh, you wouldn't find it, anyway," said Tommy. "They probably stashed it inside a cloud or something like that."

"Or maybe they employ a cloaking device like the Klingon Birds of Prey," said Hugo. "Why, it could be sitting in the back yard right now and we would never know it."

"Enough," said Sam. "Chief, we just woke up this morning and he was there. Please, what are you going to do?"

"I was just getting around to that," said the Chief. "There's a few things we might do. One, we could probably drag him to the front door. Now, I already said he's too big to squeeze through, so we would have to widen the opening a little."

"Just how would you do that?" asked Vera.

"I figure we could use our chainsaws to cut out an extra two feet…"

"Over my dead body!" Vera screamed.

"Alright, calm down, just green-lighting here," soothed the Chief, "no need to push the panic button just yet. If we can't take him out the front door, we might could take him out the window. All we got to do is pop the picture window out, build a ramp on either side and roll him out."

"You're not popping any window out and you're certainly not building a ramp on my new carpet," said Vera, balling up her fists. "And that's final."

"Well ma'am, someone suggested an alternative could be to cut a hole in the roof and pull him out with a Huey from the National Guard, but, even we knew that one wouldn't fly. We…"

A shrill voice interrupted the Chief in mid-sentence. "This is a fine use of my tax dollars, no less than seven city employees lollygagging on the lawn while criminals roam the streets and houses go up in flames. The only one here who has done anything to help is Hugo."

"Ma'am, who are you?" asked the Chief.

"Emma Medler, who are you?"

"Yuri Dickelous, ma'am. I must inform you that you're encroaching on our incident perimeter. You'll need to clear this area."

"I'm what? I'll have you know I'm a taxpaying citizen, and I'll go wherever I please. You may rest assured the Mayor will hear about this," she gasped, raising her fist.

"Hugo, will you take care of Ms. Medler," asked Hubie.

"Okie dokie. You want a sandwich, Emma? I got the makin's in the cruiser."

"Call me Em," she said, smiling at Hugo.

"Got enough to share with us?" asked Pee Wee.

"Sure do. Got some bread in the back seat and a splendid selection of sandwich fixin's from Mark's Mega Meats in the old crime stopper cooler in the trunk of the justice mobile."

"Like what?" asked Pee Wee.

"Let's see," Hugo mused, ticking off each on a stubby digit, "bologna, ham, mortadella, roast beef, salami, turkey, cheddar, gouda, jack, Swiss, American as well as the aforementioned assortment of fresh bread which I got from Big Brenda's Bakery."

"Good enough," Pee Wee said, licking his lips. He turned to the other firefighters, "Come on fellas, let's set up the canopies and some tables and chairs."

"Pee Wee," said the Chief, "before you go, I've decided to call in a code ten to dispatch."

"Right on, Chief," said Pee Wee.

"Hey Chief, what's a code ten?" asked Tommy.

"Break for lunch of course."

* * *

The firefighters worked feverishly until the Wecco's yard was dotted with bright red canopies, each proudly displaying the Bunyan Fire and Rescue logo. Folding tables were placed under each canopy and a buffet line was set up in the central tent. Under the careful direction of Hugo, the firefighters lugged the behemoth crime stopper cooler up from his cruiser. Sack after sack of deli treats were heaped on the table. Emma and Hugo made sandwiches as thick as Webster's dictionary, stacking them high on the plates. They continued feasting well into the afternoon.

Iris waited until there was a lull in the activity. "What about Big Al?"

"What do you mean, Mom?" Sam asked.

"Shouldn't we give him something to eat?"

"Well, that's an interesting question, ma'am," the Chief said.

"I think you should," said Monica. "After all, he has been in there all day. He's bound to be hungry."

"I agree with her," Hubie concurred, flashing a big smile at Monica.

"I agree with Hubie," Tommy added.

"That's Officer Strange, Tommy," chided Vera.

"It's okay, Mom," said Monica. "Hubie said we could call him Hubie. Isn't that right Hubie?"

Hubie broke into a big smile. "Yup."

"Let's not get the cart before the horse," the Chief continued. "We haven't quite figured out what he is exactly. "

"He's a grey alien from outer space," said Tommy.

"The question is, what they would do with terrorists," said the Chief.

"Say what about who?" asked Sam.

"Speaking hyperthetically, of course," said the Chief, "would you give a terrorist a sandwich if he was sitting in your living room buck naked and wouldn't come out? The answer to that may have some bearing on what we do in this situation."

"He's no terrorist," said Tommy.

"And, he's hardly your typical homeless person, either," countered the Chief. "As I see it, we have two options. One, we withhold nourishment in an attempt to starve him out, or two, we give him some food in hopes it will convince him to cooperate."

"I say we give him some food, regardless," said Monica.

"Keep in mind that I'm in charge here," warned the Chief.

"But he's our Big Al," Monica fired back. "What do you think, Mom?"

"I'm for anything that will get him out of my living room without building any ramps, tearing out any windows, ripping out any walls or cutting any holes in my roof. And it wouldn't bother me if the fireman's annual picnic which has sprung up in my yard disappeared also."

"Come on Vera, it's not all that bad," soothed Sam. "We didn't have anything planned today anyway."

"I just wasn't expecting to be eating lunch in my nightclothes with the fireman," said Vera, straightening her bathrobe. "That being said, as near as I can tell, whatever he is, he hasn't done anything but sit in there since this morning, so, I really can't say I am in favor of starving him."

"Let's put it to a vote," said Tommy.

"Yeah, Chief, let's put it to a vote. That's the democratic way," Hubie added.

"Alright then, by a show of hands, who is in favor of starvation?" The Chief looked around and not one hand was raised. "And who is in favor of fixing Big Al some grub?" A throng of hands immediately flew up. "Okay then, we'll fix the big guy something to eat!"

"Wait a minute. Does anyone know what aliens eat?" asked Monica.

"He probably has a genetically altered metabolism to allow him to consume whatever food source he may encounter on his mission," said Pee Wee.

"What in the heck does all that mean?" asked Iris.

"That means since all we got is meat, cheese and bread, someone should make him a sandwich," said Emma.

"Even more important, how many sandwiches will it take to fill him up?" asked Tommy.

"I suggest starting with mortadella on rustic Italian bread," said Pee Wee. "Mortadella is that large smoked sausage made of beef, pork, and pork fat and seasoned with pepper and garlic with a wonderful bouquet that should please the most discerning pallet."

"Gag a maggot," groaned Iris. "Can't we just settle on something that wouldn't make a buzzard puke?"

"I've got an idea," said Hugo, beaming at Emma. "I will factor in Chief Dickelous's estimations of Big Al's proportions to determine how many sandwiches he would eat and Em will select which sandwiches to give him. Sound like a plan?"

The rest ignored Hugo and continued to discuss what kinds of sandwich Big Al would like and how many he would eat. In the end, they decided to follow Hugo's plan. Emma would determine what sandwiches to offer him, primarily because no one else volunteered. Hugo was chosen to determine the number of sandwiches because he seemed the right size for it. When it was all said and done, they ended up fixing a dozen assorted sandwiches, all prepared according to Emma's precise instructions. They assigned Iris to pack them in an empty doughnut carton, while they turned their energies to deciding who should deliver the box.

They were still deep in discussion when Iris shouted, "You don't need to talk anymore. While you all were jawboning, I took him the sandwiches and a two liter jug of Big Red."

"Sam, what in the world were you thinking?' Vera wailed. "Why would you let your mother do such a dangerous thing?"

"Me? I didn't let her go, she did it on her own. Chief Dickless, you're in charge. How could you let this happen?"

"That's Dickelous, and don't look at me. Officer Strange is in charge of crowd control."

"Hugo, you're backup, what have you got to say?" Hubie asked.

"Did he eat them?"

"Tommy," said Sam, "go see what's happening.'

Tommy ran over to the window and hopped on the spigot. "Gramma, are you sure you took him the sandwiches and a full bottle of Big Red,?"

"I'm as sure as eggs is eggs," said Iris.

"Are you completely sure?" he asked carefully.

"The box was full of sandwiches and the bottle was full of pop," said Iris.

"All I see is an empty box with an empty bottle next to it."

The rest hurried to the window, crowding around Tommy to look inside.

"When do you allege you took him the sandwiches and soda?" Hubie asked Iris.

"Weren't no 'ledging about it. While you were fussin' over who should take Big Al his dinner, I decided to do it myself. He's mine, so I figured I should feed him. I put the box down with the Big Red next to it and turned right around and came back out and told you what I had done."

"Just now?" asked Hubie.

"Why, I no sooner walked out the door when you all got in an uproar."

"That's right," said Emma, "couldn't been more than a minute or two since I finished putting the last sandwich together."

"You sure the box you took had the sandwiches in it?" asked Hubie.

"Well look around," said Iris. "Do you see any doughnut boxes full of sandwiches lying around?"

"Anybody see a box full of sandwiches?" asked Hubie

"Here's the way I see it," said Sam. "There's an empty box next to Big Al. All of you agree there isn't any box with sandwiches in it to be seen outside around here, so Mom's story has got to be true."

"Why, a doughnut box that size had to hold at least ten sandwiches," said the Chief. "No one could have eaten all of them in such a short time."

"A dozen, to be precise," said Emma.

"A wonderful assortment, if I do say so myself," said Hugo. "Emma did such a wonderful job choosing the selections. Of course, we included the mortadella with gruyere and a balsamic pesto on rustic Italian bread," he said, nodding to Pee Wee. "Then we added city ham on a fine brioche. High egg and butter content in the bread gives it a rich and tender crumb. Next, we drizzled it with a nice aioli to add some interest for the pallet..."

"Hugo, put a cork in it," said Hubie.

"Right."

"If we are all agreed that Big Al polished off the sandwiches and pop," said the Chief, "and as it looks like nothing else is going to happen, I vote we eat before we do anything else."

* * *

They were just settling into their own sandwiches when a small white van buzzed up the street and pulled into Emma's drive. 'Channel 13 Big Story News' was emblazoned on its side. The driver hopped out and pulled open the side door. A young woman, dressed in a dark blue business suit and white Converse All Stars, strutted across the yard. Her blonde hair was pulled into a bun.

The driver dug around in the van, hoisted a camera to his shoulder and followed her into the Wecco's yard.

"Hello, I'm Anita Skupe from Channel 13 Big Story News. That's Jimmy, my cameraman," she said, pointing toward the driver. "We heard there was a group of wackos terrorizing this neighborhood. Are we in the right place?"

"Sorry, Ms. Skupe," Hubie responded, "but that report was inaccurate. There're no wackos here. By the way, that call went out pretty early this morning. Aren't you a little late getting here?"

"Oh, we set out from the TV station this morning to cover a coon-dog treeing contest at the Mammoth County Fair. But before we got there, a report came in about a flash mob wreaking havoc at Huge Harold's on route seventeen, so the news director dispatched us over there instead. Seems we arrived too late, however. Didn't matter anyway, turned out it wasn't a flash mob but a church group from Littleton who had a breakdown and decided to visit the breakfast buffet while their bus was being fixed."

"Yeah, we know," said the Chief.

"How do you know?" asked Anita.

"Long story," said Hubie. "You probably don't want to ask."

"I'll be the judge of that," said Anita. "Anyway, they were just finishing up by the time we got there. We decided to get

142

something to eat some breakfast before we headed back to the county fair to cover the contest. Unfortunately, by the time we got to the fair, we found out that PETA had complained, and the fair officials had cancelled the whole thing. Jimmy and I were discussing what to do for the rest of the day when the news director called to say there had been an earlier report of wackos terrorizing this neighborhood and suggested we might want to check it out. Since we had already missed everything else, we figured, why not give it a try. So, what's the story here?" she asked, looking around.

"We're just finishing up lunch," said the Chief.

"I can see that. But, why are the police and fire departments having lunch at this particular location?" Anita asked.

"Because I had the fixin's in the old justice mobile." Hugo blurted out.

"Who are you?"

"Hugo Nutts, ma'am."

"Did you say I was nuts?" Anita asked Hugo.

"Oh, don't worry ma'am, he's Nutts," said Hubie.

"That I can believe."

"No ma'am, I mean his name is Hugo Nutts," Hubie explained.

"And just who are you?" she asked.

"Hubie Strange."

"I'm warning you," cautioned Anita, "that is no way to talk to a member of the press." She looked at Jimmy. "I hope you're recording this."

"Pay him no mind, he is Officer Hubert Strange. I can vouch for him," said the Chief.

"I know I'm going to be sorry for this," Anita said, taking a deep breath, "and just who might you be?"

"Yuri Dickelous, ma'am."

"Oh, I smell a special on the 6 o'clock news." She looked at Jimmy. "You better be getting this," she shouted.

"Calm down, Miss, Skupe," said Sam. "This gentleman is Fire Chief Yuri Dickelous, a fine man of Ukrainian descent, I'm told. And before you ask, I'm Sam Wecco, that's W-E-C-C-O, not wacko. You've met Officer Strange. That's my daughter, Monica, next to him. The lovely lady with the strange hairdo next to me is my wife Vera, and next to her are our son, Tommy, and my mother, Iris. That's Emma snuggled up next to Hugo. And that's Daphne… Daphne? When did you get here?"

"Hey, Mr. Wecco. Monica sent me a snapchat of all the yummy firemen who were over here. Couldn't resist."

"Should'a guessed," sighed Sam. "Ms. Skupe, the rest are Fire and Rescue. Say hi, Pee Wee."

"Hi."

"Alright, Jimmy, you can stop recording," said Anita. She looked at Sam. "So that's it? You mean Channel 13 Big Story News sent its crack reporting team all the way over here and you're just having a picnic? This can't be the whole story. The police and fire departments don't just have picnics on people's front lawns for no good reason. Something is up and I'm going to get to the bottom of it or my name isn't Anita Skupe."

Sam felt a tug on his arm. It was Tommy. "Dad," Tommy whispered, "don't tell her about Big Al."

Anita's ears perked up. "Jimmy, start recording. Who's Big Al?" she asked.

"Oh, no one you'd be interested in. He's in our living room," Sam said. "Not much else to say about him."

"Big Al is an alien," said Hugo.

"Aha! Is this some I.N.S. operation?" asked Anita, eyes growing wide.

"No, ma'am," said Hubie, "nothing like that."

"If there's one thing I've learned in my years of journalism, it's that the phrase 'nothing like that' means 'exactly like that'."

"Big Al is a grey alien," said Pee Wee, "from outer space."

"That remains to be verified," said the Chief. "Anyway, even though he's a big rascal, I'm leaning toward the theory that he's one of them grey aliens." He put a hand to his mouth. "Oops."

"Now we're getting somewhere. How big?" asked Anita.

"About fourteen feet tall," said Pee Wee.

Anita put her hands on her hips and gave Pee Wee the stare down. "It's not nice to fool the blonde girl," she said. "You guys are getting a kick out of this, aren't you? Anyway, I believe greys are tiny, didn't you see Close Encounters? If you ask me, I think something fishy is going on around here, and I'm not leaving until I get the real story."

"Give us a minute," said Sam. He, Hubie and the Chief moved a few steps away and huddled together in conversation. After a few moments they returned.

"It's complicated, Miss Skupe," said Hubie.

"Try me."

"Sam," said Hubie, "better start from the beginning. Miss Skupe, you and Jimmy want a sandwich? This is going to take a while."

"Might as well," said Anita.

* * *

Anita was halfway finished with her sandwich by the time Sam finished his explanation.

"If you ask me," said Anita, "I think there *are* a bunch of wackos around here, and I'm sure as heck looking at them!"

"Well, you can go in there and see for yourself, if you don't believe us," said Emma.

"I think I'll do just that."

"Whoa, nothing doing," said the Chief.

"So, you're attempting to deny us our rights under the Twenty-First Amendment?"

"You do this every time," said Jimmy. "That's the one about prohibition. I believe it's the First Amendment you are thinking of."

"Let's not haggle over a few amendments," said Anita.

"What I meant to say, Ms. Skupe," said the Chief, "is that I'm not sure that's a good idea, from a safety standpoint, that is." He looked at Sam and Hubie for help. "I mean, do we think it's safe for her to go in there?"

"I don't see why not," said Sam. "Everyone else has been in there."

"Of course," said the Chief. He lowered his voice to a whisper. "but she's the N-E-W-S."

"I can hear you Chief,' said Anita.

"Sorry, ma'am. We just don't want this thing to become a circus. It's all in the interest of the Weccos' privacy. Wouldn't want all those news-hungry pirate-nazis descending on our friends. You may care about your story, but we care more about each other here."

"Word is bound to get out somehow," said Hubie, nodding toward Hugo.

"Gotcha," said the Chief, frowning at Pee Wee. "But I'm afraid we will have to ask you to refrain from taking your camera inside the house."

"Why?" asked Anita

"Active investigation?"

"Active, my eye, you all are having a picnic out here."

"I think you should let her take her camera with her," said Monica.

"Monica, stay out of this," pleaded Sam.

"What do you think, Hubie?" asked Monica, holding her phone up for him to see.

A smile spread across his face. "I agree with Monica. What could happen?"

"I don't know," said the Chief, "a lot could happen."

"Like when your firefighter took photos of Big Al?"

The Chief opened his mouth, then shut it. A smile crept across his face. "Yes, like when we took photos of Big Al." He turned to Anita. "Sure, go on and take your camera. Shoot to your heart's content."

"I'm glad you have made the right decision, Chief," said Anita. "Come on, Jimmy, I smell an Emmy." She made a beeline for the porch steps while Jimmy lugged his camera behind. As soon as they entered the house, the rest rushed to the window to watch.

Inside, the Channel 13 news duo engaged in an animated discussion. Jimmy was shooting video while Anita moved around the room setting up shots. Now and then, she would stop and strike a pose next to Big Al, making sweeping gestures with her arms and pointing to the sky. Before they left, she made sure Jimmy got some footage of her kneeling by the doughnut box and pop bottle.

On the porch, Anita said, "Forget the Emmy, hello Pulitzer Prize. Big Al is an alien alright. Jimmy, get ready to upload."

"Mind if we get a sneak peak of the news at six?" asked Hubie.

"Let them see the playback, Jimmy," said Anita. "And remember, everyone, you can say you once had lunch with Anita Skupe."

Jimmy stared intently at the camera display. He ran the video back and forth a time or two before saying, "Uh, Houston, we've had a problem."

Anita scowled. "What's that? Don't tell me the battery went dead. I don't want to shoot this all again."

"No," said Jimmy, "got plenty of battery."

"Out of focus?"

"No."

"The memory thingy's not working."

"No, it's in perfect shape."

"Well what's the problem then?"

"Nothing, unless you consider the fact that the video captured everything in that living room, *except* the big grey guy."

"Well, you can't be much of a videographer if you couldn't manage to get an alien that big in your viewfinder."

"You were standing right next to him, weren't you?"

"Yes."

"See for yourself," said Jimmy, holding up the display. Anita saw herself standing in the living room on the green carpet, pointing to an empty space. In the audio, she could hear herself saying, 'Here is the alien they have named Big Al.'

"Oh no, this can't be," she wailed. "He was there, I saw him. What did you do to the video?"

"I didn't do nothing," said Jimmy. "I checked everything before we started to shoot. The camera was working fine."

"Seems Big Al doesn't like to be captured on camera," said Hubie. "Same thing happened when Monica and the firefighters tried to take a photo of him."

"Aliens can do stuff like that," said Tommy.

"What am I going to do?" asked Anita. "The biggest story of the twenty-first century and I didn't get it on video. Well, I'll just have to get eyewitness accounts."

* * *

Anita was still trying to find someone to volunteer to be an eyewitness when a dilapidated school bus rolled up the street. It glided to a stop behind the fire truck and remained largely unnoticed until the door opened, and a large group of men, women and children tumbled out forming a picket line up and down the pavement. A pallid man dressed in a black suit was the last to leave the bus. He immediately started to walk up the Wecco's sidewalk.

"Oh, that's the last thing we need," said the Chief. "Hubie go tell them to get back on the bus. Can't they see we're here on official business?"

Hubie stepped forward, holding up his hands to halt their forward progress. "Whoa, there. Who are you and what are you doing here?" he asked the man in the black suit.

"I'm Fuller Horsterds, pastor of the True Revelation of the Incandescent Disciples of the Mystical World Tabernacle and Health Foods Co-Op. We were monitoring the police dispatch frequency when we heard a report of the demon horseman. Surely it's a sign. As the scripture says: 'Cry aloud, spare not, lift up thy voice like a trumpet, and show my people their transgression'. Isaiah 58:1. And just who are you?"

"Hubie Strange."

Pastor Fuller clutched the Bible to his chest and proclaimed, "The vexation of a fool is known at once, but the prudent ignores an insult. Proverbs 12:16."

"Hold on there, Reverend Horsterds," said Sam. "This is Officer Strange, Hubert Strange. Everyone calls him Hubie. I'm sure no insult was intended." Then he nodded at the Chief. "And this is the Fire Chief.

The chief held out his hand. "Yuri Dickelous."

"Enough of this, show some respect," exclaimed Pastor Horsterds.

"No, no," said Sam, "this is Chief Dickless, a fine man of Ukrainian descent."

"That's Dickelous," the Chief corrected.

"Oh, sorry Chief."

"Hugo," Hubie bellowed, "front and center." He stood, hands on hips, until Hugo weaved his way to the front, holding out his hand to Pastor Horsterds.

"Skip the introduction, Hugo. I don't think the Pastor is in the mood. What in the world did you tell dispatch?"

"I...ah... just told them... ah... you know... ah... about Big Al..." Hugo said, nodding toward the house. "You know. How he just appeared outta nowhere and all, and how big he was, and that he didn't have no clothes on and when Miss Monica there took a picture of him, he wasn't in the picture, but he really was there even though he wasn't, in the picture that is, and that Tommy believes he's a space alien but how you deemed him a homeless man instead, so's Fire and Rescue would have to handle it."

"That's enough, Hugo," Hubie winced, holding his hands over his ears, "You're making my head spin." He turned to Pastor Horsterds. "Sorry to disappoint, but, there's no demon horseman. For want of a better explanation we didn't know how to classify Big Al so we *deemed* him a *homeless man*, not a demon horseman. Granted, there's still a little discussion as to what he really is, but I don't mind sharing that I'm leaning toward the alien thing. Nonetheless, as far as I can see, he's not a danger to anyone. I'm sure Mr. Wecco won't mind if you take a quick look just to verify what I've told you. What do you say, Sam?"

"I guess it's alright," grumbled Sam.

"He's right up there in the living room," Hubie said, pointing to the door. "Help yourself."

Pastor Horsterds lifted his head and marched up the steps and through the door, clenching his Bible to his chest. Knowing smiles of anticipation spread across Sam, Hubie, and the Fire Chief's faces as they awaited his return. They did not have to wait very long until Pastor Horsterds appeared at the door. He had a curious look on his face and held the doughnut carton in his hand.

"I don't find your little joke funny at all," he sniffed. "In fact, it's downright unchristian. You should be ashamed."

"What do you mean?" asked Hubie.

"What I mean is, there was nothing in there but these flowers," Pastor Horsterds barked, dropping the carton to the porch.

"What do you mean, he's not there?" shrieked Anita, who shot up the steps and into the house.

Pastor Horsterds quickly called to the Incandescent Disciples. "Come, let us leave this place. The great deceiver has tried to fool us, but I have seen his treachery and will lead us from the brink," he intoned. "If we hurry, we still have time to protest that sinful coon-dog treeing exhibition at the Mammoth County Fair."

"Oh, you're too late," said Emma. "PETA shut them down,"

"Then we'll protest PETA," said Pastor Horsterds. "For as the Bible says: 'And let them have dominion over the fish of the sea and over the birds of the heavens and over the livestock and over all the earth and over every creeping thing that creeps on the earth.' Genesis 1:26."

As the Disciples worked their way back to the bus, Vera stepped to the edge of the porch and looked inside the carton. There, she saw a bouquet of flowers. Deep blue leaves feathered out from fuchsia stems, crowned with starburst petals of iridescent gold and silver.

"Where in the world did these come from?" she asked. "I have never seen any flowers like these." Sam, Hubie, and the Chief hopped up the steps and bolted through the door after Anita. The rest huddled around Vera, marveling at the strange flowers.

The Chief reappeared at the door with his arm around Anita. She was sobbing. He called out to the firefighters, "That preacher feller was right, no sign of Big Al in the living room. I don't see how he could'a got out. He was way too big to leave through a door, much less a window. It's a real mystery. You guys get in here and search the rest of the house. When you've finished that, clean up Mrs. Wecco's yard. I'll see to Ms. Skupe."

Hubie leaned from the door and called out, "Hugo, make sure nobody else comes in until we give the 'all clear'."

Hugo and Tommy took up a position at the front door, which offered them a good look into the house.

"Never seen any flowers like those," said Emma.

"Neither have I," added Iris. "Think we ought to put them in water?"

"Do they have water in outer space?"

"Never been there."

"Me neither," said Emma. She slapped her knee and laughed. "I figured if we lasted long enough, we'd find somethin' we had in common. Why don't we take these over to my house while the boys are playing cowboys and aliens and find a vase to put 'em in?"

"Sounds like a plan," said Iris.

Emma looked at Vera. "You're invited, too."

The three headed to Emma's house with the carton of flowers, while the Chief tried to console Anita.

"Can't be all that bad," said the Chief.

"Easy for you to say," sniffed Anita. "All you have to do is wait awhile for a fire to break out, then you can save the day once more. But, for a reporter, a story like this only comes around once in a lifetime."

"I'm sorry you lost out on your big story, but I'm also glad. I can't help thinking what would have happened to the Weccos and Bunyan if word of this got out. Why, our lives would never have been the same. Even as it stands now, if you were to report what you saw today, we'd really be considered wackos."

"Well, Yuri, no one has to worry. I can't go with this story without eyewitness accounts to back it up, and I don't think I'm going to get any."

"You're probably right. You know, in a way I'm glad Big Al's gone. Not that I didn't like him or anything like that. No, I don't like thinking about what the government might do to him. Lock him up in some big warehouse and poke and prod him like a Guinea pig."

"I never thought about that," said Anita, wiping the last tears from her eyes. "Maybe it is better it happened this way."

Vera, Iris and Emma returned with the bouquet carefully arranged in Emma's prized cut glass vase. They reverently sat it on the corner of the porch and admired its beauty as the golden rays of the afternoon sunbathed the delicate flowers in glowing light. Sam, Hubie, and the firefighters came out and gathered on the porch. They stood in silence, gazing at the flowers.

Finally, Hubie dropped to one knee, head just above the vase. "The preacher was right. Big Al is gone. We searched everywhere and there is no sign of him. I don't see how he got out. It's a real mystery."

"Not for an alien from outer space," said Tommy.

"You're probably right on that one, son," said Sam.

* * *

The firefighters proceeded to clean up the yard. After the last pieces of equipment were loaded onto the truck, Pee Wee hopped onto the crime stopper cooler. "Listen, everyone," he sang out, "tonight is all-you-can-eat pancakes and chili night at Huge Harold's. How about we all head over there this evening for supper?"

"But, I don't like pancakes," Iris said, stomping her foot.

"Don't worry Mom, you can have something else," Sam consoled. "They've got a menu that has everything on it. I'm sure you'll find something you'll like."

"I bet they don't have sushi sliders," Tommy joked.

"I don't like squishy spiders," Iris whimpered.

"Tommy! Put a cork in it," Vera ordered.

"Is it okay to go inside the house, Hubie?" Monica asked.

"Sure, will I see you at Huge Harold's?"

"Maybe," she smiled. Turning, she danced up the steps and lingered for a moment in the doorway, looking over her shoulder to see if Hubie was looking. A dreamy smile covered his face. "I got dibs on the shower," she laughed, as she slipped inside.

Hubie was still smiling when he felt a soft tap on his shoulder. He turned around to find Hugo standing behind him with a silly look on his face too. "What is it, Hugo?" he asked.

"Miss Emma wants to go with me to Huge Harold's. You mind if she rides with me in the Justice Mobile? She says she's never ridden in a real cruiser."

"You know that's against regulations, Hugo." Hubie paused, giving him the sternest look he could muster. "But, I guess lugging around half the contents of a Save-A-Bunch around in the trunk of your cruiser is against regulations, too. When it comes down to it, I

153

guess almost everything that happened here today was against regulations. I figure, why should we stop now? Go ahead."

"Gee, thanks, Hubie."

"Officer Strange, Mr. Wecco," the Chief called out as he trotted back into the yard from the fire truck. "We've got about everything loaded. The guys want to head back to the station and spruce up a little before heading out to Huge Harold's. Is there anything left to do here?"

"No, Chief," Sam said, grabbing the Chief's outstretched hand and pumping it energetically. "Thanks for everything. See y'all at the restaurant."

"By the way," said the Chief, "a couple of the guys have a day off tomorrow, and they are going to stop by and help put the furniture back for Mrs. Wecco. Will you be sure to tell her so she'll know to expect them?"

"Sure, Chief."

"There's one more thing. You wouldn't mind if I asked Anita to meet us at Huge Harold's, would you? After we talked, she realized it was best to give up on the story."

"That'll be fine," said Sam. "We might try to squelch a news story, but we'd never stand in the way of romance."

"Thanks. I'll send some guys over to cordon off the back room and make sure the buffet is full of chili and pancakes. We can reserve some parking near the door, if you want."

"No need, Chief, but thanks, anyway," Hubie said, giving the Chief a quick salute.

"Oh, one last thing," the Chief said, quietly leaning in. "I've asked the guys to keep a tight lip on this one. Might be hard to explain and all."

"Good idea Chief, I'll make sure Hugo knows, but I can't promise you anything."

"Gotcha. It's the same with Pee Wee."

"Mr. Wecco," said Hubie.

"Yes, Officer Strange."

"Please call me Hubie. Would it be OK if I asked your daughter out?"

"I thought you'd never ask."

"Gee, thanks, Mr. Wecco. Guess I better get going. See you later."

Sam watched the fire truck turn around and lumber down the street. Hugo cleaned the front seat for Emma before launching the old cruiser with a puff of blue smoke. Finally, Hubie gave a short hoot on his siren, waved, and disappeared down the street. Sam went back in the house and stood for a moment, looking at the corner of the living room where Big Al had been. Not even a depression in the shag carpet could be seen to give a clue he had ever been there. Sam could hear everyone bustling around getting ready. As he walked down the hall, he found Iris and Vera sitting on the floor of Iris's room talking in hushed tones.

"Vera, why did you all make Big Al leave?" Iris asked. "He was my friend, I found him."

"There, there, Mom, no one made him leave. I think he just left on his own."

"But, you were mad at him, Vera. You wanted him to go." Tears welled up in Iris's eyes.

"Oh, he just surprised me, that's all. Now, don't cry. I promise I wasn't mad at him."

"So, you didn't want him to go?"

"Well, not really, I guess."

Sam popped his head in the door. "What do want for supper tonight, Mom?"

"Liver and onions," Iris said, smacking her lips.

"Well, liver and onions it is. Come on Vera, let's get crackin'. I'm ready to get away from here for a while."

After he had showered, shaved and dressed, Sam sprawled out on the bed while Vera put the finishing touches on her hair.

"Been quite a day," he said.

"Yes, it has," said Vera.

"It was nice what you said to Mom even if you didn't mean it."

"You mean what I said about Big Al? I meant it."

"Did you mean the other things you said earlier?"

"About your job, the house vacations and everything else?"

"Yeah."

"At the time I did. But I was wrong. Everything that happened today made me realize that you were right. It's not things that are important, it's people. I came to understand that if I had to choose between you, your mother, the kids and a bit of green fabric, there is really no choice at all. I guess I just got stuck in a rut and it took something like what happened today to get me out of it."

"Too bad Anita's camera wouldn't cooperate," said Sam.

"What do you mean?"

"We could'a sold our story for who knows how much. Then, we could move to a new house, buy a new car, go on fancy vacations."

"And constantly be hiding from the pirate-nazis, as Yuri would say, not to mention that the government would probably want to study us for the next twenty years. And I don't want to think what would have happened to Big Al. No, I'm happy with the way things turned out."

"Me too," said Sam. "Monica met that nice policeman, and Mom and Emma seem to have buried the ax."

"Yeah, and we made a lot of new friends today, even if we did lose Big Al."

"So, you will miss him?"

"Oh, I don't know if I'm ready to go that far," Vera giggled, snuggling up to Sam. "There is one thing, however, Sam Wecco," she chided. "I'll never forgive you for letting me parade around all day with my hair sticking out in all directions. If I had known, I'd have been mortified. How could you let me do that?"

"Honey, you always look good to me," Sam said, pulling her close. "Besides, with so much going on, nobody noticed. Are you ready yet? I bet everyone will get there before us."

"Sam, it won't be me that holds us up," said Vera. "You forget Monica. A dime will get you a dollar we'll all be waiting on her. She'll be out to impress the young and handsome Officer Strange."

"I heard that," Monica said sticking her head in the door. Seeing her Mom and Dad on the bed, she groaned, "Ooh, get a room, you two."

"We *are* in our room," laughed Sam.

"It won't take much to impress Hubie," said Tommy, squeezing in next to his sister. "Didn't you see how he was drooling over her?"

"That's enough, you two," said Vera. "Where's your Gramma?

"She said she was going to wait for us in the living room," said Tommy.

"Listen everyone," said Vera, sitting up. She motioned for the kids to come in. "There is something I want to say, but I don't want Gramma to hear. Sit up Sam, you need to hear this too." She waited until the kids were close, then said in a soft tone, "The less said about you-know-who the better. Your Gramma was pretty upset after he disappeared."

"She must've gotten over it," said Tommy. "She's been in the living room laughing and giggling."

"That's good," sighed Vera. "Hopefully, she will get over this very quickly. Maybe she has already forgotten the whole thing."

Suddenly, they heard footsteps bounding up the hallway, followed by a raucous "Whoo-hoo!" Iris burst into the bedroom. "Hot diggidy dog," she exclaimed. "Guess what everybody? Good news! Big Al is back!"

"What?" exclaimed Vera.

"And that's not all," continued Iris.

"What do you mean, that's not all?" asked Sam.

"This time, he brought his wife and kids along."

GIMCRACK'S FANTASTIC GALACTIC MERCANTILE[5]

"Waddya going to disappoint Mom with this year?" Shereen taunted Jackie with a high whiny voice. "Not some smelly perfume like last year, I hope."

"Nah, I bet he'll get her some more earrings that will turn her ears green like the year before," chuckled Vernon. "They had to call Hazmat to get rid of those things."

"Not so," shouted Jackie, holding back hot tears. He could feel his cheeks turning bright crimson. All the while, Shereen and Vernon laughed as he grew more agitated. "She's just waiting for something special to wear them with."

"Just keep tellin' yourself that," Shereen said as she walked out of the room. "She never liked any of that junk you got her." Vernon sniggered. Jackie balled up a fist and took a wild swipe at his older brother, who deftly dodged out of the way. The force of the errant punch caused Jackie to spin out of balance and with a helping shove from Vernon, he fell to the floor. He pounded his fists until they throbbed. Then he lay still letting tears trickle along his cheeks until they fell into the carpet.

"I'll show you," he sobbed, "I'll get her the best present ever."

"Good luck with that one loser," Vernon called over his shoulder as he left.

Jackie lay on the floor until his tears had dried, then pushed himself up and went to his room. Pulling the bottom drawer of his battered, hand-me-down dresser open, he dug through clothes he hardly ever wore, until his hands reached an old shoebox. Taking it out, he sat down on the floor, legs crossed, the box in his lap. He tugged off the lid and rummaged through worn Matchbook cars,

---

[5] "Gimcrack's Fantastic Galactic Mercantile" appeared online in *Storgy Kids*, 11/24/2018.

pebbles, green soldiers, and dog-eared baseball cards until his fingers touched the envelope that lay at the bottom. He yanked it out and shoved it in his pocket before returning the box to its spot at the back of the drawer.

Jackie gingerly stuck his head out into the hall to see who was about. The hall was clear, so he began to move toward the stairs. As his room was at the end of the hall, he would have to pass both Vernon and Shereen's rooms. He breathed a sigh of relief as he discovered both doors were closed. As he tiptoed past Vernon's door, the muffled sounds of Grand Theft Auto met his ears. These were soon replaced by the pulsing beat of Miley Cyrus trying to escape from Shereen's room. Having safely negotiated what he believed to be the most dangerous portion of his trip, Jackie hopped down the stairs and made straight for the front door.

Jackie made a beeline for the road, which eventually ran into town. *I'll show them. I'll find the perfect gift for Mom, even if I have to go to the ends of the earth to find it.* He had never gone into town on his own, but no one had ever said he couldn't, so he had made up his mind to go. His mother would not get home from work until suppertime and he figured he would have no trouble finding the perfect gift and returning well before then.

A chill breeze made him sniffle as he trudged along the cracked pavement. The faint smell of smoke floated on the wind. Jackie could see it drifting up from the chimneys of the old houses that dotted the lane, grey against the blue sky. He came to a steep rise in the road. It cut through a narrow gap at the top. He trudged along until he reached the crest. The road sloped away into a broad, flat valley. Ahead, lay the town, roof tops gleaming red, green and black in the sunshine. Here and there, white plums spewing from exhaust vents shot upward, evaporating before they became clouds. He paused before he continued. *It'll be all downhill from here. I'll find the perfect gift in no time.*

Jackie had only gone a short distance down toward the town, when he spied a tiny building sitting back from the road. It was no bigger than the toolshed behind his house. As he approached, he saw a man sitting on the building's tiny porch. Above his head was a sign in gold letters on a black background which read:

Gimcrack's Fantastic Galactic Mercantile
Large Display
Of
Fancy Goods, Bibelots, Novelties, Unusual Items, And Exotic Curiosities
The assortment is unsurpassed in variety and elegance having been personally selected from throughout the universe for your consideration.
Very respectfully,
I. M. Gimcrack, Prop.

-- ----------- ----

Before Jackie could look away, the man stood up and tipped the top hat which crowned his head. He was dressed in a green velvet waistcoat and grey flannel trousers. His limbs were so thin, Jackie thought he resembled a daddy long legs spider. Then with a flourish of his right hand the man gestured toward the door. Jackie stood motionless.

"You have the look of a man on a mission, if I may be so bold, and of course I am or I would not have said so. Allow me to introduce myself," the man said, bowing from the waist. "As you may have deduced from the sign, I am I. M. Gimcrack, proprietor of Gimcrack's Fantastic Galactic Mercantile. But, that is nothing you wouldn't know if you can read, which I believe you can, as you have the look about you of someone who can read. Am I right?" Jackie stared at the man. "A simple nod will suffice," the man said.

"Uh, yes," Jackie finally managed to spit out.

"Very good then. You are in luck, as I just so happen to have an opening in the schedule to take you on a private tour of

Gimcrack's Fantastic Galactic Mercantile featuring our Planet Earth Collection. As it clearly says on the sign 'By Appointment Only'.

Jackie stared at the sign. "Where's it say that?"

"Right there under 'I. M. Gimcrack, Prop.'," he said tracing a bony finger along what Jackie had thought was a line at the bottom of the sign, "plain as the nose on your face. Come, come, time is wasting. Never can tell when someone else will come along clamoring for a tour."

"Doesn't look big enough to hold all that stuff on the sign there."

"Looks as well as words can be deceiving, what have you go to lose?"

"Well," Jackie paused, considering Gimcrack's question. "Mom said I shouldn't talk with strangers, for one thing."

"And right she is. But by now I can hardly be considered a stranger. Besides, how many strangers will you meet when you walk into one of those stores in town? If that is your concern, you might as well turn around right here."

"Oh, I can't do that, I'm looking for something. Something real special. I can't go back without it."

"My point exactly," Gimcrack said opening the door. "Gimcrack's Fantastic Galactic Mercantile awaits."

Jackie looked down the road toward the town which now looked a million miles away. He had already wasted valuable time talking with Gimcrack and he was worried he would not be able to get to town and back before his mother got home. "OK, but just a quick look," he said, as he turned from the road up the short path to the Mercantile. Gimcrack held the door until Jackie reached the opening. *He's much smaller than he appears and so is the door.* Taking a deep breath, he ducked his head and stepped inside.

To his amazement, a long hall stretched out before him. He quickly turned and stuck his head outside. Nothing on the outside had changed. He stepped back on the porch and walked to the edge of the building and looked around the corner. It looked no bigger than it had when he first saw it. Hesitantly, he returned to the opening. The bright outside light prevented him from seeing anything beyond the door. Slowly he poked his head into the shadows just inside. As soon as his eyes were past the doorway, he could see the long hallway.

"Everyone is thrown by that effect first time in," Gimcrack giggled. "Come along." Jackie's eyes quickly adjusted once the door closed. "As the sign says Gimcrack's has fancy goods, bibelots, novelties, unusual items, and exotic curiosities. Just what is it you are interested in?"

"I don't know, but I'll know it when I see it."

"You appear to be a man of high standards if not clear on specifics. Well Gimcrack's has something for everyone as I like to say. What if I take the liberty to show you some of our Planet Earth selection that I believe might be of interest to a person such as yourself? Perhaps that will help define and narrow the universe of possible items suitable to your requirements."

"Sure."

"Very good," Gimcrack said, stopping in front of a bright green door. Jackie now found the light inside to be pleasantly bright, such so that he could make everything out quite clearly. A hint of cinnamon tickled his nose. "Perhaps something gastronomic would fill the bill," Gimcrack offered as he pushed open the door.

"Gastro what?"

"Food," Gimcrack chortled. "Food, glorious food – well you know how it goes." He led Jackie onto a small balcony which overlooked an immense room. To their right stood a huge green orb. It rose ten to fifteen feet over their heads. "That my friend is the Big Apple. The uneducated believe the Big Apple to be red, but that is not the case. It is a variety of The Granny Smith and therefore green although it is yellow before it reaches maturity. You may recognize 'The Big Apple' as a nickname for New York City. It was first popularized in the 1920s by John J. Fitz Gerald, a sportswriter for the New York Morning Telegraph. He had visited the Mercantile and was so impressed with our massive *Malus sylvestris* he use the term to refer to his own city. The joke was on him though, because this specimen came from Australia."

"How do you eat something like that?" Jackie asked.

"Just like you would eat an elephant, one bite at a time," Gimcrack winked. He pointed to the right. A large harvesting basket filled with grapes sat on a tall pedestal. "There is something a little smaller, but I wouldn't recommend you pop one of those into your mouth. They are the Grapes of Wrath. Quite bitter. Never have I seen anyone swallow one. Despite my warnings, Steinbeck tried. He couldn't get the pucker out of his lips until he finished the novel about the Depression he was working on."

"Think I'll pass," Jackie said. "What's all that brown stuff back there?" he said, pointing to the center of the room. "Looks like dirt."

"On the contrary. Enjoyed by millions of people and Englishmen also. You're looking at none other than all the tea in China. You couldn't drink it all if you started today and didn't quit until you were done and there would still be more."

"Thanks all the same, and this stuff is really neat, but it's not what I'm looking for,"

"Well, let's move on then." Gimcrack led Jackie out of the room and across the hall and though an orange door. Jackie thought he detected the sweet aroma of hay as they entered. "Perhaps fauna might better suit you." They stepped out onto another balcony overlooking a cavernous room complete with a large lake. "Would something like this interest you?" he asked, nodding to the left, where a large barrel surrounded by trees stood on the lake shore. He took a long pole with a hook on one end from the wall. Reaching out from the balcony, he used it to lift the lid from the barrel. Immediately monkeys began to pop out. They jumped and rolled, climbed the trees and scampered all about. They chattered and screeched, turned somersaults. "As you may have guessed, this is the barrel of monkeys you have heard about. Quite a lively bunch. Lots of fun they say."

"Yeah, they're pretty neat, but I think a little too busy for what I am looking for."

"Well, they're not for everyone," Gimcrack said, pulling a banana from his pocket. He took careful aim and threw it straight into the throat of the barrel, upon which all the monkeys dove straight back in. As soon as the last one disappeared, he dropped the lid back in place.

"If monkeys didn't suit you, perhaps something a little quieter may interest you," he said pointing to his right. There, on a small island, stood a handsome white horse.

"He's a fine horse and all that, but there's lots of horses around."

"Watch."

"Does he do tricks?"

"Patience, patience will be rewarded." The man held his hand up to signal no more talk. They watched the horse for a few moments. Then, Jackie gasped as the horse turned a purple hue. "Patience," Gimcrack whispered. The horse took a bite of hay from the bale on the ground at its feet while turning yellow. They watched until it had finished chewing, then the man pulled an apple, red this time, from his pocket and tossed it to the horse. Down the fruit went in one gulp as a rich crimson color replaced the yellow. "That, sir, is the Horse of a Different Color," Gimcrack boasted. "George Cukor saw him and just had to have him for Wizard of Oz. Give him a carrot and he will turn orange. Oats result in polka dots."

"He's pretty and all that, but I think he's just a little big for my purposes."

"So size does matter." Gimcrack mused as he looked over the edge of the balcony into black water that stretched out as far as the eye could see. He rubbed his chin with a long finger. He opened his mouth, then paused and rubbed his chin once more. "After careful deliberation, I suggest we don't summon the Kraken. It can get very testy when disturbed. "

"The what?"

"Never mind, lots of arms, no legs, and one very, very large mouth. I only show it to serious collectors. Haven't had a taker yet. Yes, best we leave it alone." Gimcrack pushed open the door and stepped into the hall. Jackie followed quickly, not wanting to linger around the Kraken thing. "A different approach is in order. We know neither food nor zoology appeals to you. Add to that, things too busy, too big, or too testy. I know where we'll go. It just happens to be across the hall. If we're lucky we might just find what you're looking for."

Gimcrack put his arm around Jackie's shoulder as they stepped across to a blue door. "Your turn," he said, gesturing toward the door. It swung in freely as Jackie touched its smooth, cool surface. The balcony was bathed in pale blue light. Other than that, Jackie could see nothing in the black emptiness. "Beautiful, simply beautiful," Gimcrack sighed.

"I'm sorry, but I don't see nothin'," Jackie said. "Can you turn on a light or somethin'?"

"We're in luck. Look up."

Jackie looked up. Above his head a sapphire moon floated in an endless star-filled night sky. "Wow."

"After Bill Monroe saw that, he wrote Blue Moon of Kentucky."

"Wow. This might be it."

"Before we go any further, let me check something," Gimcrack said, digging into the breast pocket of his waistcoat. He pulled out a tattered copy of *Poor Richard's Almanac* and started to thumb through its yellowed pages. "This was one of Ben Franklin's personal copies, you know," he muttered as he ran a finger down the page. "Here it is. This is what I was looking for. Are you familiar with the expression 'Once In A Blue Moon'?"

"Not really, what does it mean?"

"Simply put, The Blue Moon happens only rarely, once every two or three years."

"But it's shining right now."

"In the Mercantile, the blue moon shines all the time. In the world outside, however, it must follow other rules. If you choose The Blue Moon, you will only be able to enjoy its beauty rarely."

"Oh, I don't think that will serve my purpose. You see, I need the perfect gift," Jackie said, hanging his head. "I thought The Blue Moon would be the perfect gift."

"May I ask who this gift is for?"

"Mom. Shereen and Vernon said my gifts suck. They said Mom hated them. Don't you see? I got to get the perfect gift. I can't disappoint Mom again. I just can't."

"And just who are this Shereen and Vernon that they are such experts on gifts and privy to your mother's thoughts?"

"My older sister and brother."

"Candidates for the Nobel Prize no doubt. Never mind, I think I may have just the right thing for you, sir."

"You sure got a lot of great things here in the Mercantile, but I don't think any of them are right for me."

"Giving up so easily?" Gimcrack chided. 'Surely one who could risk a journey through the wilds to town can stick it out just a bit longer."

"But it's getting late, I got to be home soon, and there is way more stuff her than I could ever look at."

"Just consider one more item. Small and easy to transport. Come with me."

"OK."

While he walked down the hall, Gimcrack began to speak. "When I asked, you said you were looking for something, something special. You did not say you were looking for a gift for your mother. 'What we have here is failure to communicate' or so the line goes. Something and a gift are very different things. Somethings are objects. Gifts are expressions of feeling. The importance of something is found in its composition – what it's made of, its rarity and the like. The importance of a gift is found in the act of giving - a feeling shared between the giver and the recipient. Few gifts are perfect. They don't need to be. Let it suffice to know a gift given with love is a wonderful gift." He stopped in front of a plain white door at the far end of the hall. As he opened the it, Jackie expected to see another balcony. Instead, it was a small closet with a single shelf on which a tiny cardboard box sat.

"Open it," Gimcrack said.

Jackie took the box and lifted the lid. He thought he saw a tiny glint of light. He tilted the box back and forth in his hand. Each time he moved the box, he saw a glint of light. "What is it?" he asked.

"The Twinkle In Her Eye."

"What's that?"

"A symbol. A symbol that tells you she has received a wonderful gift."

"What do I do with it?"

"There is a card in an envelope on the shelf. Take them home with you and write to your mother, telling her how you feel about her. Tell her how much you love her, because it is obvious you do. Put the card in the envelope along with the contents of the box. Then give them to her with whatever gift you choose. When you see The Twinkle In Her Eye, you will know you have given her a wonderful gift. From then on, whenever something wonderful happens for her, you will see it. Your task is to make that happen as often as you can."

"Gee, thanks Mr. Gimcrack. How much do I owe you?"

"All I ask is that you use what you have received wisely. Think you can do that?"

"Sure, it's got to be easier than that Kraken thing."

Gimcrack smiled. "Don't forget, make it happen as often as you can."

"I won't."

"We have reached the end of the hall as well as the allotted time for your visit." Gimcrack opened the door. "Time for you to go home now." Jackie stepped outside, expecting to be at the rear of the building. Instead, he found himself on the tiny porch looking ahead at the road. He looked back at Gimcrack who said, "Saves a lot of steps this way."

"When can I come back?"

"Everyone who comes to Gimcrack's Fantastic Galactic Mercantile gets what they need. Limit one to a customer."

Jackie nodded and walked up the path to the road. He turned to say goodbye. But before he could say a word, the Mercantile shot straight up and disappeared through the clouds.

.

COSMIC LIGHTNING BUGS

It was almost dusk when Uncle Peck said, "Here," motioning to the left with a gnarled finger. It was the first thing he had said since Tommy picked him up from his apartment in Springfield. Uncle Peck had called saying he wanted to take a ride out by the old farm. Tommy turned off the road and nosed the truck up to the gate.

"Now what?" asked Tommy.

"Open it up."

"It's locked. Besides, don't you remember, you sold the farm. We can't be riding all over someone else's fields."

"I didn't sell all of it," said Uncle Peck, holding out a key. "I held this place back."

Tommy paused for a moment. "You sure?"

"Got the key, don't I?"

"Well, if we get arrested, you're paying the fine." Tommy unlocked the gate, then pulled the truck into the field. Scrub trees and bush honeysuckle poked through the weeds.

"Up there," Uncle Peck said, pointing to a huge walnut tree. "Stop when you get to the rocks."

Tommy eased the truck up the hill until they reached the remains of a stone foundation. The walnut tree had grown up through its middle. Ahead, the field dropped away into a shallow holler with a small creek running through its middle.

"What's this place, Uncle Peck?" Tommy asked.

"Come on. We'll sit awhile," he said, climbing out of the truck.

Tommy checked his watch. "Uncle Peck, it's gonna get dark soon, Don't you got to get back?"

"We'll know pretty soon if they's coming," said Uncle Peck. He picked a stone block overlooking the holler and sat down. "Now, sit down and be quiet."

"What're you talking about?" Tommy asked, as he plunked down next to Uncle Peck. "Who's coming?"

"I first seen 'em before you was born. Used to work this field back then. Wasn't good for much, but I tried. I was finishing up just about this time of day when I seen 'em. All bright and floatin' over the field."

"I don't understand. You mean lightning bugs? We come out here to look at lightning bugs!" groaned Tommy. "We coulda done that back in town."

"I'd seen enough lightning bugs to know they weren't no bugs. They was perfectly round, big as bowlin' balls and full of all different colors. Like the colors in the opal necklace I gave your Aunt Lu when we got married."

"I remember that necklace," said Tommy.

"I seen 'em different places on the farm, but they always seemed to like this little holler the best. That's why I'd come up here ever' chance I got. That's why I held this spot back when I sold the farm."

"Well, I spent a lot of time on this farm, and never seen like what you're talking about. But then again, I don't remember ever coming to this field." said Tommy, "So maybe I missed it."

"Only person I ever brought up here was Lu, but she could never see 'em, neither. Didn't seem to bother her none. Said she just liked sitting up here with me. Maybe they can only be seen by certain people. Maybe some of us got brains tuned to a certain frequency which lets us see 'em, while the rest of you can't. You know, Lu understood, though. She believed I could see 'em. Said she could tell by lookin' at my face. She called 'em my cosmic lightning bugs."

"I still don't understand. What exactly are they, then?"

"Who knows what they are, Tommy. Cosmic lightning bugs is as good a name for 'em as anything. Maybe they're the souls of the dead. Maybe they're swamp gas or aliens playing tricks on an old man. Maybe God put 'em here for nothing else than to provide a moment of beauty and wonder. Kinda like your lightning bugs. Who's to say God wasn't sitting around after a hard day's work and decided to float a bunch of tiny lights over ever'thin? Then, seeing how beautiful it was, He, in his infinite wisdom, figured out how He could stick them lights up a beetle's backside so folks could enjoy 'em forever."

"But ain't lightning bugs just part of nature or evolution, or whatever? Don't they pollinate flowers and such?"

"I don't know about that, but don't you think God could figure out how to give 'em something useful to do besides bein' beautiful?"

"Yeah."

"Well then, don't you think God coulda created cosmic lightning bugs if he wanted?"

"Well, I guess," said Tommy. "So, these things just float around?"

"No, they fly all around like they know where they's goin'. Kinda like hummingbirds do. You know, back and forth, up and down, zippin' all over the place. Sometimes they'd come right up and hover in front of my face like they was studyin' me. They shined so bright, you coulda read a book by the light they give off. Any sudden move, though, and they'd fly away so fast they'd be at the other side of the holler before I could blink an eye."

As the light faded, they watched the lightning bugs rise up, filling the holler with twinkling lights. A doe and her fawn stepped out from a copse by the creek. The crickets and grasshoppers started chirping and zizzing, while the bullfrogs serenaded in basso profundo. Suddenly, the deer bolted back into the trees and the holler fell silent.

Uncle Peck held up his hand. "They're here," he whispered. "Be still."

Tommy searched the holler, looking for any sign of the cosmic lightning bugs. Nothing. The only thing he saw was the twinkling of the regular lightning bugs. He opened his mouth to speak when he felt Uncle Peck's hand on his arm. Turning, he saw Uncle Peck's smiling face, bathed in light. Tommy understood.

HETTIE JOHNSON AND THE ORB RIDER[6]

Hettie Johnson clamped her pipe between her teeth and sat down in the rocker on her back porch. She set her glass of sweet tea on the table, smoothed her apron and struck a match. She waited for the flame to settle down before touching it to the tobacco, then took a long draw, filling her mouth with warm smoke. She moved her glasses from the bridge of her nose to atop her white hair and looked out across the fields. To the west, the sun was touching the ridge and the sky was taking on a deeper blue on the other side of the valley. The birds were concluding their daytime chatter before returning to their nests for the night, not to be caught out when the owls began to hunt.

At the far end of the valley, a ball of light swooped down from the sky, leveling off above the ground at the tree line running along Reins Lick Creek.

"Humph, what we got here?" she muttered, exhaling a plume of blue smoke. "I seen you before." The light flitted around like a butterfly in a patch of wildflowers for a while before coming to rest above the tall second harvest fescue. "Seen that too. Now, off you goes."

Hettie took a sip of tea, waiting for the ball of light to bounce over the trees and out of sight. Instead, it approached the house. It moved purposely, not in the random fashion she was used to seeing. As it neared, she could see its perfectly round, glistening surface. It steadily advanced, finally coming to rest at the base of the porch steps. It appeared about five feet in diameter. A thin slit, running from top to bottom appeared. As it widened, Hettie leaned forward peering into the dark opening.

A face appeared, followed by a body. Hettie studied the smiling, diminutive woman who stepped out onto the bottom porch step. She had a flawless, pale tawny complexion. Curly bronze hair

---

[6]"Hettie Johnson and The Orb Rider" appeared online in *All Worlds Wayfarer*, 3/18/2020.

framed her long thin face and bright amethyst eyes. She was dressed in a plain white jumpsuit.

"Good evening, Hettie Shaw Johnson," she said, bowing her head. "I hope I have not given you cause for alarm."

"Dear, I'm a hundred-an'-five-year-old black woman an' most likely lived through more than you could ever think of. Ain't much gonna upset me, unless you're from social services an' come here lookin' to take me to the retirement home." Hettie pulled her glasses down, staring intently at the woman. "Well?" she asked.

"I assure you; I am not from social services."

"That's good," snorted Hettie, "but I 'spect you've got somethin' in mind or you wouldn't be standin' on my porch step. You can start by tellin' me who you are an' what you wants."

"Call me Solasta. I am an orb rider."

"A what?"

"An orb rider," Solasta replied matter-of-factly.

"Orb? Is that what you call that thing?" Hettie asked, nodding toward the ball of light.

"It is a word from your language to signify the form you perceive. You could not comprehend our name for it. Similarly, you could not comprehend my real name. I use the human sound *Solasta* to signify the form I have chosen to present."

Hettie, pointing a thin, gnarled finger at the gleaming ball, asked, "Where'd you get that thing? Up at Walmart?"

"No, the orb and I come from elsewhere. Think of it as an extension of me and I of it. The orb and I are inseparable."

"Hmmm, I think social services might be lookin' for *you*," said Hettie. "You sure you didn't wander away from somewhere you wadn't supposed to?"

"It is true I wander all about, but it is for a purpose," Solasta replied.

"Uh-uh. Now I know the boys in the white coats are sure to show up any moment," Hettie said, shaking her head. "You ain't dangerous, are you?"

"Hardly. I am what you would call an observer. I ride the orb throughout your universe, observing and recording what happens."

"What for?" asked Hettie.

"We are inquisitive beings and this universe has much to interest us."

"What do you mean when you says 'this universe'? Sounds like you're trying to say you ain't from around here."

"As I said, I am from elsewhere. Yet it is not distance that separates us. The place I come from exists alongside this one, although undetectable. Your scientists would call it a parallel universe. It has certain similarities to this universe but remains fundamentally different. The orb allows me and my fellow orb riders to travel between our universes."

"I don't rightly know if I understand all what you're sayin'. Why don't you sit down, and I'll get you some sweet tea while we waits for the padded van? We can visit awhile. Not many folks come this way no more; just the Jehovah Witnesses and them fellers wantin' to sell me winders."

"Thank you, Hettie Shaw Johnson," Solasta said, bouncing up the steps. She sat down on a rocking chair on the other side of the screen door.

"No need to call me by all them names. Hettie will do. My given name is Henrietta Jones Shaw. I married a Johnson. Everybody's called me Hettie since I can remember. I was named after my father, Henry Shaw."

"As you wish, Hettie."

Hettie eased up from her rocker and pulled the screen door open, causing the old spring to cry out in pain. She filled a tumbler with ice cubes, followed by sweet tea. The ice crackled. She wrapped a napkin around the glass and went back out on the porch.

"Here you are," she said, handing the glass to Solasta. "Better drink that up, before they comes and takes you away."

Solasta took a sip of sweet tea, savoring its flavor. "Delicious. You take your water straight from the earth," she said, "no contamination from chemicals detected."

"That's my secret for livin' as long as I have. That and eatin' a good breakfast of bacon and eggs ever mornin'." Hettie laughed, then slapped her knee. "Oh, an' not goin' to doctors. That's key. Don't go to no doctors. They always got to find somethin' wrong, even if you feel jus' fine. I've lived on this farm all my life, 105 years, like I said. The water from that well has always been pure and sweet, never run dry, even though some mighty bad droughts. You looks like a healthy young lady. Bet them doctors has had a field day with you."

"We have no doctors."

"So's the better for you, sounds like my kind of place."

"Hold out your hand, Hettie," said Solasta, "I have something to show you."

Hettie wiped the condensation from her hand on her apron, then turned her palm upward, holding it a few inches above her knees. Solasta pointed toward the orb. It shimmered slightly. Drifting up the steps toward Hettie, it shrank to the size of an orange by the time it came to rest above her waiting hand.

"No need to worry," said Solasta. "You may hold it if you wish."

"Well don't that beat all," Hettie whispered, staring at the orb for a moment before closing her fingers around its smooth, cool surface. It was solid and very light weight. She sensed a slight tingle in her fingertips. Shoving her glasses to the top of her head, she brought the orb close to her face. Eddies of the palest colors of the spectrum gyred over the surface. A tear welled up in her eye.

"All shrunk down, this here thing reminds me of my Mama's special Christmas ornament. She used to do laundry for old Mrs. Luttinger. That was way back before I was born. She said one Christmas, Mrs. Luttinger gave her the ornament. Said it was hand blown, come all the way from Germany." Hettie pulled up the corner of her apron and dabbed at her eyes. "She wouldn't let nobody touch her ornament but her. She always picked out the perfect place on the tree to hang it. Kept it wrapped in tissue in a shoebox in her cedar chest. Then come World War II. My brother, Henry Junior, enlisted in the Merchant Marine. He was a mess attendant on the Dorchester Troopship when it got sunk by a German U-boat. There weren't no survivors. That was February 3rd, 1943. Next Christmas, when we went to decorate the tree, Mama smashed her ornament in the fireplace. Said she didn't want nothin' what had to do with the Nazis. That's what the Germans was called."

Hettie fell silent for a moment. "You better take this thing back before I drops it."

"You cannot break the orb," said Solasta. She made a gentle sweeping motion with her hand and the orb lifted from Hettie's grasp and returned to its former size and position at the base of the porch steps.

Hettie remained motionless until the tingling in her fingertips subsided. "You know chile, I don't know why, but I likes you. Guess if you was going to rob me or chop me up into tiny pieces you'da done it by now. So while you probably ain't got any mischief in mind, I 'spect you've got some reason to be sitting on my porch."

"Indeed, Hettie," said Solasta, " I have come to ask you to ride with me."

Hettie raised her eyebrows, turned her head and stared at Solasta for a few moments. Then, she slapped her knee again before flopping back in her rocker, laughing. "Chile, you sure had me going there for a minute." She took a deep breath and started to laugh again. "Sure enough. You want to take this old woman for a ride in your Christmas ornament." She rocked back and forth, puffing out blue smoke between laughs. "An' just where did you have in mind for us to go?"

"Out there," Solasta calmly answered, gesturing toward the sky, "beyond your sun, beyond your galaxy, to the farthest star you can see. Out there, wonders await."

"Chile, I ain't even been out of Kentucky. Never had no cause or desire to. What makes you think I'd wanna hop in that bouncy ball and fly off to God knows where? Besides, that thing don't look big enough for two to ride comfortably."

"As you have seen, the orb can assume the size it needs to accomplish its task. As for why, I would be grateful for your companionship. I understand this is an unexpected and fantastic proposal. Maybe we could go on a test ride of sorts. To some close place where you can get a sense of what orb riding is like."

"Where would that be?" asked Hettie.

"We can leave that up to you," replied Solasta.

"You's serious ain't you," said Hettie. Solasta pointed to the orb. The slit reopened. "Just a short ride?" asked Hettie.

"Yes."

"Anywhere I wants to go?"

"Yes."

"You ain't gonna ab-duck me or nothin?"

"No."

"You'll gonna bring me right back?"

"Yes."

Hettie studied Solasta for a while. "Chile, I don't know why, but I feel like you is being straight with me. Only been fooled one time in my life. That was back in 1929 when I married Lester Johnson. He was passin' through lookin' for work. That was the Depression time, you know. We was doin' okay on the farm. Anyway, Lester said he loved me and if we got married, he'd come work on the farm for Daddy. Should'a knowed better. He was a city boy, all talk and not much else. Well, our daughter Frances was born in 1930 an' by the time 1931 rolled around, Lester had done got his fill of farm life an' fatherhood. He disappeared and we never seen or heard from him again. As for my baby girl, she died of the croup in 1935."

Hettie slumped back in her rocker. She pulled the pipe from her mouth and knocked the spent tobacco from the bowl. Shoving it into her apron pocket, she asked again, "Anywhere?"

"Anywhere."

Hettie stood up, untied her apron and hung it on a nail by the screen door. "I ain't got no idea why I'm doin' this, but let's go before I comes to my senses." She motioned to Solasta, "You first."

Solasta walked down the steps and stepped through the slit in the orb. Hettie followed, stopping on the bottom step to peer inside. She could see Solasta few feet from the opening, surrounded by a thin mist. She beckoned Hettie forward. Hettie pushed her right hand through the opening, then quickly withdrew it. She examined her hand, wiggling her fingers.

"Well, alright then," Hettie said, stepping through the opening. Inside, the mist disappeared. Behind Solasta, she could see the entire farm just as if she had stepped off the porch on a crystal clear morning. She turned around to an unimpeded view of her back porch. She extended her arms in an attempt to find the side of the orb.

"The orb does not have an inside boundary," explained Solasta. "It is autogenous. That means it adjusts to the needs of the rider. For instance, the orb senses we need a flat surface on which to stand, so it provides one. Otherwise we would be standing in the dirt. To find the side, you will have to want a side."

"So, if I wanted a side right here," Hettie said reaching out, "this thing would make a side?" Immediately, her hand touched an invisible barrier. "Well, I'll be. How'd it know that?"

"The orb senses our needs and provides."

"Can it provide me a chair; cause I don't think I can take all this standin' up."

"Wait here," said Solasta. The orb rose so they were standing level with the porch. An oval of mist formed. Solasta stepped through and went to the rocker. She picked it up and returned, placing it behind Hettie. "I think you will be more comfortable in your own rocking chair. Now, let's take our ride before all the light is gone."

"Wait jus' a minute," Hettie said, sitting down. "You ain't gonna stand over me while we flies around in this thing are you?"

"Well, I usually float in my natural form, which looks like something similar to a jellyfish. I can return to that form if you desire."

"No... no, no, no. You looks just fine, but I don't wants you standin' over me or floating around neither, so go get that other rocker and sit down."

"As you wish, Hettie." She retrieved the other rocking chair, then asked, "Where would you like to go?"

Before Hettie had finished saying, "Duncan Bend Cemetery," the orb lifted away from the porch and whisked over the ridge. In an instant it came to rest among rows of weather-beaten headstones.

"That didn't feel like we was movin' at all," said Hettie.

"The laws of gravity and inertia do not apply while we are in the orb. What that means is no matter how quickly we start or stop or how fast we go, it feels as if we are standing still."

"Guess that comes in handy," laughed Hettie. Her voice turned somber as she looked at a group of grave markers. "Been a while since I been here," she whispered. "All my folks that I knows of is buried here. In the back is my Grandmother, Agnes. She was born a slave in 1857. Escaped to Ohio on the Underground Railroad. Lived a hundred an' nine years. Next to her is her son, Henry. He's my Daddy. Died in 1937 while working cleanup on the gymnasium the WPA was building up to Trenton. Roof truss fell on him. Next to him is Mama. She died in 1968. She was only ninety-seven. My little Frances is right down there in front next to Henry Jr. Already told you 'bout them. When my time comes, they gonna put me in that empty spot in the corner."

Dusk was settling in. Hettie leaned forward looking at the mottled, lichen-covered limestone markers in the thinning light. Grass and weeds were growing up the sides. "They don't keep up this side of the cemetery like they does for the white folk," she said. "I'll have to get out here soon and pull them weeds." She sat back in her rocker. She folded her arms in her lap and said, "We can go now."

The orb retraced its path, settling softly at Hettie's porch. The sun had slipped below the ridge and the sky on the opposite side of the valley was turning indigo. The faint twinkle of stars could be detected.

"What is your decision, Hettie?" asked Solasta.

Hettie looked at the stars now visible above her head. The orb shot straight up into the night sky. Now, surrounded by star encrusted blackness, she looked down to see a blue and green sphere shrinking from sight. "Is that what I think that is?" she asked in amazement.

"Yes, that is what you call Earth," said Solasta. "Among the many worlds in this universe, it is small and relatively insignificant, but beautiful none-the-less."

"Did I do this?" asked Hettie. "Didn't mean to. I was just wondering what it'd be like. Didn't think we'd go flyin' off like this. You better take over and tell this thing where to go before we runs into a star or somethin'."

"As you wish," said Solasta.

Forgetting what Solasta had said about gravity and inertia, Hettie braced herself, waiting for the orb to lurch forward. Instead, the stars seemed to blink and the next thing she saw was a large red sun.

"This is the Ellista system," explained Solasta, "seven habitable planets, orbiting this red star." Another blink and a planet wrapped in swirling pink clouds, popped into view. "This is Calindra," she continued, "the fourth planet."

Below the clouds, Hettie could see grey and garnet continents, surrounded by smooth turquoise oceans. They continued their descent until the orb was engulfed by the roseate mist. An instant later, they emerged above the gently rolling blue-green water. Their descent leveled off and they continued toward land until they could see a vast city perched at the edge of the water.

"Before you is Coneste, capital city of the Ellista System," said Solasta. "and home to Wasruob, the grand market, where the inhabitants of the seven planets converge to sell, buy, and trade. They have been doing this for a thousand earth years."

The orb glided over the water until they reached the coastline. Below, Hettie could see Coneste, its domes gleaming red-yellow in Elista's sunlight. Along the shore, thousands of ships with tall sails that resembled dragonfly wings were moored. Far inland, an array of strange looking craft, some suspended in air, some resting on the surface, surrounded the city. They skimmed over the concentric rings of domes, separated by narrow streets which were intersected by larger avenues. They followed one of the large boulevards toward the center of the city until they reached a vast circular plaza.

"Wasruob," said Solasta.

Hettie edged forward in her rocker, gazing down on the plaza filled with a jumble of tents and booths of every imaginable color and shape. Throngs of market goers snaked along in winding queues from one vendor to another. The orb was now close enough for Hettie to see them clearly.

"My, oh my, I guess I thought they'd look like us," gasped Hettie.

"A natural expectation," said Solasta. "We all seek the familiar."

"Sure ain't much familiar about the looks of them folks," laughed Hettie.

"The ones with two ears that look like wings are the Rhüln and the ones with the purple scales are the Zhakrill," explained Solasta. "The Tolu are covered in thick red fur. Their planet, being furthest from Ellista, is very cold. Then there are the Quizans, recognizable by their prominent orange dorsal crest. The Silurusa, who live on a water world, are the ones with the bright yellow gills. If you see tall and graceful beings with pale green skin, they are the Jurápha. The Calindrans are short with bright blue facial spots."

Hettie studied the hustle-bustle of the market for some time. After a while, she said, "You know this is kinda like the 8th of August celebration. That's our big homecoming when all the family and friends that had gone away come back to be with them who never left. When I was a girl, folks would come on the trains and busses or hitchhike to get to the celebration. Now they comes in cars and airplanes. There was barbecue and fried chicken, horseshoes and baseball, not to mention the music and dancin'. I goes to the one in Allensville. They say they been celebrating the 8th of August there for 150 years. That's where my Grandfather Joseph met Grandmother Agnes. She had come down from Ohio.

"Well they got married and started sharecroppin'. After Henry, my Daddy, come along, Grandfather Joseph started stillin' moonshine to make some extra money. Must'a been pretty good stuff cause Grandfather Joseph made enough money sellin' shine to buy our farm. When I was six, he took a batch over to Hoptown. He never come home, though. The Christian County Sheriff said he probably run off with the money. Grandmother Agnes never believed that. She heard tell from a good source that some local moonshiners robbed him, then threw him down a ravine for cuttin' into their territory. No matter, we never seen or heard from him again."

Hettie sat back in her rocker. "You ever been?" she asked.

"Been where?" Solasta inquired.

"To the 8th of August celebration."

"No."

"Well, chile," said Hettie, "you need to go at least one time. It ain't as big as this thing, but there's plenty to keep you interested."

"Of that I am sure. We can stay here as long as you like but there is something else I would like to show you and time is of the essence. "

"I think I've seen enough here. If you got some other place in mind I'll be happy to go. Just let me know before you start this thing up."

"We go now," said Solasta. This time, Hettie was ready when the plaza blinked out of site. She was not ready when two planets came into view, growing in size and looking very much like they were on the verge of collision. "These are the planets Lokono and Aketi of the Teebia System. Most of the time, their orbits keep them far apart. However, once every twenty-seven orbits they come in close proximity to one another. So close, in fact, that lifeforms can freely move between the two. Over the millennia, their respective ecosystems have evolved to rely on this migration. It is wondrous."

"Chile," Hettie huffed, "I only understood about two words of what you jus' said. Any chance you could say that in plain talk?"

Solasta remained silent for a few moments, then said, "It's like the bees pollinating the flowers."

"Well, why didn't you say that in the first place?"

"It begins."

Hettie watched the planets approach. Glowing swirls appeared on the surfaces nearest each other. Suddenly, countless spores of light erupted, rushing to bridge the void between the two planets. The orb lay dead center.

Solasta placed her hand on Hettie's arm, assuring her, "Do not be afraid, no harm will come to us."

In an instant, a vast glowing jumble of winged, diaphanous creatures caught up in the migration between the planets whorled about the orb in a chaotic eddy. So dense were they, Hettie thought the orb may be swept away or worse crushed.. This swarm continued for quite some time before the flow of creatures dissipated and the last few drifted to the surfaces of their new homes.

"Didn't look like no damn bees and flowers to me," Hettie muttered, letting out the breath she had been holding. "Chile, next time, you gots to give me some kinda warning when somethin' like that's gonna happen, otherwise you gonna have a mess to clean up."

"Forgive me Hettie, said Solasta, "I forget how it feels to experience this for the first time."

"I'll have to admit they was sure sumpin' to look at. I don't mind tellin' you they had me goin' there for a minute. Thought we was goners." She shook her head and sighed. "You know this here reminds me of when I was a little girl and saw fireflies for the first time. I was out back right after sunset and all of a sudden, all these little yellow lights started coming up outa the grass. They was flying all around my head, I could feel 'em on my arms an' in my hair. I let out for the house an' didn't quit hollerin' till I had the covers pulled over my head. Well, they all had a good laugh, but it wadn't that funny to me. But then, Mama took me back out and told me all about fireflies and they wadn't scary no more."

"Hettie, I have something to discuss with you," said Solasta.

"Go ahead chile. But make it quick. It's been a long day. We best be getting back 'fore I gets too wore out."

"Certainly," said Solasta. "Hettie, in about two weeks your scientists should discover a gravitational anomaly deep in space. Eventually they will conclude that it is a small primordial black hole hurtling along on a near-earth trajectory. This small black hole is only about the size of a marble, but its extreme gravity will ultimately have devastating effects on your planet. It will pass close enough to rip away your planet's atmosphere and a significant portion of its oceans. It will also fracture the earth's crust and set off a chain of super volcanic eruptions. These will cause cataclysmic environmental devastation resulting in the extinction of all lifeforms."

Hettie sat in stunned silence. She closed her eyes, burying her face in her hands. She took several deep, steady breaths before she said, "Chile, I don't understand none of this what you're tryin' to tell me, 'cept that last part about extinction. It don't sound too good, no ways. Are you tellin' me we ain't got long before we all gonna die?"

"Yes, but you do not have to go back. You can stay with me."

"Stay with you?"

"Yes, become an orb rider. Today, you have seen only a very few of the wonders in this universe. Think of all there is to discover. There are marvels out there that make what you have seen pale in comparison."

"Hold on," said Hettie. "This is a lot to spring on an old woman. Give me a minute to think on all this." She leaned back in her rocking chair and stared at the stars. It was some time before she asked, "Can't you do somethin' to make that black hole go somewheres else?"

"No, the orb can do many things, but moving a black hole is beyond its capabilities. Besides orb rider are observers. We cannot interfere in the happenings of this universe."

"So's if a whole planet goin' to blow up, you won't do nothin'?"

"The risks are too great," explained Solasta. "Diverting the black hole could lead to the destruction of a different inhabited world or even an entire galaxy."

"Well, mebbe so," sighed Hettie. "Answer me this: can this thing take me anywhere?"

"The orb has unlimited capability to travel. You can even visit other parallel universes if you wish."

"Alright then, I got one question for you. Can this thing take me to see God?"

"Which one?"

"Chile, don't be blasphemin'." Hettie snorted. "We's got along jus' fine up till now, but I won't tolerate that kind'a talk."

"I apologize, but beings in this universe believe in countless deities in a multitude of forms. On the desert planet, Arda, for instance, the Krayiri worship the river, Déran, as the giver of all life. The orb could take us there. On Segomo, the Uhuans believe their world sits in the eye of their god, Yeom. When Yeom is awake, it is daytime. When he sleeps it is night. They believe the stars are his dreams. The orb could take us there."

"Them are places. I'm talking about going to see *my* God. I want to see if He'll make that black hole thing go somewheres else. Seems to me He wouldn't want something like that to ruin His handiwork. I could be wrong, it's happened before. I knows it might not make a difference if I saw Him in person, but it couldn't hurt to try."

"Would not your concept of prayer accomplish the same thing?" asked Solasta.

"Of course, I jus' thought asking in person might help move things along."

"The orb can do many things and go many places, but it cannot travel to a belief, even one as strong and sincere as yours."

"Do you believe in God?" asked Hettie.

"I am convinced there is a power greater than all the universes," Solasta replied, adding, "I do not profess to understand it, but I believe this higher power guides all things."

"I 'spect this thing don't go there neither, does it?"

"No."

"I figured as much." Hettie rubbed her jaw. "Let me ask you somethin'. Outta all the people in the world, how come for you to ask me?"

"I was one of those fireflies you encountered as a little girl, and I do apologize for frightening you so. Since then, I have felt a special kinship with you. Over the years, I have visited you many times. I was sincere when I said I would be grateful for your companionship."

"Well, now what about all that you was talking about not interferin'? Ain't taken me along with you interferin'?" Hettie asked.

"You would stay with me within the orb. The overall impact on your universe will be the same whether you perish on earth or ride the orb."

"Why not take some young person. I ain't got much time left."

"It is not about age," said Solasta, "It is not about saving the human race. Ii is about the chance to spend a brief moment with someone I greatly value. If all life on your planet was not on the verge of extinction, I could not even consider such a thing. An extraordinary opportunity such as this may never occur again during my travels. Will you not come?"

"Thank you chile," Hettie said, "I'm flattered an' all, but I think I'll pass. I'm sure everthin' you said is true and I likes you jus' fine too. I think, though, I'd like to be home in familiar surroundin's when my time comes. How long before that black hole does its thing?"

"Approximately one earth year."

"So, I'll have time to go to the 8th of August celebration, and have one more Christmas, won't I?"

"Yes," answered Solasta, then added, "and you will see the fireflies one last time."

"All of a sudden, I'm feelin' real tired," said Hettie. "I think it's time to go."

The stars winked out and Hettie's back porch appeared. Solasta stood up and held her hand out for Hettie. She stood up as the oval of mist formed. Solasta led her onto the porch.

"Chile, will I ever see you again?" asked Hettie.

"I have it on good recommendation that I should go to the 8th of August celebration."

"That's right, come back a while to be with them who is stayin'."

Solasta stepped into the mist and returned with Hettie's rocker, then turned back toward the orb.

"Wait jus' a minute," Hettie said, lightly touching Solasta's arm. "Where you goin'?"

"Well, I was going to retrieve the other rocking chair."

"No... no, no, no. I won't be needin' it. You keep it so's you won't have to be standin' up or floatin' around all the time."

Solasta smiled, "As you wish, Hettie." She reached through the opening and gathered a large swirl of mist from the interior of the orb. She cupped her hands around it as it coalesced, forming a shiny ball the size of an orange. "For your Christmas tree," she said, handing it to Hettie.

"Well, don't that beat all," Hettie whispered, closing her fingers around its smooth, cool surface. She sensed a familiar tingle in her fingertips. "Thank you chile, I'll find the perfect spot for it. An' when I sees the fireflies next, I'll think of you."

MULDED[7]

Hack leaned on the counter watching the late afternoon heat shimmer off the flat, parched ground. The motor of the refrigerator chest hummed, laboring to keep the beer cold in the searing Arizona summer heat. A rolling ball of dust moved swiftly up the road. When it got close enough, Hack could see it was one of the Wrangler JK's they rented back in Dooley to adventurers from the city who wanted to rough it in comfort. It slowed, pulling off the road into the gravel parking lot, tires scrunching as it came to a stop. Some dust, not willing to give up the chase, wafted by the Wrangler toward the screen door of the weather beaten building.

A young man hopped out of the Jeep, pulled out his cell phone and took a selfie before following the dust through the door. He squinted as he looked around the interior of the store. There were a few old tables in the center, banked on either side by glass display cases. An old time saloon bar ran across the back of the store.

"Is this Mulded mister?" the young man asked.

"It's pronounced Mule Dead," answered Hack. "Story is that Elmore Shouse came here in 1880 lookin' for gold. He had jus' found some when his mule up and died. Thought that would be a good name for the place. Apparently, he weren't much of a speller cause when he filed his claim, he wrote out Mulded. The name stuck. Turns out his claim petered out right fast, so he decided there was more money to be made in selling whisky, beans and shovels to the would-be miners. Anyways, that's how the story goes. Call me Hack. What they call you?"

"My name's Leland Lowe. I'm an amateur ufologist. I've been over to Roswell, Alamogordo, White Sands and Spaceport

---

[7] "Mulded" appeared in print in *Anthology Askew, Volume 006: Askew Horizons* published by Rhetoric Askew, 10/1/2018.

America. Before I leave for Area 51, thought I'd check out the place where the Mulded Maiden incident took place. Is this it?"

"Sure is. Back in 1955. I was there."

"You're telling me you were here when she landed? How do I know this ain't some yarn you tell the touristas to sell a few trinkets?"

"See for yourself." Hack turned and grabbed a large picture frame from amid the bottles on the shelf. He took a towel and gently wiped the dust from the glass, then studied it a moment before laying it on the counter.

Leland walked up to the bar. The picture frame contained a yellowed newspaper clipping. The heading read: **Local Men Claim Female Alien Visits Local Grocery!** Beneath it was a grainy photograph of several men in front of the bar where he was now standing.

"Don't hardly seem like it was sixty three years ago," said Hack. "I was sixteen. Ed Spivey owned the store back then. He'd got it from Elmore Shouse himself. When he died, he give the store to me." Hack tapped a gnarled finger on a boyish face in the photo. "That's me right there. We posed for the reporter from the Dooley Sentinel who come down to get our story. I'm the only one left. All the others have passed on." He wiped at his eyes with a bar towel. "Do you see the name 'Hack Boyd' underneath the photo? That's me. How 'bout somethin' to drink while you read the article?"

"Sure," said Leland. "What do you have on tap?"

"Nada. All I got is Miller or Bud - in longnecks."

"Let me have a Bud."

"How about a burger to go with that?" asked Hack.

"Do you have a menu?"

"Nope. Jus' with or without."

"With or without what?" asked Leland.

"Cheese."

"With."

"Oh, you get chips with that. Pick a bag from the rack," Hack said.

He pulled a longneck from the cooler and laid it on its side, rolling it across a stack of napkin-like papers, neatly covering the slippery sides. He inserted the bottle in an opener mounted on the end of the counter and popped off its cap which fell with a soft clinking noise into a can below. He placed it on the bar in front of Leland, then walked over to a dingy refrigerator and retrieved a stack of hamburger patties from the freezer and a pack of sliced cheese. He turned on the gas to the flattop and tossed on a patty.

"It'll take a bit for the flattop to warm up." Hack said.

"Not much left around here but the store, I see," said Leland.

"Yeah, the rest moved out years ago."

Leland took a draw on his longneck. "I take it they thought you all were pulling a hoax. So, tell me what really happened."

"Well, let me start out by saying all that Mulded Maiden stuff is a bunch of hooey made up by some shady businessmen up in Dooley. Thought they could make this thing into a big money makin' tourist attraction. After a while, the story got so outlandish, no one believed it and it all blew up in their faces. Only, we were the ones forever branded as hoaxers."

"Got to expect stuff like that if you're going to go around claiming female aliens stopped by."

"It ain't a claim. It happened, and it was only one."

Leland took another draw on his longneck. "Well, I'm listenin', at least until my burger's done."

Hack studied the young man for a moment before starting. "Well, it was late in the afternoon on a Saturday jus' about this time of year. The Morgan twins, Bob Wiley and big Frank Peavey, were already here when I arrived. Ed was frying up burgers. I ordered one and got a cream soda out of the cooler. 'Ida Red Likes The Boogie' by Bob Wills was playing on the jukebox. I had no sooner sat down when this loud rumbling noise commenced and the whole place started to shake. Bob shouted, 'Earthquake!', and we all headed for the door, stumblin' out into the parking lot."

"That's when the mothership landed?" asked Leland.

"Weren't no mothership," growled Hack. "That's one of them lies those boys up in Dooley made up. It's the stuff like that made us a laughin' stock. We got out to the parkin' lot jus' in time to see the strangest thing. It looked like one of them fancy hydroplane racing boats, but it wasn't in no water. It was floatin' down out of the sky, all smooth and shiny silver colored. Then it jus' hovered about a foot above the ground. By then, all the rumblin' and shakin' had stopped. It had a canopy of sorts on top which slid open and the most beautiful gal you ever saw got out."

"So let me get this straight," asked Leland, "a galactic race boat flew down from the sky and the most beautiful woman you ever saw got out?"

"Does a coyote crap in the cottonwoods? You bet your life it happened…"

* * *

Hack stood alongside the others in the dusty parking lot, staring at the woman who had just emerged from the sleek silver machine. She was tall, with curly, chestnut hair and lavender eyes. Nice figure. Despite the fact that she had just dropped out of the sky, her friendly smile immediately put Hack at ease.

"My name is Aubrina," she said. "You boys got anything cold to drink? Flying across the galaxy sure makes a girl thirsty. I could do with something to eat, too."

Ed led her into the store. "How about a Miller," he said, searching under the bar for a glass. "Ain't fancy, but they do call it the champagne of bottled beer."

"What more could a girl ask for?" laughed Aubrina.

Ed looked in the refrigerator. "Humph. . . as for somethin' to eat, I can cook you up a cheeseburger or I got some chicken salad if it ain't gone bad."

"Cheeseburger. You got a music maker in this place?"

Ed pointed to the jukebox. "I'll get some quarters from the register," he said.

"Don't worry, I got it," she said, waving her hand. Jukebox started right up.

* * *

". . . Hell," Hack said, shaking his head, "we pushed back the tables and took turns doing the two-step with her. When she wasn't dancin' or singin', she was eatin' cheeseburgers. Must'a ate half a dozen. She would sing softly in your ear when you held her close. She smelled like the white desert wildflowers that pop up in the spring. An' she was light as a ball of cotton and just as soft. She kept that old jukebox playin' most of the night while we all took turns dancin' with her. The thing was, it seemed like it didn't make no difference to her that we was jus' ordinary fellers. She jus' made you feel good. I fell in love with her that night. We all did..."

* * *

Hack held Aubrina closely as she sang the last refrain of 'The Tennessee Waltz' in his ear. It was 3 am.

"Boys, I hate to say it, but it's time for me to go," she said. "I've had a wonderful time."

". . . Well, she waved her hand," said Hack, "and the jukebox fell silent. She asked Ed to fix her a cheeseburger to go. The rest of us walked out into the parking lot with her. She motioned toward her ship and the canopy slid back. Along about then, Ed came rushing up and handed her a sack with her cheeseburger in it. She gave us all a hug and a kiss on the cheek, then hopped back in her machine. Everything rumbled and shook again before it shot straight up, disappearing into the starry night sky."

Hack checked the burger which had begun to sizzle. He smashed it down with his spatula, then flipped it over. He retrieved a sack of buns from atop the refrigerator before unwrapping a slice of American and depositing it on the burger.

Leland waited until Hack was finished before asking, "So that's the story? A woman flies down to earth and you guys spend the night drinking beers and dancing to the jukebox. You fall in love with her, then you send her off into the sky with a cheeseburger! I've got to say that's a hard sell even for the 50's."

"Can't change what happened cause folks is expectin' to hear something different," said Hack. "You want any mustard or catsup on your burger? Got some dill pickles too."

"Just some mustard."

Hack grabbed the cheeseburger and a squeeze bottle of mustard and set them on the bar in front of Leland. He tossed two more patties on the flattop.

"Maybe I should get this to go," said Leland.

"Stay where you are kid," said Hack. "Enjoy your cheeseburger. You ain't hurt nobody's feelings."

"Does the jukebox work?" asked Leland.

"It's temperamental," said Hack. He fished a quarter out of the register and tossed it on the bar.

Leland walked over to the jukebox. "This is an antique," he said.

"Same one that was here in '55."

Leland wiped the dust from the glass and peered at the song selections. "These songs are antiques too."

"Ed never wanted any others after that night. Neither did I."

Leland put the quarter in the slot. It clinked through the chutes and dropped into the coin box with a muffled clink. "What's a good one?"

"I like 'em all. But I'm partial to 'The Tennessee Waltz'."

Leland searched the playlist until he found it and pushed the button. No response. He tried it again. Same result. He tried a different song, then another. The Jukebox remained silent. Instead, he heard a soft rumbling in the distance. It was growing louder. As it grew, the windows began to rattle.

Hack stepped out from behind the bar and made a beeline for the door. "Better get a move on boy or you'll miss out."

"Miss out on what?"

"Not what. Her, stupid! The female alien, The Mulded Maiden, Aubrina."

"No way I'm falling for that," Leland called out. The rumbling was increasing. "It's got to be a helicopter or something like that."

"Suit yourself," Hack yelled back.

Leland could feel the rumble in his chest. "Wait for me," he hollered and bolted for the door. He found Hack standing in a whorl of dust looking up and waving his hand. Leland joined him as a ruby red craft descended. Then, the rumbling and shaking faded away. As the dust was carried off by the evening breeze, Leland could see it was floating motionless about a foot above the gravel. The canopy slid back and the most beautiful woman he ever saw stepped out.

"That can't be her, can it?"

"Sure is," said Hack. "She ain't changed a bit since I first saw her."

"Thought you said her ship was silver."

"Oh, she changes the color of that thing like she changes her nail polish," laughed Hack.

* * *

Aubrina, Hack, and Leland ate cheeseburgers, drank beer and danced until the wee hours of the morning. Patti Page was singing the last refrain of 'The Tennessee Waltz' when Aubrina said, "I hate to say it boys, but it's time for me to go. I had a swell time."

Hack and Leland walked her to the spaceship. She gave Leland a kiss on the cheek. "It was my pleasure to meet you."

"The pleasure was all mine," he said.

Aubrina motioned to her ship and the canopy slid back. She took Hack's face in her hands, kissed him on the forehead, hugged him, then stepped back and looked into his eyes. A tear rolled down her cheek.

"Hack, you're dying," she whispered.

"Yeah, the docs say it won't be long," he said.

"Such fragile creatures your kind are. You bloom like spring flowers, then you are gone."

"Oh, I've had a good run. I danced with the Mulded Maiden you know." Hack fell silent for a moment. "You got room in that thing for two?" he asked.

"Yes."

He held up a sack. "Got a couple of cheeseburgers to go. I was wonderin' if you would take me up there with you for a while, like you done with the others." He looked up at the sky. "I've always wanted to see what it's like and this is my last chance. As you know, it won't turn out to be a long ride."

"I know," said Aubrina. She took his hand and led him up to the canopy. It slid back as they approached. When they reached the opening, Hack fished a ring of keys from his pocket and tossed them to Leland.

"What's this for?" he asked.

"The store is yours, kid. If you want it. I got no use for it now. Everything you need to know is written on the side of the refrigerator. If you're smart, you won't say anything about tonight. And don't fret, she'll stop by and see you again."

IVELISSA'S BOOK[8]

"Tell me the story again, Papa," said Elina, "like you did when I was a little girl." She paused, bending down to pick a blossom of Sweet William. Lifting the soft blue-lavender petals close to her face, she inhaled their pleasant fragrance. She held it out for her father to smell, then tucked it behind the ash blonde tresses above her ear.

"You're still my little girl. You always will be," William said, wrapping his arm around his daughter. He drew her close, kissing her on the forehead. "Can you wait until we get there? Right now, I would like only to enjoy our walk. If we're quiet, we may see a deer."

Their path, paralleling a small creek, led them upstream between steep ridge slopes. They continued walking for some time, listening to the birds flitting through the treetops and the occasional rustle of leaves made by some foraging squirrel. They did not speak again until they arrived at the waterfall, a horseshoe ledge of limestone about ten feet above their heads. The water tumbled over the edge, dancing momentarily on the rocks below before resuming its course.

"Your mother believed places like this were full of energy," said William. "Let me go first."

He stepped over to the grassy bank and sat down, feet dangling in the air. Scooting over the edge, he descended, stepping on exposed roots and stones until his feet were firmly planted on the gravel of the creek bed. Elina followed.

"Used to be there were some old railroad ties set into the bank to form steps. They rotted out and washed away years ago," he said. "You know, I'm not exactly a young man anymore. With the steps gone, that bank seems to get higher and steeper every time I come here."

---

[8]"Ivelissa.s Book" appeared online in *CommuterLit*, 3/10/2020.

"Please, Papa. You said you would tell me the story when we got here. Now please, before it's time to go."

"Alright, alright. You could say I was a confirmed bachelor," William started. He looked about, finally settling on a fat length of tree trunk lurking along the creek bank. "Still unwed at forty-five years of age and with no prospects, I had certainly given up on marriage."

Elina moved close to the waterfall, sitting down on a smooth table of bedrock comfortably beyond the reach of the splashing water. She opened her backpack and pulled out a dog-eared book.

"I see you remembered to bring Ivelissa's book. It always reminded me of Carroll's 'Jabberwocky'. There were words I understood and then there were those that baffled me. And it was the same way when she spoke at first. Her fairy talk, I called it. But she was a quick study and in no time at all she could carry on a conversation like she had lived here all her life. She tried to teach me her strange lingo, but I never could catch on. You, on the other hand, picked it up as soon as you could talk."

"Papa, the story."

"Okay, okay, indulge your old man. It was some twenty years ago. I was a bit leaner back then and I still had still had some hair on the top of my head."

"I think a bald pate makes a man look distinguished," laughed Elina.

"As I was saying," William continued, "I was renting a small cottage on the edge of town. It backed up to a large field of fescue dotted with copses. I had hopped over the rock fence for a walk. I was spry enough to do that sort of thing back then. It was a late May evening. The sun was a fat red coal on the horizon and the lightning bugs were on the rise, flashing to attract their mates. The birds were singing their twilight songs. I approached a thicket of honeysuckle, hoping a soft breeze would come up to carry its sweet aroma my way. I was almost there when I heard a faint rustling sound, like a feather would make brushing your ear. It was not like any sound I had ever heard. It wasn't coming from any distinct direction but seemed to flow around and through me. This was immediately followed by a tingling sensation. I looked up. Beyond the honeysuckle, an iridescent haze coalesced, wispy like the morning mist. It filled the space before me like a curtain made of damselfly wings, stretching beyond my field of vision. It glowed pink in the last rays of the sun."

"That must have been something to see," said Elina. "Weren't you just a little scared?"

"Whether from fascination or fear, I was unable to move, watching the thing creep inexorably toward me. As it advanced, to my surprise, I could tell it was very thin with a smooth surface. Like a soap bubble, colors swirled on its surface. I could see through it, but everything looked a bit jumbled and out of focus. Just as it reached me, it meekly evaporated. In its wake, your mother, my beloved Ivelissa, stood before me, her Jabberwocky book in hand. She was so beautiful and not much older than you are now."

"And was it love at first sight, just like in the fairy tales?" asked Elina.

"On my part, most certainly. I thought she must surely be a fairy princess, come to beguile me." He paused for a moment before asking, "While you two were having one of your private chats in that fairy talk you used when you didn't want me to know what was being said, did you ever ask your mother what she felt that day?"

"Of course," answered Elina coyly.

"What did your mother say?"

"She said you were the most beautiful man she had ever seen."

"Pish posh. Most likely I was the first man, of this world anyway, she had ever seen," William said. Tears welled up in his eyes. "I miss her dearly."

"As do I," said Elina. "I wish she was here with us."

"I wish that book could have warned her about the accident," William said bitterly.

"Me too, but that's not how it works."

"Your mother and I came here often before you were born. This place was important to her." He looked at his watch. "Are you sure about the book?"

"Mom trusted the book, and look what happened," said Elina. "She travelled between universes to find you. Wouldn't you say it all worked out for the best?"

"For me, it did. I cherished every minute of my life with your mother. I'd like to believe the same was true for her...and you."

"Then you must trust, and we must follow her wishes."

"I know, I know," said William, shaking his head. "Oh, how she tried to explain it to me. She was always going on about parallel universes and how sometimes they brushed up against one another; convergences, she called them. And when that happened, if the universes were very much alike, one could simply step from one universe to another, as she did from her universe to this one. And if that wasn't fantastic enough, she had this book with a timetable of when such things happen. If you knew how to read it, of course."

"It's not a timetable," said Elina. "You make it sound like the book is a bus schedule and you can look up when the next universe arrives. The book enables us to interpret and recognize the harbingers of convergences." She stood up and walked over to her father. "And most importantly, the book reveals to us in which universe we will find our true love."

"That is the most confounding aspect of the whole thing," said William. "It sounds so nonsensical. She wanted desperately for me to comprehend, but my poor brain was just not up to it. You must know, I couldn't figure out the Father, Son and Holy Ghost thing much to the chagrin of the poor nuns and I fear I'll never understand how a book can do everything your mother claimed. Perhaps if Stephen Hawking had been walking through that field instead of me, she would have found someone who could have understood. Me, I just wanted to believe I had found my fairy princess."

"And who is to say in her world, she wasn't a fairy princess?" Elina whispered into his ear.

"Well, you have a point there," William said, looking at her face. "You remind me of her." He stood up, pulling Elina close. He hugged her, tears streaming down his cheeks.

"And do you regret that she came here to find you, her true love?"

"Of course not!"

"The point is," Elina said, touching her hand to his cheek, "you put your doubts aside and accepted her beliefs because you loved her, and for that, she loved you all the more."

"Yes, she did. Maybe I didn't want to believe that the book could do what she claimed because I was afraid if it was true, there was a chance it would tell her to leave me. I thought I couldn't live if that happened, finding love so late in life. It never occurred to me a drunk driver would take her away. And now there's you."

"It's time, Papa." Elina kissed him on the cheek, then walked back to her spot on the rock.

Though he had not heard it in twenty years, William immediately recognized the faint brushing sound and felt the familiar tingling sensation. He knew the moment had finally arrived.

"Good by Papa. I love you," Elina called. Behind her, the veil of damselfly wings appeared.

CARL AND LEE'S YARD SALE[9]

"Whose bright idea was this again?" Lee asked, wiping the August afternoon sweat from his eyes. He pulled the lid up on a battered cooler and retrieved a beer. "We been here four days and ain't sold a damn thing."

"Just takes one good sale to make it worth all the trouble," Carl snapped back. "Throw me one a them whilst you got your hand in there."

Lee grabbed a can, gave it a shake and tossed it to Carl. "Mucho gusto," he said.

"Thanks a lot," Carl muttered.

From deep inside a pile of rusty and dusty junk sitting on a rickety display table, a clock began to chime. The table was really a sheet of plywood resting on two sawhorses. The weight of the junk caused the plywood to bow down so everything wanted to migrate to the middle. Overhead was a makeshift canopy made from a bright blue tarp and some poles. Carl ticked off a finger for each strike, making it through both hands and three additional fingers before it fell silent.

"Hope that thing don't act up whilst a customer is here," Carl said. "Might be bad for sales."

"What customer?" asked Lee. "When've we seen a customer? How far from the road do you think we are?"

"No more than a half a mile or so."

"How would you know, we can't even see the road from here," said Lee, looking at the two gravel-filled ruts that trailed from the back of their pickup and disappeared over the hill. He dug a cellphone out of his pocket and held it up in the air. "We're so far

---

[9]"Carl and Lee's Yard Sale" appeared online in *Spank The Carp*, 2/1/2020. It was voted most popular story of Issue 55.

off the beaten path, there ain't even service out here. What'll we do if an emergency arises?"

"Don't lose faith, brother," soothed Carl. "I got the feeling someone is gonna be along anytime now."

"Mebbe we can get them to help us pack all this stuff up." Lee checked his watch, then carefully slipped a finger underneath the beer can's tab. He slowly pried it up until the thin aluminum gave way. He waited for the hiss to stop before opening the tab completely. "I'm here till three, then you'll be lookin' at my hip pockets."

Their dog, Tick, ambled over, looking at Lee's beer with sad eyes. "Don't he ever learn? He comes over here ever time we pop a top and the result is always the same." Lee held the can down for his dog to sniff. Tick licked some of the foam that had spilled over the side. Snorting, he returned to his shady spot under the display table. Lee took a sip of the beer. "I agree with Tick. I been chokin' this swill down for three days. Where'd you get this stuff?"

"Over at Wily's Discount Beer Barn."

"Well, don't go there no more." Lee grimaced. "This stuff is rancid. How much did you pay for it?"

"Let's just say I was cognatious of our limited resources."

"Wily shoulda paid you to cart this stuff off."

"I'll propose that to him next time," said Carl.

"Better not be a next time if it means drinkin' this."

"Well, you buy the beer next time. Jeez, try to save a dollar and this is the thanks I get."

"So, did you apply the same logic to renting this patch of cow pasture as you did for buying the beer?" asked Lee.

"I thought we came here to make some money, not spend some money," snapped Carl.

"Sure we did, but ain't you ever heard of the phrase, 'You got to spend money to make money'?"

"Of course, but I don't see how that applies to The World's Longest Yard Sale. Most everybody here just done what we done -

clean out their attics and garages and hope to sell it to them yard sale crazies. Why, there's over 690 miles of folks' leftovers and can't-use-no-mores strung out from Michigan to Alabama. And ever' one sellin' somethin' is waiting to make the big sale so's they can pay off their bass boat, and ever' one buyin' is lookin' for that rare antique or something to stick in their garden."

"Yeah, and in the meantime, the only folks guaranteed to make money are the convenience stores and Wily's Discount Beer Barn," muttered Lee.

"Well, Wily has a right to make a livin' don't he?"

"Mebbe, mebbe not if it means sellin' that stuff. Anyway, I thought we come here to try to make some cash to help out Momma and Daddy, not discuss the finer points of beer," said Lee.

"All I'm sayin' is mebbe we could've just found some extra payin' work to do around home instead of hauling all this junk up here," said Carl.

"That's all fine and dandy, but Daddy needs some cash now. If there was payin' work around home, he'd be workin'. Have you forgot his paycheck from the coalmine bounced?"

"No, I ain't forgettin'."

"Well then, why are we arguin'?" asked Lee.

Tick stepped out from under the table and barked, interrupting their discussion. Carl and Lee looked up to see a huge swirling ball of dust next to their battered and rusted F150 truck. As the dust thinned, they could see a huge RV in the center. It emitted a whirring sound like a vacuum cleaner when it is turned off. As the noise faded, the dust drifted to the ground, flowing outward in a large circle. Once the dust settled, the afternoon sun radiated off the RV's gleaming metallic surface.

Tick snorted and resumed his position under the table. Carl dug an elbow in Lee's ribs. "What'd I tell ya? Bet ya a dollar to a dumplin' them there are bonafried customers. And by the looks of that rig, with big pockets and little knowledge of antiques, or lack thereof."

Lee studied the RV for a few moments, then said, "Carl, am I not seeing things or does that rig not have wheels?"

"It's got to have wheels," Carl said. "How else could it get back in here?" Then, he looked closely at the RV. Its body was sitting flat on the ground. He studied it some more before he let out a yelp. "I'll be daggone, Lee, must be some kind of low-rider RV. I ain't never heard of such a thing, much less seen one, but that's what it's got to be."

"A low-rider RV? How many of them bargain brews have you had?"

Before Carl could answer, the driver's side door of the vehicle swung open. A set of steps folded out, touching lightly on the ground. "Look. Somebody is gettin' out. Get a load of that outfit," Carl chuckled. "Now you let me do the talkin'."

A squat cowboy appeared, then descended the steps, spurs jingling. He was dressed in full Western regalia, complete with chaps, pistols, and a large, broad-brimmed hat with a high, rounded crown. He teetered from side to side on stubby, bowed legs as he walked toward them.

"Let you do the talkin'?" asked Lee. "You speak cowboy or somethin'? I thought you wanted us to sell something."

"I do. That's why you need to keep your trap shut and let the expert handle this," said Carl.

"Expert? Where are you hidin' him, or did you have a mind to let Tick handle the negotiatin'?"

"Never you mind. Hey, they's two of them," said Carl. A tall woman had appeared in the RV doorway. Her stiletto heels rapped sharply on the metal steps as she followed the cowboy. She was wearing a clingy, red sequin gown with matching arm length evening gloves. Atop her head was a swirl of blue hair which looked like a huge spin of cotton candy.

The cowboy stopped a few feet from Carl and Lee. He drew his pistols.

"Whoa, whoa, whoa!" shouted Lee. "Easy there, we ain't got but fifteen dollars between us."

The cowboy smiled and proceeded to spin the pistols like the movie cowboys. After performing a few tricks, he tossed the guns over his shoulders before returning them to their holsters. "Just like John Wayne, pilgrim," he said with a Texas drawl.

"Yeah, and Randolph Scott and Roy Rogers, too," said Carl."

The cowboy produced a bullwhip. "Now, how about a little Lash LaRue."

"We believe you," said Lee. "But mebbe you ought not to right now, it might scare our dog, Tick."

"Put it away, mon chéri," admonished the woman. "We come here to buy zee artifacts, non? Not to scare zee country folk. "

"Yes ma'am, that's right," said Carl. "We're sure happy y'all stopped by today. You ever been to The World's Longest Yard Sale?"

"No, pilgrim," said the cowboy. "This here's our first time around these parts."

"I bet you watch a lot of John Wayne movies," said Lee.

Digging a knuckle into Lee's kidneys, Carl snarled under his breath, "Shut up." He then smiled and pointed to the tarp. "Our display area is right over here, ma'am. We got a fine selection of rare and innerestin' stuff for you to choose from."

The woman had to duck her head so her hair could clear the tarp. Tick watched them closely from his spot under the table. He leaned his head forward and sniffed the air. Satisfied, he stood up, stretched then lay back down.

The woman picked up a round object about the size of a cantaloupe. "Qu'est-ce que c'est?"

"Kiss what?" asked Carl.

"No, mon ami. I mean to say, what eez thees?"

"Oh, that's somethin' specially rare," said Carl. "What you got there is a Prinzsound SM8 Space Ball. It plays 8-track tapes. They was a popular way to play music back in the 70s. Belonged to my Uncle Ray."

The woman held it up. "Space Ball, musique, s'il vous plaît."

"What's she sayin' Lee?"

"I don't know," he muttered, then he addressed the woman. "Ma'am, you got to plug it in. See that cord? You plug it in, then you put in your 8-track and then you listen."

"Plug?" asked the woman.

"Lee! Go start the generator up," said Carl. "I think the lady wants to hear some music."

Lee hustled over to the generator sitting on the tailgate of their F150. He gave a mighty pull on the starting cord and the generator roared to life. He made sure the extension cord which ran over to the display table was plugged in, then gave the thumbs-up to Carl.

Carl plugged the player in and turned the knob to 'Tape'. He looked under the table and found a battered box. "Ma'am, you're in luck. Contained in this box jus' might be the best collection of 8-track tapes on the North American Contingent. And they's only two dollars each with the purchase of the Space Ball." He reached in and pulled out an 8-track entitled "K-Tel's Music Machine". Blowing the dust off the cartridge, he shoved it into the Space Ball's waiting slot, then turned up the volume as "Play That Funky Music" blared over the tinny speakers.

Immediately, the woman stepped into the sunlight and began to dance. She undulated, arms flapping wildly like an air dancer in front of a used car dealership. The cowboy joined her, hopping from one foot to another as if he was walking barefoot on hot blacktop. With each hop, his hat sunk lower on his head.

By this time, Lee had returned from the F150 and joined Carl and Tick watching the woman and cowboy dance. The song finished and "Gonna Fly Now" started.

"Say, wasn't her hair blue?" asked Lee.

Carl looked at the woman whose hair was now bright orange. "I thought so, mebbe it changes color when exposed to the sun."

"And isn't the guy wearing boxing gloves an' a robe now instead of that cowboy getup?"

"Maybe he had the gloves and robe under his hat."

"Well, where'd his hat go? Carl, I don't think these folks are from around here."

"You might be right on that."

The woman and man continued to dance, going through a variety of hair colors and wardrobes, not stopping until all eighteen K-Tel selections had played. Carl pulled the 8-track out and unplugged the Space Ball.

"I take it you enjoyed the music," he said. "You gonna buy it?"

The woman, now wearing formal riding attire, complete with a bowler hat precariously perched on top of her purple hair asked, "Dahling, what are you ahsking for this chahrming bauble?"

"If you buy the Ball and the box, which only makes sense unless you got some 8-tracks laying around your low-rider, how about three hunert?" asked Carl.

"We must decline your offer, old chap," said the man in a thick British accent. He was now donning a top hat and tails. He carried a short walking stick which he was twirling.

It was Lee's turn to bury a knuckle in Carl's kidneys. "How's about fifty?" he asked.

"Again sir, we must decline," said the man.

"Okay, thirty-five," said Lee, "but that's as low as we can go."

"Dahling, you misunderstahnd," said the woman. "We want to know what price you are ahsking for everything."

"Everything?" asked Carl.

"Of course, everything," said the woman.

"I told ya!" exclaimed Carl, slapping Lee on the back. "Ma'am, how about fifteen hunert for everthin' and we'll throw in the Space Ball and 8-tracks for nuthin'?"

"Marvelous, we'll take the lot," said the woman and man in unison.

Carl held out his hand. "Shake." The woman and man began to quiver. "No, no. I mean we gotta shake hands to seal the deal. Like this." He grabbed Lee's hand and shook it furiously. The woman and man stopped quivering, then grabbed each other's hand and began pumping.

"That's alright," said Lee, extracting his hand from Carl's grip. "We can dispense with the shaking. You folks want some help totin' all this over to your RV?"

"No need for that, old chap," said the man. "If you would be so kind as to wait here." The man and woman went back to the RV.

"Must be gonna get their money," said Carl. "Bet they got all kinds of loot in there. I shoulda asked for two thousand."

"I got a strange feeling about those two. Something ain't right. Didn't you think they's jus' a bit weird?"

Carl shrugged. "The World's Longest Yard Sale attracts all kinds."

"But what about them changing their clothes at the drop of a hat - no pun intended - and that woman changing the color of her hair?"

"Prob'ly bought some old magician props or such." Carl paused. "So, you can apologize anytime now."

"Apologize for what?" asked Lee.

"Doubtin' I was an expert salesman."

"I don't think this qualifies you as an expert," said Lee. "If he'd a-wanted, Tick could've sold his fleas to them two."

"Well, you was the one that was goin' to let the Space Ball go for thirty-five bucks. That ain't necessarily inductive of a sales genus."

The RV began to hum. Soon, the noise grew into a roar as a cloud of brown dust roiled up around it. "Look, they's leavin'," cried Lee. "We've been snookered." They watched in disbelief as the RV shot straight up, disappearing in the clouds.

"Did you see what I just saw?" asked Carl.

"I don't know what you saw, but I think that damn beer has given us hallucinations."

"I don't think so. Wily says he drinks that beer all the time."

"My point exactly," Lee said. He paused. "But seriously, did you see that RV thing shoot up into the clouds?"

"Yep. So, I don't think we's hallucinatin'. I think we had us an encounter with a UFO. Say, I got an idea. Mebbe we could sell our story and make some money."

"I'm sure they're goin' to line up to hear how two aliens in a low-rider RV visited The World's Longest Yard Sale in the middle of nowhere, Kentucky, but left without buyin' nothin'."

"Weren't there those women who run up on a UFO over to Stanford, Kentucky? That ain't but about 30 miles from here. They became famous."

"But that was back in 1976, and they weren't at no yard sale."

"1976? Well maybe we done encountered the same aliens what got them. Could be why them two liked that K-Tel 8-track so much. It was released in 1976. Why those women could'a been listening to that very tape when the UFO swooped down and took 'em."

"All that ain't what really matters, though," said Lee.

"Whaddya mean?"

"I mean, we have gone an' spent the last few hours of our last day of the yard sale watching aliens, or whatever them two were, dance to "Play That Funky Music" and didn't sell one blessed thing. Now, the yard sale is over an' we got to go back empty handed with nothin' to help out Momma and Daddy."

"I wasn't thinkin' of it that a way. I guess we done failed in our mission," said Carl.

"Yeah, all we can do is pack up all this stuff an' sell it for scrap. We'll be lucky to get twenty bucks. We spent more'n that on gas, beer and rentin' this patch of cow pasture." Lee shook his head, then looked up, searching the sky. The ground began to tremble and the hair on his arms stood up.

"What's goin' on?" cried Carl. "They ain't goin' to attack are they?"

Before Lee could answer, a thick mist welled up from the ground, accompanied by a throbbing high-pitched whine. The whine reached a crescendo, then fell silent. When the mist cleared, Carl and Lee found themselves standing in the middle of an empty field, save for Tick, who was still lying in his spot where the display table had been.

"Don't that beat all," said Lee. "Not only did them two crawfish on the sale, they come back and stole everythin' - even our truck. There's no call to steal a man's truck and leave him stranded in a field."

"I don't know what we done to deserve this, but it sure don't seem fair," said Carl. Tick ambled over and nudged his hand. "Least, they didn't get you," he said patting Tick's head. "And even though it looks like you ain't much of a guard dog, we're happy they left you with us."

"Come on," said Lee, "let's get back to the main road and see if we can pick up some cell service or catch a ride or sumpin'."

A small ball of mist appeared on the ground in front of them, accompanied by a loud "Thwappp." Tick growled. "You're too late

Tick," said Lee. The mist melted away, revealing a pirate's chest about the size of a shoebox. "What now?"

"Should we open it?" asked Carl.

"I guess so. If they'd wanted to hurt us, I think they'd a done it by now." Lee picked up the chest and flipped back the lid. Inside, he found a note which read:

As agreed, please find payment of 1500 for everything.

Lee lifted the note from the chest and gasped. "Carl, look here. Are these what I think they is?"

Carl grabbed the chest and looked inside at a cache of brilliant diamonds. "Hot damn!" he exclaimed. He held one up to the sky. The sunlight sparkled inside the stone with such intensity it hurt his eyes.

"Lemme see," said Lee. Carl tossed him the stone. When Lee held it up to the sun, it was so bright he had to turn his head away.

"Lee, them two turned out to be alright. I take back ever bad thing I said or thought about 'em."

"Me too."

"Do you think there is 1500 diamonds in that chest?" asked Carl.

"I guess if you believe they's diamonds, you got to believe they's 1500 of 'em in there."

"How much you think they's worth?"

"A lot more than everthin'," chuckled Lee.

"Who's the expert now?" asked Carl, puffing out his chest.

"Well, have you considered that diamonds to them might be like pennies to us?"

"Hadn't thought about it in that way. They might be up there right now laughin' about what a great deal they made."

"Don't make no difference, anyway," said Lee. "The important thing is that now we can set Momma and Daddy up for life."

"For sure. That'll be nice."

"And mebbe have enough left over to buy us a couple of new trucks."

"I hear that," said Carl.

A larger ball of mist appeared in front of them accompanied by a loud grinding sound. The mist melted away revealing their battered cooler.

"What now?" asked Lee. He pulled up the cooler's lid and found a note inside. It read:

You can keep the beer!

APPENDIX
INTRODUCTION TO INVERSION

Inversion - Not Your Ordinary Stories, is all about speculative fiction. From my viewpoint, this form of fiction places us in a world where the *Laws*, those regularly occurring or apparently inevitable phenomenon that govern what happens to us, operate differently than what we would expect. In the speculative fiction world, the rules as we know them do not always apply. Or could it be the rules as we thought we knew them?

Speculative fiction aims to explore our world as it would be altered by posing the question *What if?* The most appealing and freeing aspect of speculative fiction is that, like the worlds it creates, it is not bound by the traditional genres of Science Fiction, Fantasy, and Horror. In fact it is not bound by any genre. It is free to adventure anywhere it likes as long as anywhere is a creation of imagination and speculation.

Inversion means turning upside down or inside out; reversal of a normal order or relation. What better title for a collection of speculative fiction stories? When you ask *What if?*, the result is not your ordinary story.

Some of these stories have been previously published, either in print or on line. They have been identified throughout. I wish to express my appreciation to those editors who were willing to publish my work and encourage the reader to visit these other publications.

I would also like to thank the members of the Danville Writers Group, who have read many preliminary drafts of these stories and offered their feedback and assistance.

Finally, I would like to thank Joan Stansbury, affectionately known as the *Queen of Commas*, for her editorial assistance.

Paul Stansbury

ABOUT THE AUTHOR

Paul Stansbury is a lifelong native of Kentucky. Now retired, he lives in Danville, Kentucky. He is the owner of Sheppard Press. He is the author of *Inversion - Not Your Ordinary Stories, Inversion II - Creatures, Fairies, and Haints Oh My!, Inversion III - The Lighter Shades of Greys,* and *Down By the Creek – Ripples and Reflections,* all published by Sheppard Press. His novelette, *Little Green Men?* was published by The Society of Misfit Stories.

His stories appearing in print/e-book anthologies:
- "A Game Of Tag" and "Dark Meat" appeared in Brief *Grislys* published by Apocryphile Press
- "Sigaforgas" appeared in *Neo-Legends To Last A Deathtime* published by KY Story
- "The Ghost Eye" appeared in *Frightening* published by SEZ Publishing
- "Takers" appeared in *Out of the Cave* published by MacKenzie Publishing
- "Phantasmal" appeared in *In Media Res, Stories From the In-Between* published by Writespace Houston
- "Under the Wolf Moon" appeared in *Nocturnal Natures* published by Zimbell House Publishing
- "Spirit Painter" appeared in *Book 3: 30 Authors - 30 Stories* published by Flash Fiction Magazine
- "Exiled" appeared in *See Through My Eyes: A Ghost Mystery Anthology* published by Fantasia Divinity Magazine
- "Selkie Cove" appeared in Mirrors & Thorns - An OWS Ink Dark Fairy Tale Anthology published by Catterfly Publishing (A Division of OWS Ink. LLC)
- "Little Green Men?" appeared in *The Society of Misfit Stories Presents...Volume One* published by Bards and Sages Publishing
- "The Girl In The Harvest Moon" appeared in *Autumn's Harvest: An Autumn Fantasy Anthology* published by Fantasia Divinity Magazine

- "Mulded" appeared in *Anthology Askew 006* published by Rhetoric Askew
- "The Scroll And The Silver Kazoo" appeared in *The Rabbit Hole, Weird Tales Volume 1* published by The Writers Co-op
- "Word Of Mouth" appeared in *THEMA Vol. 21, No. 2 Summer 2019* published by the THEMA Literary Society
- "Do You Know Why You Are Here Today?" appeared in *Hallucination* published by pacificREVIEW, a San Diego State University Press Journal 2019
- Do You Remember How To Fly?" appeared in *Mad Scientist Journal Summer 2019.*
- "Yovido, in the Ivaldi System", "The Usual Conclusion" and "The Red Star" appeared in *Our Universes* - a Boyle County Public Library Chapbook published through Sheppard Press, 2019.
- "Mangalo" appeared in *The Weird and Whatnot November 16, 2019.*
- "A Thanksgiving To Remember" and "I Can't Believe I Fell For This One", appeared in *Memories Worth Remembering II* - a Boyle County Public Library book published through Sheppard Press, 2020.
- "Ndoto Vumbi", appeared in *Going-Off-The-Grid: Down in the Dirt - March 2020, Volume 169.*
- "Unnoticed" appeared in *The Rabbit Hole, Weird Tales Volume 0* published by The Writers Co-op, 2020.

His work has also appeared in a variety of on-line publications. His poetry has appeared in The Rising Phoenix Review, Young Ravens Literary Review, Strange Poetry and Kentucky Monthly.

He is a contributing writer for the Danville Advocate Messenger Newspaper, Scheduling Coordinator for The Jeanne Penn Lane Celebration of Kentucky Writers, and a member of the Board of Directors of Scarlet Cup Theater.

BOOKS FROM SHEPPARD PRESS

Down By The Creek – Ripples and Reflections by Paul Stansbury
ISBN 978-0-9986516-0-6 paperback
ISBN 978-0-9986516-1-3 e-book

Inversion – Not Your Ordinary Stories by Paul Stansbury
ISBN 978-0-9986516-3-7 paperback
ISBN 978-0-9986516-4-4 e-book

Inversion II – Creatures, Fairies, and Haints Oh My! by Paul Stansbury
ISBN 978-0-9986516-5-1 paperback
ISBN 978-0-9986516-6-8 e-book

Inversion III – The Lighter Shades Of Greys by Paul Stansbury
ISBN 978-0-9986516-7-5 paperback
ISBN 978-0-9986516-8-2 e-book

By George – A Collection Of Childhood Experiences and Anecdotes by George Herbert Stansbury, Jr.
ISBN 978-0-9986516-2-0 paperback

Migrant Times and Other Musings by George Boursaw
Available only at Lulu - https://www.lulu.com

Memories Worth Remembering by Various Authors Available only at Lulu - https://www.lulu.com

Our Universes by Various Authors
Available only at Lulu - https://www.lulu.com

Memories Worth Remembering II by Various Authors
Available only at Lulu - https://www.lulu.com